BED OF STONE

ADVANCE UNCORRECTED PROOFS
NOT FOR SALE • REVIEWER'S COPY
Original Paperback • October 2007 • $12.95

AVOCET PRESS INC
New York

Published by Avocet Press Inc
19 Paul Court
Pearl River, NY 10965
http://www.avocetpress.com
mysteries@avocetpress.com

Copyright ©2007 by Letha Albright

All rights reserved. No part of this book may be reproduced or transmitted in any form or by any means, electronic or mechanical, including photocopying, recording, or by any information storage and retrieval system, without written permission from the author, except for the inclusion of brief quotations in review.
This novel is a work of fiction and each character in it is fictional. No reference to any living person is intended or should be inferred.

Library of Congress Cataloging-in-Publication Data
Albright, Letha, 1952-
Bed of stone / by Letha Albright. — 1st ed.
p. cm.
ISBN 978-0-9725078-7-5
1. Women ex-convicts—Fiction. 2. Widows—Fiction. 3. Missing children—Fiction. 4. Depressions—1929—Oklahoma—Fiction. 5. Distilling, Illicit—Fiction. 6. Oklahoma—Fiction. I. Title.
PS3601.L34B43 2007
813'.6—dc22
2007005026

Cover design by Mike Watters
Printed in the USA First Edition

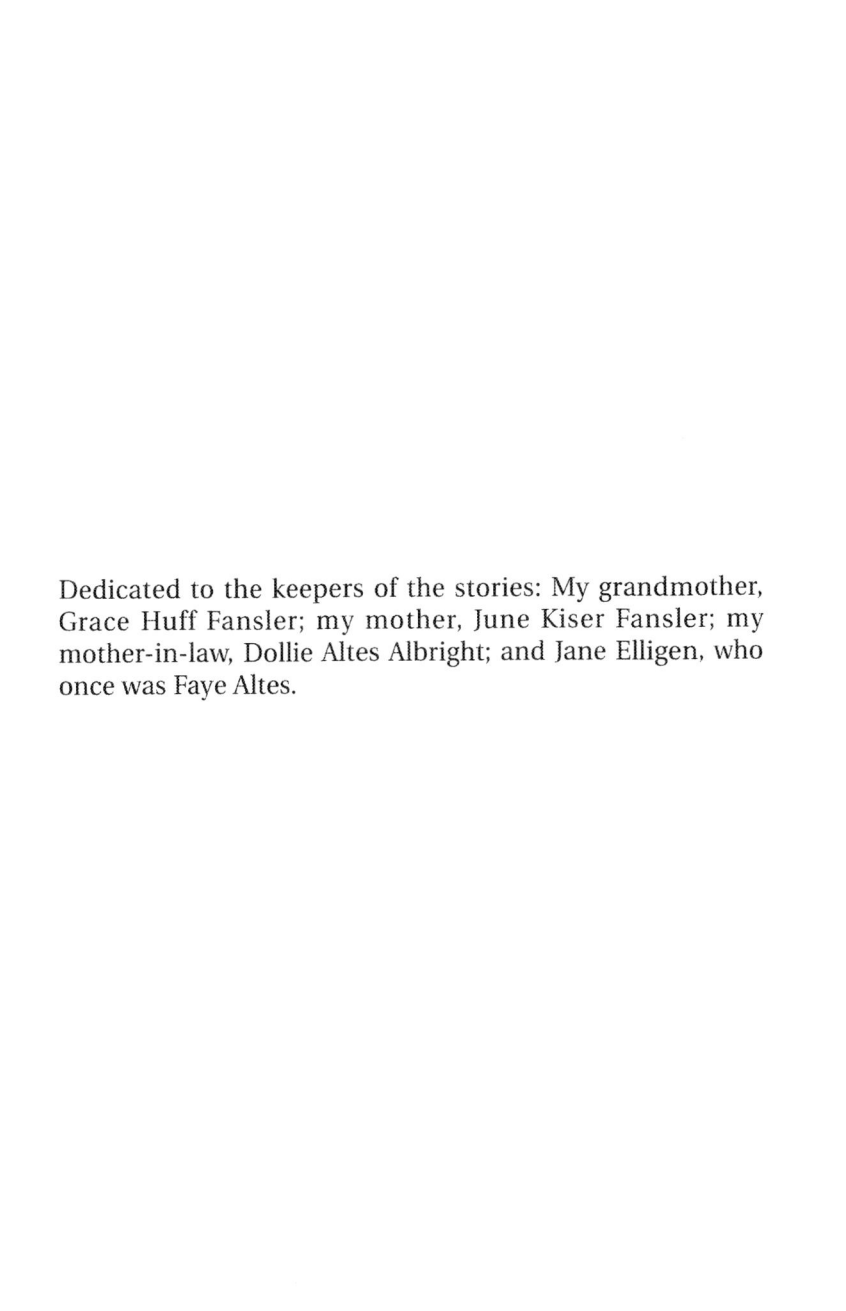

Dedicated to the keepers of the stories: My grandmother, Grace Huff Fansler; my mother, June Kiser Fansler; my mother-in-law, Dollie Altes Albright; and Jane Elligen, who once was Faye Altes.

"Go up into Gilead and take balm, O virgin, the daughter of Egypt: in vain shalt thou use many medicines; for thou shalt not be cured.

"The nations have heard of thy shame, and thy cry hath filled the land: for the mighty man hath stumbled against the mighty, and they are fallen both together."

Jeremiah 46:11-12

1

It was a perfect day for a hanging. A perfect day to escape Missouri's bone-chilling cold and enter the warmth of the hereafter. Those were Johnny Crow's thoughts as he was led out the back door of the Jackson County jail toward the scaffold. He tried to hold onto that attitude; it was all he had.

The February wind cut his face, and the weak sun was a cruel whisper. Not long, he'd be out of it—beyond all earthly pain while the sonsabitches running this show would be shivering in the cold, and the inmates lined up to witness his punishment praying for their own release.

Crow stumbled on the rough ground, and the deputy's hand on his elbow jerked him back upright. Deputy Enos Richards, chief sumabitch. Richards murmured in his ear, "Feeling it, ain't you?" It was said with the same cheer as when he'd entered Crow's cell the day before.

"Crow bait!" he had said, running his keys across the bars so they made a rat-a-tat-tat. "You've got an appointment with your tailor."

Crow rose slowly from his bunk, feeling the pain shoot to his hip—a reminder of the ass-kicking Richards and Stretch had given him a week earlier. Not that it had satisfied them. Because of Crow, a brother-in-arms was dead.

Crow held out his arms for the cuffs, and then Richards and another guard led him through a maze of corridors to a small room with bars on the window. On the other side of the bars, Crow saw a black bird cut across the sky.

The tailor turned out to be the hangman, a small man with a thin scalp and the palest blue eyes Crow had ever seen. His voice was matter-of-fact. "We're going to have us a good hanging," he said. "I need to take some measurements to get it right."

He gestured at Crow to stand on a set of scales.

Richards stood by the door and watched. "Lots can go wrong in a hanging, ain't it, doc?" His tone was conversational. "Take the rope, for instance. It's gotta be greased and stretched just right. A loose catch, and our wild Injun will be gasping like a fish out of water. If you drop him too long, his head could pop right off. We wouldn't want that, would we, chief? That's why doc needs your weight." His laughter bounced off the limestone walls.

Crow kept his eyes on the window, watching for more birds to fly by.

The hangman licked his pencil stub and made a notation on a small pad. "We're done here," he said.

Richards grabbed Crow by his shirt collar and pushed him toward the door. On the long walk back to the cell, he kept up a running commentary.

"They'll do some dry runs this afternoon with that trap they built. Just so's no one will lose any sleep over you, they set up four different levers that pull a pin. Four levers, four men. Only one of 'em drops the trap, but they'll never know which one done it.

"If everything goes right, and I damn well hope it don't, chief, your neck will be broke when you drop and you'll go into shock. You'll be brain dead in six minutes and heart dead in eight. Anyways, that's what they say."

His voice was implacable. "I hope in those six minutes you get to relive ever miserable thing you done in your life and think on the hellfire waitin' on you."

Nine steps led up to the gallows. A rope dangled from the crossbeam; the noose below looped on a nail. The scaffold had been built in a small enclosure behind the jail, protecting it from onlookers.

All the day before, Crow had heard the hammers as the prison work gang constructed the gallows. Other than the steady echo of the hammers, the building had been unusually quiet.

The hanging was set for 8:30 a.m., but Crow was awake long before that. Just after four, he asked for the lights to be turned up and paper and pen brought so he could write letters. But then he sat with the pen poised over the paper on his knee, and no words came to him.

What words are there to express a lifetime of ruin and longing? Who knows the words to make actions any different than their outcome? My dear wife and darling daughter, he wrote. He paused and thought—*my dear Virginia, my darling Isabelle*—but nothing came. In the end, he folded the paper and placed it on the unmade bunk.

At the top of the steps, the hangman and the sheriff waited. The witnesses—twelve white men—sat on hard benches before a screen that separated the scaffold from the rest of the prison yard. Crow recognized a few of them: his lawyer, Benjamin Johnson. A journalist who had interviewed him the week before. A preacher from a holiness church who had prayed for his soul. The others were strangers. Behind the witnesses, the inmates stood in loose ranks, dressed in their black-and-white striped prison garb. They looked miserable in the sharp wind, a fact Crow found vaguely comforting.

One of them shouted, "Johnny Crow!"

"I told you I'd try to be here, boys," he called back. His voice was strong, but inside he felt weak as a kitten. Weak as his baby girl the day she was born.

From behind, Crow felt the warning squeeze of his captor. "We don't need no circus," Richards said.

But the damage was done. The inmates hooted and stamped their feet and chanted "Chief, chief," until guards with rifles stilled them.

The sheriff's mouth was a thin line. He wanted it over. Crow could see that. In fact, he saw everything with unusual clarity. Colors so bright they burned his eyes. Blue sky, yellow sun, white clouds. A black hearse beyond the cracks in the slat fence.

For a brief moment he closed his eyes, and then he mounted the steps. At the top, he stood facing the sheriff, Richards hard behind him. Crow felt any man's equal today. He had been allowed to dress as he chose, and he wore a white shirt with black piping on the cuffs and collar. A black Stetson sat atop his jet-black hair, and on his feet were black Tony Lama boots, freshly polished.

It wasn't only the clothing that bolstered him, though; it was the deference with which he had been treated on this day. As though they all realized there was nothing more they could do to him, no pressure they could bring to bear, no threats they could make. For a brief time, this was what freedom felt like.

The sheriff's cheeks were red with cold, and the wind ruffled the sideburns below his hat. He held up a paper and took a deep breath before reading the charges.

"Johnny Crow, of Oklahoma City, Oklahoma, you have been found guilty of causing the death of Kansas City deputy Edward Mahoney while in the commission of a crime. You are ordered by Jackson County Circuit Court Judge Titus Frailings to hang by the neck until dead. By the power vested in me by the court and the state of Missouri, I hereby carry out the commission of that sentence."

He lowered the paper and looked Crow in the eyes. "Have you any last words?"

Crow felt dizzy and out of focus—like that night four years earlier when he first saw Virginia. He had had too much bootleg to drink that night, and when he spotted her across the dance floor, his legs went weak.

It was Virginia he thought of now. Virginia he had no words for. Virginia and Isabelle. There were no words.

He heard the sheriff's voice. "May God have mercy on your soul."

The sheriff stepped back and nodded at the hangman. Behind the hangman's hood the blue eyes were all Johnny Crow could see. The man stepped forward and removed the Stetson from Crow's head and handed it ceremoniously to the sheriff. Then he nudged Crow over the trapdoor and efficiently strapped his legs together and his arms to his body. Finally, he pulled a black hood from his vest pocket and slipped it over the condemned man's head.

As the hood descended, Johnny Crow felt calm settle over him again. Inside the hood, he felt his breath expel and envelop his face in warmth. It suddenly seemed quiet. So quiet. As though the entire world were breathless.

He felt the noose slip over his head and the knot being tightened behind his right ear.

The prisoners began singing:
When the trumpet of the Lord shall sound
And time shall be no more,
And the morning breaks
Eternal bright and fair…
Closer than the sound of singing was a metallic clicking,

like a ratchet counting turns.

    Johnny Crow took a deep breath and sent a final message.

    Virginia, forgive me.

2

"When they let you out?"

The cabbie, eyes narrowed through the smoke of his hand-rolled, looked in the rear-view mirror at Virginia Crow.

"What?"

He rested an arm on the back of the seat and half turned to face her. A ragged scar ran like a zipper across one cheek. He smiled, and his teeth were yellow and uneven. "I know the look," the cabbie said. "Me, I did county time, state time. Been mostly legal five years now. Ex-cons, even lady ex-cons, have a look."

The residential street was wide, as were most streets in Oklahoma City, and the afternoon traffic sparse. Virginia smoothed her dress over her knees—a black wool traveling dress, so soft compared to the gray serge she had been forced to wear the past year and a half—and stared out the window,

In the pocketbook clutched under her arm, Virginia had thirty-seven dollars and change and a picture of her daughter.

"You'd best keep your eyes on the road," she said. "I'd like to get to my daughter in one piece."

The cabbie winked at her and paused long enough to show no woman could tell him what to do before turning back to the steering wheel.

"Daughter, eh?"

The idle inquiry set her nerves on edge. Isabelle was none of his business. She pursed her lips and looked out the side window at the towering elms lining the street. Behind the trees, ochre in their winter nudity, ash clouds dusted the sky.

Virginia's thoughts were a continuous prayer. Please God, please God. Please let my baby be all right.

Since her release the day before from Prison Farm No. 1 in Jefferson City, Missouri, the worry she had managed to suppress for eighteen months took root like a weed. You can't survive in prison if your mind is other places. You do the time, you keep your nose clean, you don't raise a ruckus just because your baby's in someone else's care.

If only her own mother had been alive to take charge of Isabelle. If wishes were horses...

But why hadn't Iona Tweedy responded to her letters these past three months? Had something happened to Isabelle? Isabelle was so tiny, so helpless. She needed her mother's care.

Virginia remembered the last time she had seen Isabelle. The baby's dark curls bounced as she tottered along with one hand on Mrs. Tweedy's horsehair sofa. Isabelle's little cry of surprise and delight at standing alone enchanted both Mrs. Tweedy and Virginia.

"She'll be walkin in no time," Mrs. Tweedy had said.

Please god, please god.

Virginia told herself she was lucky to be alive, lucky to be free. Lucky to be returning to Isabelle, the baby she had left behind eighteen months earlier.

The cabbie shrugged off his passenger's silence. Didn't bother him. Let her stew in her own juices. The cab passed spidery oil derricks that rose behind pretentious mansions and then turned south toward Capitol Hill and its modest close-set homes. With each turn, Virginia's heart beat faster. She felt like she might be sick.

They had almost reached the address Virginia had given when the cabbie spoke again.

"I know where we could get some action. A handsome

woman like you must have some catching up to do." He shifted his eyes once again to the mirror and looked at her. Broad face and arched eyebrows—heavy and not plucked to slender threads the way so many broads were doing these days. Hazel eyes and hair like a mink's pelt. He wondered what lay beneath that demure dress.

Virginia ignored him, staring out the window at the house they had just pulled up to.

Please god, please god.

Behind those doors was her daughter, so much older than the baby she left behind. She tried to imagine Isabelle walking and talking, a miniature person. Would she even remember her mother?

The cabbie stopped the car along the curb. In the steel-gray light he saw a run-down rooming house. Paint peeled on the porch balusters; a broken window marred the smooth face of the plaster exterior. Tree limbs were strewn like body parts across the dry and cracked yard.

Virginia paused with her hand on the taxi door. Now that she was so close to the realization of her dreams, she felt exhausted, like a marathon runner who must drag herself across the finish line. It had been a long journey.

Her mind rushed back to the last time she had seen this house.

Eighteen months earlier: A weekend whiskey run to Kansas City with Johnny. Isabelle had just passed her first birthday, and Virginia was ready to cut loose from motherhood for a few days. Not something she often did, but she felt the need for a little adventure, and Iona Tweedy, their landlady, said she would take good care of Isabelle. Iona was like a grandmother to Isabelle, Virginia told herself. Her baby would be in good hands.

Johnny sang as he drove down the highway. Some song about the sweetest gal he ever saw was down in the Ar-kan-saw. They were in the Pontiac Johnny claimed was once owned by Jelly Nash. By then, Virginia had learned to doubt most of what Johnny told her, and this statement was more suspect than most since Nash had been on the run for more than three years after escaping from Leavenworth in 1930. Just when would he have driven this almost new car that had somehow fallen into Johnny's hands?

The trunk was filled with wooden crates that cradled jugs of premium whiskey.

In Kansas City, Johnny said he had to make a delivery before they went to the Reno Club for barbecue, and Virginia said "Don't be long, Johnny." She waited in the car while he went inside a red brick building on Paseo.

The cop was by the door when Johnny came out, and Johnny reached inside his jacket like he was going for his wallet. He pulled out a gun. The sound it made was sharp and quick, as if someone had punched a hole through the crust of the earth.

If there was one moment Virginia could take back, it would be that second before Johnny Crow pulled out his gun and fired. In the months past, it replayed in her head like a newsreel. The glow from the streetlights reflected in the puddles like a hundred lesser moons. The scream as she leaped from the car and left her husband to deal with his final mistake. The young cop's look of surprise that so quickly slid into the blank, impersonal mask of death. It was that second that changed everything.

For good luck, Virginia touched the envelope that held Isabelle's baby picture—a small round face, serious brown eyes, scrubby hair like smudged ink. The picture was nestled among the few precious notes she had received from Iona Tweedy in those long months. "Baby has croup. Kept me up half the night. She's gitting better. Ate her oatmeal this morning and hollered for more."

And this one six months later: "Can't keep little Belle in clothes. She's growing like Topsy's calf. I want to get me one of them new music masheens."

But the notes had stopped coming two months ago.

Please god, please god.

Virginia tipped the cabbie more than she should have; she felt giddy with hope and fear.

He looked at her cynically. "It's not what you think," he said. "Life on the outside."

Virginia rushed up the steps, the cabbie already a fading memory, and opened the front door. The dark hallway stank of boiled cabbage and bacon. On the left, a narrow staircase led to the rooms she used to share with Johnny and Isabelle.

"Mrs. Tweedy!" she called. "Mrs. Tweedy? Isabelle?"

Above, a door opened and a pale face peered over the railing.

"She ain't takin in boarders no more."

"Mrs. Thompson? It's me. Virginia Crow."

The old woman clucked her tongue and slowly made her way down the stairs. Mrs. Thompson wasn't dressed for the day, even though it was afternoon, and the hem of her cotton housecoat dragged on the stairs behind her. With her head cocked sideways, she looked like a wizened bird gone all white-feathered.

The old woman studied Virginia through the thick lenses of her spectacles. "Virginia Crow? I thought you was in prison somewheres."

"They let me go. I've come home." Virginia looked around for signs that Isabelle had recently played on these dirty steps or in the parlor with the broken window glass scattered across the stiff carpet. And what had happened to the furniture? The room had been stripped of tables and lamps and chairs. The first confirming flutter of disaster crossed her heart.

"What's happened here?" Virginia said. "Where's my baby?" She couldn't keep the panic from her voice.

Mrs. Thompson drew her collar around her throat. "Mrs. Tweedy took the money and left."

"What? What are you talking about? Left where?"

The woman took a step back, her hand on the stair rail. "She said you knew. You owed back rent. You signed the papers."

"Where's my baby? I didn't sign any papers." Virginia was breathless, as if she had been running.

"Your husband killed the Laws. You can't never pay your debt to society. She did your little girl a favor."

"Where is she?" Virginia grabbed Mrs. Thompson's arm. "Tell me where she is!"

Fear distorted Mrs. Thompson's face, but spite, also. "I heard 'em talkin. I don't see so good, but my ears are keen. They gave her top dollar for your little girl. Four hundred bucks. She said you signed the papers all proper."

"No!" It was a drawn-out howl. "No. No. No."

Virginia released the woman's arm and sank to her knees in the hallway. "I never saw any papers. Mrs. Tweedy sent me letters about Isabelle, how she was starting to say words and learning to climb the stairs. Where's my baby?"

"They was a respectable couple. The woman had a nice cloth coat, and the man wore a good hat. Looked like a businessman. Drove a new car. They weren't no spring chickens, neither."

"Where is she? Where's Mrs. Tweedy?"

"She's sellin this place. Already sold her belongings and left. Said she was going somewheres the wind don't blow." Mrs. Thompson rubbed her arm where Virginia had gripped it and then scrabbled like a crab back to her room.

Virginia—rooted to the floor - felt her body turning to stone. It crackled through her like the spread of ice across a winter pond. Time itself slowed, and every movement was dipped in thickening seconds and minutes and hours.

Her thoughts were chaotic. She would go to the judge. She would call the police. She would find Iona Tweedy and cut the woman into small pieces and feed her to the dogs. No one had the right to sell her child.

The shadows deepened into night. Virginia Crow searched the empty closets and the barren rooms for clues to where her daughter had gone. On the top floor, Mrs. Thompson locked her door and refused to let Virginia enter.

In the rooms where Virginia and Johnny and Isabelle had lived, all she found were dust and cobwebs. The furniture Virginia had scraped together was gone: the brocade sofa, the walnut side table, the double bed with the carved oak headboard. Where was the wedding china, the baby crib, the carefully preserved layette?

Late in the night, Virginia stretched on the glass-strewn carpet in the parlor and fell into an exhausted stupor, where in her waking dreams the past, present and future collided and burst apart. In her hands, she clutched Isabelle's photo like a drowning woman would cling to a piece of debris.

3

Four months after Isabelle's birth, they had spent a dreamlike month at the ocean, Isabelle and Virginia. Day after day, Virginia divided her attention between the baby and the waves that crashed against the California shore. She left the cottage above the beach only to buy food at a neighborhood grocery. Amidst the mewling cries of Isabelle and the seagulls, the ocean beat a soothing percussion.

Isabelle's birth had been difficult. Day after day, Virginia lay in bed with the tiny, red-faced creature, listening to the baby cry and feeling too wrung out to so much as get up and feed herself. Johnny Crow was flush with luck and new fatherhood in those days, and he decided it would be best to send his wife and daughter to the ocean. He would have sent her home, but her parents had died the winter before, and only her sister, Carolina, was at the family farm with a girl of her own to care for.

So Johnny took Virginia and Isabelle to Union Station in Oklahoma City and saw them off to San Diego. As the miles melted away in the fresh January sun and the clackety-clack of the train lulled the baby to sleep, Virginia felt herself relax for the first time since she had learned she was going to have a child. Motherhood was the scariest thing she had ever experienced, and once begun, it was a runaway horse that you dare not jump off.

It wasn't the discomfort and pain of childbirth that had her so undone; it was instead the overwhelming sense of responsibility. It was as though she alone had brought this new soul into the world, and she alone had to see it fed and clothed and nurtured. She hadn't expected to become this tiny child's prisoner, but she was. Their destiny was intertwined, and anything that happened to Isabelle would happen also to Virginia.

Isabelle was a beautiful baby, with curly black hair and dark eyes that seemed wise and ancient. Everything about her was perfect: her miniature hands and feet; her grimacing smile; her rosebud lips. But the best thing was her smell. To Virginia, from the sweet folds in Isabelle's fat neck wafted the odor of the beginning of creation.

When Virginia and Isabelle returned to Oklahoma City, it was spring. The season of change. It also was the beginning of the end. When Johnny Crow's carelessness would catch up to him and bring them all down—Johnny and Virginia and Isabelle.

4

The law was no help in a case such as Virginia Crow's. At the Oklahoma City police station, her situation was made clear. A woman just released from prison whose husband had been hanged for killing a cop claimed the landlady had sold her child? The police said Virginia gave them nothing to go on. Their lack of sympathy was as transparent as window glass.

To Virginia's surprise, she found she had few concrete things to tell them about Iona Tweedy. And yet, she had entrusted the woman with the care of her child. On the surface, Mrs. Tweedy had seemed perfect: grandmotherly, warm and generous. But she had vanished, and Virginia learned that the things she had known hadn't been important after all. Who were Iona Tweedy's friends? Where was her family?

Virginia had been enwrapped in her own world, a world that held only her husband and child. She had somehow thought that everything that brushed against her world was made of the same elements. That iron was iron and trust was trust.

Iona Tweedy quilted. She drank tea with milk. She took Isabelle downstairs so Virginia could rest, and she fed Isabelle sugar cookies. She spoke often of her dead husband. Those things Virginia knew. As for the concrete details of Iona Tweedy's life, she had never thought to ask.

The agent who was handling the sale of Mrs. Tweedy's rooming house was no help. He muttered something about keeping his business to himself and closed his office door in Virginia's face. When she pounded on the door in helpless fury, he yelled that he would call the law on her.

Virginia slept in the deserted parlor and watched her money dwindle. Some of it she spent at the corner drugstore where the proprietor remembered her. She would carry her refilled flask to the rooming house, and the whiskey's harsh magic would stun her into restless sleep.

During the days, she went from house to house in the streets that led from Iona Tweedy's rooming house, asking residents if they knew the woman. If they had seen her baby. She held Isabelle's picture in her hand, and if the person who answered the door consented to look at it, Virginia said, of course she's older now.

"They grow, don't they," said one woman, wiping her hands on her apron. "Yes they do now."

The city had changed. The people who answered the doors were suspicious and unfriendly. Store windows were boarded. The bank Virginia had once used was a heap of ashes. She tried to find Johnny Crow's old associates, but they, too, had vanished. All but one.

On a blustery March day near Union Station, Virginia saw Jack Chandler sitting at the counter in a diner. His stringy blond hair had grown over his collar. He was nursing a cup of coffee, and she saw as she drew closer, a hangover.

She slipped onto the stool beside him and said, "Jack Chandler."

He looked at her without turning his head and then looked again. "Virginia Crow," he said. "They let you go."

"They let me go."

Chandler offered her a cigarette, and she inhaled the smoke like a sacrament. She had no money for cigarettes these days. She crossed one ankle over the other to hide the hole in her stockings.

Chandler was handsome in a rakish way. Wide-set gray eyes that were now bloodshot. A challenging stare. A tall, thin body that moved with unconscious ease. Older than Johnny Crow, Chandler was the unofficial leader of the small band of what Johnny called his "associates." Their business was gambling, moonshine and other things Virginia didn't want to know about.

"Shame about the Chief," Chandler said.

The waitress, a dark-haired fluff with a pot of coffee, hovered near, but Virginia waved her away. "Yes, it's a shame about Johnny," she said. "A shame he was ratted out."

Chandler didn't move, but she sensed his body stiffening. "I asked around," he said. "After. Don't think it was any of the boys around here. But the Chief did some business back in the hills."

Virginia remembered a night not long after she and Johnny moved to Oklahoma City when they went out dancing with some of Johnny's new friends. Champagne, chandeliers, chiffon. It had all seemed so sophisticated. The sense of longing that had haunted Virginia ever since she could remember abated. This was the bigger life she had yearned for. Bigger than Gilead, Oklahoma, bigger than her classroom of students at Honey Springs School.

Become a schoolteacher. That was what young women did when they wanted to strike out on their own. She had tried that. A year at Normal School in Tahlequah and then a classroom of her own. A little one-room school at the end of beyond. It hadn't satisfied. She had been left with a deep sense of something missing that she couldn't satisfy, an urge that led her into Johnny Crow's arms and then into a world of gin parties and the delicious feeling of wickedness.

She had danced with Jack Chandler that long-ago night in Oklahoma City, she remembered. She had been heady with champagne and orchestra music.

What an innocent fool she had been. Virginia pushed her hair back as though she were wiping off memories. "None of that matters now," she said. "Who set Johnny up. It's done, and there's no more to be said. I need help, though, Jack Chandler. I don't know where to turn."

His shoulders relaxed now that he knew she wasn't there to fix blame. "Is it money? I can spare a bit."

His cuffs were frayed, and his shoes needed shining. Virginia could see that he, too, had fallen on hard times.

"Money? Yes, I need money. More than anything, though, I need my child."

Chandler listened politely while Virginia told him about Isabelle and Iona Tweedy. His eyebrows knitted in outrage, and his mouth pulled down in disbelief. However, it was apparent even to Virginia that his mind was on something else.

When she was finished talking, Chandler pulled out his billfold and handed her some bills. "To tide you over," he said.

He pulled at his moustache and said he might have a job for her. "Hear me out," he said. "Jobs are scarce. Most everyone I know has moved on to greener pastures. But I have a little business going, and there's a place in it for you. Just till you get back on your feet, mind you."

"I'm a hard worker," Virginia said. "But my first job is to find my child."

"Just something to keep the wolf away from the door."

His evasion finally awakened her instincts. "What are you thinking?"

Chandler's eyes skated away. "Sometimes there's big meetings here in town: farm equipment salesmen, bankers, lodge men. They're looking for a bit of female companionship while they're here. Easy money."

Just a few months earlier, Virginia would have slapped any man who made such an offer. But that woman—the one who turned away from off-color jokes and pretended not to hear men's catcalls - was a skin Virginia had shed. Instead, she now fought the urge to laugh while she went through the motions of outrage.

"Just because I've been in prison doesn't make me a chippie. I thought you knew me better than that, Jack Chandler." She said it in her schoolteacher voice, the one useful skill she had acquired during her time as a teacher.

"No offense meant," he said. "Business proposition. That's all."

Virginia stood. "I'd best be going." She tucked the wad of bills in her pocket. The money was for Isabelle, she told herself. It didn't make her beholden to Jack Chandler.

Chandler put a hand on her arm. "Wait. I know someone who might could help you."

She was skeptical, but she could not afford to leave any stone unturned. Not if it might lead her to Isabelle.

"Detective name of Ned Bender. Clever man. He does the odd job for me now and again. Good tracker."

Chandler scribbled an address on a scrap of paper and handed it to Virginia. "I'll call him right now. He'll help you."

5

Ned Bender reminded Virginia of a banty rooster her mother used to have. Small and aggressive. "Well, Mr. Sir," her mother would say to the rooster while scattering cracked corn to the flock, "you're feeling mighty prancy this morning."

Bender leaped to his feet when Virginia walked through his office door and threw his shoulders back. Even so, he was half a head shorter than Virginia.

"Come in, come in." He pointed to a chair. "You must be the woman Mr. Chandler spoke of."

Virginia had never been in a private detective's office, and she was disappointed. Ned Bender's agency was a single room above a Chinese restaurant in downtown Oklahoma City. The odor of garlic wafted up from the restaurant. Dusty piles of paper covered the desk. A telephone and a bottle of ink hinted at conversations of import.

Other than the ladder-back chair Virginia sat on and a similar chair that Ned Bender now stood behind, the desk was the only piece of furniture in the room. The windows were fly-specked. A fan in front of one of the two windows stirred the soupy air.

Virginia decided to suspend judgment. Jack Chandler had recommended this man; she had nothing else to hold to.

She saw that Ned Bender was taking her measure, too. His small black eyes snapped, and he smiled at her before pulling a bottle and two glasses from the desk drawer.

"Drink?"

She shook her head, and he shrugged. "My wife said I drink too much, but that was before she ran off with a Bible salesman, so to hell with her." The drawer made a snicking sound when he closed it.

"Can we get down to business?"

Ned Bender made the sound of a laugh - heh, heh - but there wasn't any humor to boost it up to the real thing. He sat at the desk, dipped his pen in the ink jar and held it over a piece of paper.

"Spill," he said to Virginia.

While the fan swished in the background, Virginia told her story, and Ned Bender took an occasional note, asking for the spelling of names and clarifying dates.

Virginia felt grateful. For the first time, someone was interested in her plight. Action was being taken.

"About that drink," she said when she had told him everything she knew about Iona Tweedy, "I think I would like one after all."

Something passed over Ned Bender's face, some kind of satisfaction, and he set his leaky ink pen down and pulled the drawer open.

They drank in silence, with concentration.

Virginia's appetite for whiskey had been building ever since she returned to this city with its memories that crowded every turn. Memories of Johnny Crow and memories of Isabelle. They ambushed her at parks and in stores. They waited on street corners and in city buses. They haunted the hallways and stairs of the rooming house. Virginia told herself that things would be different when she found Isabelle. She would wipe the whiskey off her lips and put the drinking behind her. She would become again the model mother that she had been before the trip with Johnny to Kansas City.

Ned Bender tilted the bottle toward her and Virginia held her glass out for a refill.

Eventually the question of payment came up.

Virginia handed over what was left of the bills Jack Chandler had given her.

Bender's eyes narrowed. "This puts me on your team," he said, "but it won't get the ball out of the park."

"I'm looking for work. I can pay you week by week. You'll see."

"It's not me," he said, smiling thinly. He patted the desk for emphasis. "It's my colleagues. Job like this I have to call in people I know in other cities. Woman skipped town. We have to look other places. They want money up front. Simple really."

Virginia felt the world slipping from under her. "How much?"

Bender looked at the ceiling where the single light bulb hung from a wire. "Oh. Two hundred should get it started."

"Two hundred!"

His eyes trained on her. "You have family don't you? A mother and father and such? A rich uncle maybe? There's not many people can't come up with a couple of centuries."

Virginia's mind cataloged her family one by one. Her father, the solid Finis Watts. Her mother, Araminta. They had died within two weeks of each other the winter before Isabelle was born. Influenza. Fear had kept Virginia from their funeral in order to protect the child who was growing in her belly.

Her brother Charles. He had gone west before his eighteenth birthday, and no one had heard from him since.

And then there was Carolina. Virginia's mind flinched when she thought of her older sister. Carolina had always been difficult. A mama's child, a prig, a spoiled girl who always must have her way.

Maybe Virginia could someday forgive her for that. But she

could never forgive Carolina for what she had done the one time she saw Isabelle. Virginia had taken the six-month-old infant to Gilead by train to visit her parents' graves. She regretted that she hadn't been able to say goodbye. She wanted to show them their granddaughter, even if only their spirits saw.

So Virginia had made the pilgrimage and had been met at the train station by her sister and by her sister's daughter Eva. Eva was a pretty girl, shy and silent. She stayed in the background while the sisters sparred and picked up threads of their family ties.

It was the moment, though, when Virginia offered her baby to Carolina to hold, that could never be taken back or forgiven. Carolina had lifted the blanket off the sleeping Isabelle's face and looked at her tiny dark features and said, "Why, she's a nigger."

It was no secret that Carolina thought Virginia had disgraced the family by marrying a man who was half Cherokee. A breed. And now she had brought this little breed child into the family.

Virginia had believed in her heart that when Carolina saw what a perfect and beautiful baby Isabelle was that she would finally understand. But all Carolina could see was the dark hair and the high cheekbones and the stain of miscegenation.

Virginia snatched Isabelle from Carolina's arms as though her sister's bile might burn through the hand-sewn blanket that swathed Isabelle. Carolina and Eva watched her leave. And she hadn't seen them since.

"Family," Virginia said to Ned Bender. "I don't have any family that can help."

His eyes were calculating. "Property then. Must be something you can sell off."

Yes. There was that. Virginia felt a sudden spark of excitement. The family farm. Her father had told her once—years after Charles disappeared—that she and Carolina would inherit equally. She hadn't thought about it before, but half the farm was hers. And what about her mother's jewelry? The rings had to be worth something. Virginia remembered a brooch with a glittering purple stone surrounded by small diamonds. It was a family heirloom, her mother had told Virginia. She would gladly give up any shiny trinkets to regain her child.

All she had to do was go home and take her share from Carolina. All she had to do was go home to Gilead and claim what was rightfully hers.

The thought weighed her down like a stone.

6

Virginia lost track of the number of days she was on the road. From Oklahoma City through Witcher, Arcadia and Luther in a hay truck. A night spent in a farmer's barn with an old horse for company. Wellston, Warwick and Chandler with a seed salesman in a new Dodge touring sedan. He put his hand on Virginia's leg and then quickly withdrew it when he saw the look in her eyes.

"No harm meant, lady," he said, his eyes darting away. He stopped the car to let her out and gave her a pack of factory-rolled cigarettes.

Virginia walked the seven miles from Chandler to Davenport; the cars and trucks whipped past her on Route 66. She carried a lumpy burlap bag, and her steady pace ate the miles. The late March sun was warm. As she walked, a cloud of red dust rose around her ankles and worked between her toes.

In Davenport, she pumped water at the city park to drink and to wash her face and feet. The trees had leafed out, but they hung dull and listless in the dry heat. The parched grass was thin and scraggly, and no children played on it. A constant wind picked up the dust and dropped it in new places.

Outside town, an Indian driving a Model A gave her a ride. They traveled without speaking across grasslands and past clumps of scrubby oak and blackjack through Stroud, Milfay, Depew, Bristow. The land buckled into small hills. Blossoming redbuds stained the creek banks crimson.

The Indian said he felt bad that he couldn't take her to her destination. A woman shouldn't be alone on the highway, he said. Heyburn, Kellyville, Sapulpa. His family was waiting for him, though. A stomp dance up to Pawhuska.

They crossed the Arkansas River, and the water, dirty with Colorado snowmelt, boiled beneath them.

The tall buildings erected by Tulsa's oil barons scarcely marked Virginia's attention, nor did the vast refineries with their ranks of white tanks and smoke-stained stacks that belched black clouds. The forest of derricks and oil rigs sucked from holes in the earth and spewed their black treasure, and Virginia looked at her large hands clasped in her lap and waited.

The Indian took her out of his way east of Tulsa to Broken Arrow where, he said, she could get a ride with farm folk. He gave her a silver dollar when he dropped her, and she bought a loaf of bread and a can of Vienna sausages at a small grocery. An auction bill posted on the store's wall advertised a farm sale. The headline at the top said, "Forlorn, Dejected and Mortgaged to Beat Hell." Virginia laughed, a short, harsh sound. The proprietor, an old man wearing overalls, frowned at her.

"They're tractorin them out," he said. "Farmers that come here in the first land run. It ain't nothin to make fun about. Soon won't no one be left but the bankers and the buzzards."

Virginia picked up her purchases from the counter. "The beauty of the world has two edges, one of laughter, one of anguish. That's what some woman writer said. From where I stand, it's the same edge."

The man scowled and turned away. "Ain't nothin to make fun about."

The sun was low in the west, and its slanting fingers bathed Virginia's face. She sat on a discarded wooden box beside the grocery and ate the Vienna sausages with her fingers.

A farmer tied his horse to the watering trough next to the store and tipped his hat to her before he entered. The horse nuzzled the water to clear the surface dust then drank deeply.

Virginia dropped the can on the ground and put the leftover bread in the burlap sack with her other few belongings. While she watched the cars and trucks roll by on the highway, she smoked a cigarette. Occasionally an overloaded truck passed by, laden with down-and-out sharecroppers headed west. A small girl with auburn curls rode in the front seat of one car, and Virginia made a small sound as though the air had sucked out of her.

She walked down the road and spent the night in the shelter of a fallen sycamore. Before dawn, the creeping cold roused her, and she stood and brushed the dust off her clothing as best she could before walking east. She kept to the back roads. After the sun came up, the land awakened: a farmer and his mule tilled a dust-dry field. A woman carried a basket of eggs into a shanty. A boy and girl walked to school, clutching lard tins.

The land was poor from lack of rain. Virginia felt a kinship with it, as though she were dry bones walking through a land from which all life had faded.

Just before she reached Oneta, a farm truck stopped and picked her up. She squeezed in the cab beside a young woman holding a baby. The husband was little more than a child himself. He wore a cloth cap pushed back on his head, and his cheeks were smooth. He smiled shyly at her as he put the truck in gear and said, "We can take you far as Coweta."

"Obliged."

They shared cold biscuits and a thermos of coffee with Virginia. The baby cooed and tried to reach the brooch pinned to Virginia's hat. She caught a sudden whiff of wet diapers and spilled milk, and the odor was like a knife that probed at a tender place deep inside her.

They dropped Virginia off east of Coweta, and soon a sheriff's car pulled beside her. The sheriff was a tall, thin man, and he wore a gun strapped to a Sam Browne belt, like a soldier. At first his questions were friendly, but when it became clear that Virginia wasn't a local woman and that she had no money, he turned hostile. "We don't like vagrants here," he said, turning his head and spitting on the ground. "We got enough folks on relief. Can't handle no more." He gave her a ride to the county line just past the confluence of the Verdigris and Arkansas rivers near Fort Gibson. He sat in his car and watched her until she disappeared over the distant hill.

She was beyond caring. The home where she was born was just a few hills away. The Cookson Hills rose in the east, taller and deeper than the country in which she had been traveling.

By dusk, thirsty and footsore, she stood within sight of her destination. Now that she had made it this far, she found that her desire to end the journey had faded to a shadow of the will that had driven her here. On the other side of the valley lay her sister Carolina and her daughter. On the other side of the valley lay a narrow-minded, spiteful woman and a niece she hardly knew.

Virginia stood in the warm dusk on the brim of the hill. The dusty road curled below her across a narrow valley and snaked up the other side. She drew a deep breath.

The fading light sketched the valley below with deep hues: tawny untilled fields, a creek bottom choked with blackhaws and chinkapins. Beside the creek lay a small cemetery lined by a stone wall. Headstones leaned randomly, as though they marked the attitudes in which the dead had fallen.

The ruins of a once-grand mansion stood atop the ridge where Virginia had stopped. Only the thrust of a crumbling chimney remained. The grounds were overgrown with brambles and poison ivy. Grapevines tied the oaks together like twining snakes.

On the distant hilltop stood the farmhouse where Virginia had grown up. Its outline was softened by the fading light. Smoke threaded out the chimney, and giant elms ringed the house like sentries. Behind the house stood a barn, a smokehouse and a windmill. From the direction of the farm, a dog barked, and then silence reclaimed the valley.

Virginia felt as if a huge hand weighed her down and kept her from moving. Her black traveling dress was gray with dust, her stockings torn, her hair greasy under a black cloche. Her open face was empty with fatigue.

"One foot in front of the other," she said aloud. The mail road sunk between fencerows of briars and dusty buglevines. When she came to the stone-walled cemetery at the bottom, Virginia paused, but she didn't pass through the iron gate. The headstones of Virginia's parents stood at the edge of the enclosure, and enough light remained to make out the inscriptions: Araminta Watts, March 1, 1932; Finis Watts, March 18, 1932. The burial ground had a name, the Old Taney Grove Cemetery, but no one tended the graves, and no map marked its location.

The sky deepened above. All around, the woods were dark, and when Virginia came to the low-water bridge across the creek, she remembered her father's long-ago warning: If you're in the woods at night and hear the footsteps of a ghost behind you, try and reach a stream of running water, for if you can cross it, no ghost can follow.

There was no running water. The creek bed was dry. Virginia stopped on the bridge and listened. She remembered summers when they swam in this creek, she and her brother and sister. From deep in the woods came the dark, lonesome call of a whippoorwill, and the dog from the house on the hill barked. Other than those noises, all was silent. She knew that the sudden fear that cloaked her was of her own making, but it was a fear that harked back to her earliest childhood, ever since her father had told her the story of the ghost in the Old Taney Grove Cemetery.

7

Finis Watts had been a storyteller of local renown—storyteller, moonshiner, horsetrader and fiddler—and on cold winter nights after the horses were bedded in their stalls and the supper dishes washed, he would gather his wife and three children and hone his tales.

He began with a ceremonial cleaning of his briarwood pipe. With his pipe tool, he scooped out the old tobacco and tapped the ashes into the stove. Finis Watts' face was as gnarled and lined as the briarwood, and he frowned in concentration while he shook fresh tobacco into the bowl, tamped it down and sucked on the pipestem while holding a match to the bed of tobacco.

The smoke wreathed his shaggy white hair, and he settled back in the rocker, his belly stretching the seams of his overalls.

His speech, when he talked to the neighbors or to a customer, took on the patterns of the hill speech, but when he launched into a story, he suddenly sounded like the pages from a book—more learned and refined than his rough surroundings. It had earned him the nickname of Doc.

On this night, he didn't talk of long ago wars and betrayal in far-off places that no one had heard of, like Peloponnesus. Instead, the subject of his story was as close as the other side of the valley.

"Listen to me, children," he said. "Many years ago, during

the War Between the States, there lived in the house on yonder hill a woman and her two sons. They were of royal blood. The woman's father had been a great chief back in Georgia before the soldiers pushed the Cherokees out and forced them to march in the dead of winter to this land. As you know, many died on that Trail of Tears."

He fixed a fierce eye on his children at this point to make sure they understood the gravity of the tale he was telling. Only Virginia's mother, Araminta, was allowed to occupy herself with other things while a story was being told, and her knitting needles flew and clicked against each other. Carolina, the eldest child, sat with her hands folded, a look of false piety on her face. Charles, the ever-restless middle child, had been chasing an acorn with his toe, but under his father's eye he stilled. Virginia sprawled on the rug in front of the open stove and watched the flames lick the logs. But her ears were tuned to her father's voice.

"The family fared well in this new land," Finis said, "and their livestock multiplied and their crops grew and they built a fine home. After many years, the father died, but the sons were old enough by then that they could take over the work. The two boys were handsome and hard-working, but ever since they were small, they had vied with one another for their mother's affection. The mother favored the older son, and it was no secret that he would inherit the greater part of her fortune.

When the war came to Indian territory, the Cherokees divided into two factions: the Keetoowahs, who fought on the side of the Union, and General Stand Watie's men, the Knights of the Golden Circle, who defended the rights of the secessionists. The two boys, who had never agreed on anything, found themselves on opposite sides in the war. The older son joined the Union Army, even though his mother was loyal to the South. She told him that if he fought with Lincoln's army, he would no longer be her son. He was a proud man and filled with strong convictions, so with a heavy heart, he left his mother's house.

The two boys marched off into battle, and the mother was left alone in her mansion with only her field hands and an elderly house servant to defend her. She was a fearful woman, and when her younger son was wounded and sent home to recover, she was relieved to have him with her.

But she constantly worried about her older son despite her vow to disown him, and when word came that he had been killed in battle, she would not be comforted.

The younger son was secretly glad to hear of his brother's death. Now he had no rival for his mother's affection or for her property.

Months went by, and one day when the younger son was riding his horse across the fields, he was accosted by a man he didn't at first recognize. It was his brother, but he looked years older. His hair was long and tangled, a scar disfigured his face, and his uniform was tattered and dirty.

"I have deserted," the older brother told the younger. "It is not our war, and we should not be fighting it. I want to come home, but I fear what our mother will say."

The younger brother embraced his older brother as though he was overjoyed to see him, but inside he was seething with anger. He told his older brother that he would return that night and together they would decide what to do.

That night, he brought his brother a fine red cloak, for the nights were cold, and he brought him a white horse. "I have fixed it with our mother," he told his older brother. "Here is what you must do. Ride up to the house on your white horse and walk in the front door as though you had never left."

Now in that lawless time, a band of outlaws terrorized the land, and their leader was said to wear a red cloak and ride a white horse. The older brother knew nothing of this for he had been gone long from the land.

The younger man said to his brother that pressing business required that he travel to a nearby town, and he took his leave. He had told his mother the same story, saying nothing of the son she thought was dead, and he had left her in the parlor with a loaded shotgun in her lap, because she feared being alone.

The field hands were in their shacks asleep when the older brother rode up to the mansion on the fine white horse. The sound of the barking dogs drew the mother to the window, and when she saw the stranger dismounting from the white horse, she remembered the stories she had heard about the outlaw band and their leader. She had no time to latch the door because the stranger's boots sounded even now on the porch.

With her heart beating fast, she waited for the door to open. She raised the shotgun to her shoulder as her younger son had taught her. The door opened slowly, and she saw the red cloak. She fired, and the man fell to the floor dead.

When she saw that she had killed her own son, she went mad with grief, and she set the house on fire and died that night with him."

Finis Watts paused for effect.

"The mother's sorrow knows no end," he said. "She walks these woods at night. Sometimes a mist rises from the graveyard down yonder and you can hear her moaning."

The children stirred as if waking from a dream.

"I'm glad I ain't got no brothers," Charles said.

"Don't have any." Araminta's correction was automatic.

"What happened to the bad son?" Carolina asked. She always missed the point.

"I seen her," Virginia said. "The mama. One night I was walking to the outhouse, and I seen her out in the field. She was like a woman-shaped cloud." She had seen something, a lighter smudge in the darkness, and now she was sure it had been the ghost of the grieving woman.

Carolina started crying and ran to her mother. "I ain't going to the outhouse no more at night," she said.

"Father," Araminta said severely, "tell your children it's just a story."

He knitted his fierce eyebrows and looked at her. "I'm many things," he said, "but I'm not a liar." Then he turned and stomped out the back door.

8

The whippoorwill called again, and Virginia stirred. No mist rose from the graveyard, but the ghosts of the past were enough to prickle the hairs on the back of her neck and speed her across the bridge and up the hill.

She slowed again when she came to the farmhouse porch. The old hound checked its bark and came out to greet her, his tail wagging. Absently, she said, "Red, you good old boy," and petted his head.

In her memory, the house hadn't been so worn, but now it seemed to be sinking into the earth. It was built of red oak leveled on flat rocks stuck below a base plate. The planks had warped over the years. Two coonskins stretched on wooden frames hung on the porch.

Through the dusty windows, Virginia tried to see into the parlor and the front bedroom, but the rooms were dark. She glimpsed movement through a doorway that opened to the kitchen.

She went around to the back stoop. Through the door a crack of light shone, and she smelled frying pork.

She took a deep breath to compose herself and opened the door.

"Carolina," she called, stepping into the kitchen. "I've come home."

A girl whirled away from the stove, her eyes wide and startled. She grabbed a knife and held it high.

The girl stopped, still holding her knife at ready, and stared at Virginia.

"Aunt Virginia?"

"Eva? I didn't mean to give you such a start."

"I almost wet my pants." The girl dropped the knife on the table and looked at her aunt. "Some folks knock," she said, suddenly sullen.

"I guess it kinda seems like I still live here," Virginia said. "Where's your mama?"

"I've been tellin folks she's up to the city seein to her sick sister." A pause. "That would be you." Eva sank into a kitchen chair and said dully, "That would be you."

The pork sizzled and popped in the skillet, and Virginia automatically tended to it before turning to Eva.

"What happened? Where's Carolina?"

"She got sick. She got the dropsy and was all swoled up like a circus balloon, and then her heart gave out sudden-like."

"She's dead?" Virginia sank into a kitchen chair. "Your mama's dead?"

"She was doin fine," Eva said. "But awhile back that picture of great-grandma Pyatt fell off the wall. Mama knew what that portends. But she couldn't just leave it on the floor."

Virginia glanced toward the hall that led to the front of the house. The photograph of Grandma Pyatt hung next to the doorway where it had always been. The old woman's expression was severe. She wore a black coat and hat, and she clutched a large purse.

"That's an old wives tale." Virginia's voice was as sharp as a needle. "People don't die because pictures fall or mirrors break, and the Devil doesn't sit a-straddle the rooftop when sassafras pops in the fireplace."

Carolina had been Virginia's last hope. She had swallowed her pride and come home; she had nowhere else to turn. No, the Devil wasn't a-straddle the rooftop; he was in Virginia's chest clenching tighter and tighter until it was hard to know if it was rage or grief that she felt.

Virginia looked at the girl opposite her. Eva had grown up. She must be at least fifteen. Her breasts swelled against the flowered cotton dress, and her face had lost its baby fat. Her blond hair was cut in a stylish Greta Garbo bob like all the young girls were wearing now, and her brown eyes were large and doe-like. There was no innocence in her eyes, though. Now, they looked right through Virginia.

"Mama didn't have no one to turn to since granny and grandpa died. Not you, that's for sure."

"I'm here now," Virginia said.

"Where's my little cousin?"

Virginia ignored the question. Her mind was racing. She would need to see the family lawyer, Ben Whitman. Perhaps he could help her sell the place and raise the money she needed to pay Ned Bender.

And her mother Araminta's jewelry? What had become of the rings and the brooch? Eva's hands were bare, and fresh on the heels of learning about Carolina's death didn't seem like a proper time for Virginia to bring up such things.

The smell of smoking fat filled the air.

"Your supper's burning," Virginia said.

Eva flounced to her feet and slapped the pork into a plate. She cut a piece of bread from a loaf and placed it alongside. Then she sat down and began eating.

"I wasn't expectin company," she said. "There's more side meat in the smokehouse."

Virginia cut a hunk of bread from the loaf on the table and chewed it slowly. The loaf had a blue spot on it. The sight of the molding bread awakened pity in Virginia.

"You've been through a time, kid," she said to Eva. "Losing your mother, then having to take care of the funeral and all that by yourself."

Something flickered at the back of Eva's eyes.

"What?" Virginia said.

Eva frowned as if she was performing a difficult calculation. She swallowed the food that was in her mouth and said carefully, "If they knowed I was alone here, they'd put me in a home."

"What?" Virginia said again. But the idea was slowly taking hold. She just didn't want to see it.

"I ain't goin to no home." Eva held her knife and fork low to her side as though they were weapons. "They ain't locking me away like they done you."

In the sudden silence, the only sound was the popping wood in the cookstove.

"Where is she?" Virginia finally asked. "What did you do with your mama's body?"

Eva didn't answer. She walked out the back door into the darkness. Virginia followed. Eva was looking toward the barn.

"It ain't all that bad," Eva said. "I washed her good then I wrapped her in one of granny's quilts."

Virginia lit her last factory-rolled cigarette. "We have to take care of her," she said. "Folks can't just dig a hole in the orchard and drop people in it anymore. There's laws. We have to report her, and we have to pay the undertaker."

"We, I, ain't got any money."

Now was the time, Virginia thought. The time to bring up the jewelry that was now rightfully hers. "Your grandmother had some trinkets," she said. "I remember she had rings and such." She watched Eva while she talked.

Eva looked down and drew a line in the dry earth with her toe. "They went long ago, before the beasts. We sold granny's jewelry and then we sold the cow and calf. We sold until there wasn't a thing left to sell."

Virginia felt another hope falling away. If what Eva said

was true, then coming home hadn't brought her any closer to finding the money to reclaim her daughter. If anything, it had taken her further away. She felt sick. She was in a place she had vowed to never return, saddled with an orphan niece and not a penny to her name.

"I reckon we're paupers. We'll have to give your mama a county burial."

"She's in the barn," Eva said. "She's in the corn crib so animals can't get at her."

Eva twisted her hair into tendrils, and in the moonlight she was a changeling child, both fairylike and innocently evil.

9

In the end, burying Carolina wasn't difficult.

The name of Finis "Doc" Watts still carried weight in the community. The undertaker remembered him, and he knew how much land the man had owned, and it was on that strength that he let Virginia sign a note saying she would pay him forty dollars.

On a gray April morning, Carolina's body was placed beside those of Araminta and Finis. A slab of flint rock marked the place where she lay, and the wind caught at the newly loosed earth. The small knot of mourners paid their respects and went away.

Burying Carolina was easy; inheriting the property was not.

Ben Whitman, Gilead's only lawyer, explained the problem to Virginia. "When a person don't leave a will," he said, "the courts decide how to divvy it up."

Virginia sat stiffly on the edge of the chair in front of Whitman's desk.

The office was small and dirty. The only decoration on the walls was a yellowed law-school diploma in a cracked frame. Stacks of dusty books and papers covered the flat surfaces, and flies buzzed against the window panes, trying to find a way into the bleak day.

"There's only the two of us," Virginia said. "Eva and me."

Looking in his eyes was like trying to see inside a mirror. His eyes bounced off hers while he maintained a genial smile.

He had once been a candidate for the state legislature, but his opponent's friends had been more powerful. Now he just pushed papers around on his desk and drank too much from the bottle in the bottom drawer.

"It's complicated, Mrs. Crow." Whitman slid a hand through his thin hair and pulled at his suspenders. "You and ... ah ... the deceased are married women, and your husbands have rights, too."

"Haven't you heard? I'm a widow, and Carolina's husband hasn't been seen for more than 10 years."

The lawyer absorbed the information and plowed on.

"And who's going to see to Eva's interests? Are you her guardian?"

Eva's guardian? The girl had no one else. Her grandparents were dead. Her father was a traveling man; Virginia had seen that from the first time Carolina had brought Clayton Wilder home to dinner. Did that mean she was now responsible for Eva? A small piece of her heart warmed as an image flashed by of Eva and Virginia having heart-to-heart talks and choosing a wedding dress when Eva married, as she surely would soon. Yet, an almost-grown girl like Eva couldn't take Isabelle's place.

Virginia felt the walls closing around her, the doors clanging shut. Her voice came out in naked desperation. "I have to sell the place, Mr. Whitman. I need the money."

The lawyer's shuttered eyes blinked. He reminded Virginia of a toad sitting in the sun.

"Even if the courts award you the property, which will take time," he said, "you might not be able to sell it. Folks all over the state are pulling up stakes and moving west. No one's buyin right now. The Dunlap place is one of the finest spreads in these parts. It's been up for sale a year now, and they can't find a buyer. You're better off waiting."

"I can't!"

He looked at her over the top of his glasses. "Al Bucklin down at the hotel is looking for a woman to help out. It'll keep body and soul together. You work there while I look into your situation."

The Monday morning traffic in Gilead was sparse: a farm truck laden with hay chugged around the corner; a horse stood head down in its harness in front of the feed store. Two women, both gray-haired and stout, stared at Virginia from the door of the general store. They had been at Carolina's burial, and afterward one had asked Virginia about her baby and husband. She had turned away as though she didn't hear.

Now she sensed them talking about her. Most everyone knew the story. Parts of it anyway. The scandalous schoolteacher who ran off with the half-breed moonshiner. The jailbird who had returned home without her baby. The black sheep come home to bury her sister.

It wasn't so much that she minded being talked about. But she couldn't bear the thought of pity. Better that they look at her and say, "There's a woman who's been through hell and kept on going with her head held high." She had made so many mistakes, and now it seemed to her that all that was left was the ability to hold her head high. That had to count for something.

The business district was small and drab. The gravel road was filled with potholes. The bank had failed, and someone had broken the windows. Down the street, the weathered sign on the hotel reminded her of the job she would begin the next day.

Virginia didn't see any choice. She was broke. She couldn't just go off and leave an orphaned girl behind while she chased after her own child. She felt trapped. Just until she got back on her feet, she told herself. Just until she figured out what to do next.

The hotel owner had been one of her father's customers. Back in those days, Al Bucklin had purchased a jug of moonshine every week, which he watered down and sold to his guests. She remembered overhearing her father say to her mother, "You can tell when Al Bucklin's lyin. His lips are movin."

Earlier, when she had presented herself at his office door to ask about the job, he sized her up with his gimlet eyes and named the price he would pay her to clean the rooms. Next to nothing. "But we might work a little raise in later," he said. "For services rendered." The way his eyes never wandered above her neck made it obvious what services might be rendered. She told herself that he was a man she could deal with if need be.

On the street, the wind whipped the hem of Virginia's dress and threw sand against her legs. Her legs were bare. The stockings she had worn when she left the prison were torn beyond repair, and she could not afford new.

Even the dress she wore wasn't hers; she had gone through a cedar chest in the front bedroom where she had been sleeping the past few nights—Carolina's former room and before that their parents' room—and found the shapeless black dress. She remembered her mother wearing it to church on Sundays. It was too short to be fashionable, but it would do.

She had dug deeper in the cedar chest, hoping to find some overlooked bit of her mother's jewelry that might be sold. There was none, not even a silver chain - and made a find that tore at her heart: a half-finished baby blanket. It was knit in pale pink yarn, and the ball of yarn and two needles were rolled inside. Araminta must have been knitting it for Isabelle when she fell sick, and someone had tucked the abandoned project in the cedar chest. How had she known to choose pink? Her mother always had a way of knowing these things.

Virginia pulled the blanket out and lay it on the bed. It seemed a sign of some sort, one that fell to her to decipher its meaning.

In the very bottom of the chest, she found an old worsted suit her father had worn. The inside pocket of the suit jacket held a pouch with nearly two dollars in silver. The two discoveries—the unfinished blanket and the money—were a reminder of how quickly the influenza had taken her parents.

The money, though... the money she could put to use. Virginia stood in the street outside the Gilead post office, fingering the coins.

Finally, she went inside. She recognized the young woman at the telephone switchboard. Pearl Whitesides, her name was.

Pearl looked up, and her eyes widened. "Miss Watts... Mrs. Crow!" She blushed. "Why, Mrs. Crow, I didn't expect to see you!"

"How are you Pearl?"

Pearl smiled widely, revealing a large set of teeth the color of tea stains on a tablecloth. "I'm helpin Mrs. Dunham out. When she goes to lunch, I mind the post office, and I can place long-distance calls for folks, too."

"That's why I'm here." Virginia touched the coins again. "To place a call."

Pearl hadn't finished her say, though. "You made me stay in school until I finished the eighth grade, Mrs. Crow, and that's why I come to have this job."

"You were a good student, Pearl. Can you place a call for me now?"

"You were a good teacher, Mrs. Crow. You told us we could do anything we set our minds to."

Virginia's days as a teacher seemed as though they had happened a lifetime ago. She bit her lip. "You do me proud, Pearlie. Now can you place that call for me and give me a little privacy?"

The switchboard telephone at the post office was probably the only phone in town that wasn't on a party line. Virginia remembered times when so many people listened in that some kind of power drain seemed to take place, and the voice on the other end faded in and out like a weak radio signal.

Pearl looked disappointed that she wouldn't be able to hear at least one side of the conversation, but after the connection was made, she yielded the office to Virginia.

The voice on the other end was oily and smooth, like smoke through a hookah. "Ned Bender Personal Investigations."

Virginia gripped the receiver so hard that her nails bit into her palm. "This is Virginia Crow," she said. "Remember I came to your office a few days ago? Do you have any news about Iona Tweedy and the other?" That was the only way she could talk about her daughter right now. "The other."

She felt something sticky and looked at her hand. Blood seeped from her palm onto the hard, black Bakelite. She switched the phone to the other hand and pressed her wounded palm into the hem of her dress.

"Ah, Mrs. Crow. I may have a line on what you're looking for. Little dark-haired girl with an older couple" —the pause was long and meaningful—"but there is the matter of a bill."

"I promise I'll pay you. I've come into some money," she said. "Just tell me."

"No pay, no play," he said. "When I receive your payment, we'll talk." He hung up the phone.

Virginia stumbled out the back door and fell to her knees on the dusty earth behind the post office. Her chest heaved, but no sound came out.

Virginia's job at the Gilead Hotel began at sunrise. The work was mindless drudgery. Hard times had fallen on the place, just like hard times had fallen everywhere. The world was on hard times.

In Virginia's childhood the stately two-story building had always been freshly whitewashed, and in the bright Oklahoma sun, it had shone like angels' robes.

Now the building provided lodging for a handful of old men and the few people who ventured through Gilead on their way to somewhere else. The smoke-stained lobby held sagging leather sofas and chairs, cigar ashes littered the floor, and Matt, the ancient bellhop, wore a soiled uniform.

Virginia began work early each morning before the kitchen opened to sweep up the dining room and to mop the kitchen floor. The sky was dark when she left the house, the morning birds calling from the shadows.

Eva would be sleeping. Virginia had no idea what the girl did during the day. She sometimes had a light meal on the table when Virginia got home in the evening, and she washed the dishes afterward. Beyond that, there was no evidence that Eva ever stirred.

One afternoon, she saw Eva standing in front of the mirror in the parlor. The girl didn't know Virginia was watching, and she preened and pouted in front of the mirror and swept her hair on top of her head and thrust her breasts out like a movie queen.

Virginia had laughed, and Eva whirled, anger flushing her pale face. "Sneak up on a body why don'tcha?" she said. Then she darted into her room and slammed the door.

Instantly, Virginia wanted to take back her laughter, and she headed toward Eva's room to apologize. She stopped at the door, the words stuck in her throat. They weren't the right words, anyway.

The effort of getting Eva to warm up to her seemed like

scaling an insurmountable wall. The wall that separated adults from almost-adults. Eva needed a mother, someone to guide her. Someone with a delicate touch. Virginia saw the need, but it was more than she had to give.

Teenagers were a separate species, Virginia told herself, and drawing on the memories of her own adolescent years didn't help one bit. Rebellion, confusion, angst. What cure other than time was there for such extremes?

Surely mothering a teenager wasn't the sort of thing one could step into midstream. That's why children started out as infants, and as their needs grew, so did the experience and knowledge of their mother.

If Virginia wasn't qualified to take Carolina's place, she told herself, the least she could do was let the girl play her harmless games without making fun. Let Eva have her little Hollywood fantasies.

The closest thing to a movie queen Gilead ever saw came to the hotel the day after Virginia saw Eva vamping in the mirror. The woman wore a cap of platinum blonde hair and a fur coat, which she slung over one shoulder. Her lips were as red as ripe strawberries, and she held a cigarette in a long holder.

The wind, which had been rattling the branches of the sycamores all day, whipped up the tail of her skirt as she stepped out the passenger side of a long Packard. Her legs were white as marble above her silky stockings.

The man with her unloaded three heavy bags. He wore a blue pin-striped suit and a fedora with a snap brim, and he treated the woman with a kind of exasperated deference.

Virginia had been preparing to go home when the woman and man arrived, but the woman complained about the dirty sheets in the room, and Al Bucklin yelled at Virginia to put fresh linens on the beds as though it weren't his policy to change sheets only after they turned gray.

Virginia hung a clean towel next to the washstand and was leaving the room when the woman came in.

"Excuse me, miss," the woman said to her as though she held the rank of age in addition to wealth. "Any place in this burg a lady could get something to drink?"

"I can bring you a bottle," Virginia said.

"I'd be forever grateful. And some ice." The woman handed her some money and then pulled her gloves off one finger at a time. She turned to see Virginia still watching her. "Any time today," she said.

Virginia slept late the next morning, and the couple in the Packard were already gone by the time she showed up for work. Truth be told, she had bought two bottles and kept one. The man and woman had the means to buy plenty more. And, god knew, no one needed a drink more than Virginia.

The stuff was vile, like drinking coal oil. Nothing like the stuff her father had made. Finis Watts had prided himself on his whiskey-making skills. He aged his moonshine in white oak barrels until it turned a rich amber color. It had a reputation for going down like smooth fire.

When she tasted the stuff Al Bucklin was peddling to his customers, she knew exactly where it came from. The shock hit her harder than the sting of the whiskey, and she choked on it. What was it Johnny had said when he first poured her a glass? "Drink about half a pint of this and get bit by a snake, and hell, it'll be dead in thirty minutes."

She had laughed then. It didn't seem so funny now.

It meant Slick and J.P. were back in business somewhere in these hills. She remembered Jack Chandler's words in the Oklahoma City diner: "I don't think it was any of the boys around here. The Chief did some business back in the hills."

And while Johnny's former partners ran free and sold rotgut whiskey to Bucklin, Johnny was dead.

She wondered if the Laws had given them a reward for turning in Johnny.

She tossed back the drink and poured another shot. It wasn't so bad after all. She felt the bite of the whiskey in the back of her throat, and soft warmth suffused her. The chair she was sitting in, an overstuffed relic of the last century, enveloped her in its arms. The threadbare fabric had once sported hunting dogs and horses and white-wigged men in red coats; now it was faded to a shadow.

The walls were fading to shadows, too. Eva hadn't lit the lantern before retreating to her room, and Virginia was drinking by herself in the last of the dusky evening light - holding Isabelle's photo in her lap, as gently as she would have held her sleeping baby. She was thinking about Johnny Crow and his former partners. There wasn't enough whiskey in the world to forget them.

The next day when she showed up late for work and Al Bucklin barked at her, she made a suggestion about what he could do to himself.

Her head felt like it had been crushed between two rocks, and her voice came out soft and squishy, in direct opposition to her words.

"What did you say to me?"

Bucklin was in her face. His little eyes shone with malice.

Virginia needed the job, she needed the job. God, her head hurt.

"I didn't mean anything."

The old men in their chairs on the front porch of the hotel watched the exchange with pleasure. They accepted anything that relieved the monotony, whether it was mating dogs, milk deliveries or hungover employees getting the what for. Usually, nothing happened but morning, noon and night. Their whittling knives stilled, their pipe smoke floated away, they elbowed one another.

Virginia held Bucklin's eyes until he turned and spat. "You're no good," he said. "From stem to gudgeon just like your father."

Later, looking back on it, Virginia wondered if that was the turning point - the point where she began to think that some people should be beyond the protection of the law, beyond the protection, indeed, of society. There were so many places she could point to, though, and say, "That. That was the moment that changed everything."

Later, after the blood, after the money, after the fear, she wondered just when that turning point had come.

That day, she didn't have the advantage of distance. She only knew that she had to find a way to get out of Bucklin's hotel and out of Gilead and back into her own life. Every day seemed to take her farther from Isabelle. Everything she had been through was bearable. Except that. Not that.

While she swept the stairs and filled the coal bucket and hung the laundered sheets, she thought about money.

Money was the only thing that held her here. The lack of money. Others had it. She had to find a way.

Honest labor? What a laugh. Men who were lucky enough to find work toiled from dawn to dark building roads, plowing fields, mining lead and breaking their backs in a hundred ways for a buck or two a day. Women earned less.

If she wanted money, she would have to take it. It made her feel all crawly inside. Virginia had been in prison with thieves and murderers and whores, but she had never considered herself one of them. She had been with the wrong person in the wrong place at the wrong time. She wasn't a bad person, she told herself, but she was for sure a desperate one.

Every day, Isabelle's memories of her mother grew dimmer, and her new life seemed more and more like her real life. Isabelle's mother would be the woman who held her when she cried, who taught her to say her prayers at night. The thought nearly drove Virginia mad. How long did Virginia have before any memory Isabelle held of her real mother was wiped away?

She needed money, and she needed it now. Nevertheless, could she take someone else's money, knowing it made her a thief? Virginia promised herself that if it came to that, she would pay it back when she was able. After she found Isabelle and they started a new life far away, she would stop drinking, and she would pay restitution if owed. Then she wouldn't be a bad person, would she?

In the room where the platinum-haired woman had spent the night, Virginia found a Photoplay magazine that had fallen between the mattress and the wall. She picked it up and studied the cover. An almost life-size photo of Marlene Dietrich stared at her. Long black lashes fringed her big blue eyes. Her skin was milky pale. Except for the color of her eyes, she looked like an older version of Eva.

Bucklin laid claim to anything left behind by the guests. Carrying the magazine, Virginia walked down the stairs to his office. The door was ajar. She had lifted her hand to knock when she remembered she didn't owe Al Bucklin anything.

She turned to leave, but a small rustling stopped her. She peered through the crack in the doorway and saw Bucklin stuff something into a canvas bag. He snapped the clasp shut and placed the bag in his bottom desk drawer. He locked the desk and pocketed the key. Then he looked toward the door with a sudden furtive expression.

Virginia froze, hoping he wouldn't glimpse her through the crack. Her dress was dark and the hallway behind her dimly lit. She must have blended in because after a moment, Bucklin turned away and bent to his ledger book.

Virginia hurried down the hall, the magazine rolled in her hand, her heart thudding. Money. Al Bucklin kept money in his desk drawer.

10

The thought of money—so close, so available—carved a groove in Virginia's brain. No matter where she was or what she was doing, money was at the back of her mind. She had worked out a budget, one based on superstition. Seven was the perfect number, so the Bible said, and she divided her needs accordingly: $200 to pay Ned Bender to find her daughter; $200 for a car; $300 to start a new life far, far away where she and Isabelle could get a fresh start. Seven hundred dollars. That was what she needed.

Sometimes late at night, when Virginia smoked cigarette after cigarette and stared out her bedroom window into the darkness, she knew there were holes in her thoughts. First and foremost: Where would that money come from?

Without a known reason, hope was welling inside her, telling her that all she had to do was bide her time and the answers would come. It was hard to wait, though. It was hard to not get up and walk out the door and set foot on the road to Oklahoma City, walk all the way if necessary, and hunt down Ned Bender and force him to tell her where to find Isabelle.

But where would that leave her? Much better to wait. To come up with the money she knew she needed.

This much was certain. Al Bucklin was buying moonshine from her husband's former partners Slick and J.P., and he was selling it to hotel customers and perhaps to others as well. He was making money that he couldn't entrust to a bank.

She started staying later at the hotel and watching the movements in and out the back door. Some deliveries Al Bucklin took care of himself. Others were accepted by Beulah Stivers, the cook. Bucklin seemed to trust Beulah or at least feel confident that she wouldn't cross him. Sometimes they disappeared together upstairs, and later, when Virginia was cleaning the rooms, she'd come across a rumpled bed in a room that hadn't been rented since the last time she'd cleaned.

Virginia wondered if Bucklin's wife knew what went on at his hotel.

Beulah, wide-hipped and uneducated and older than Virginia, was a superb cook. Her buttermilk biscuits were light and golden, her fried chicken crisp and tender, her pies sweet-pierced and fruity. Sometimes Beulah would wrap up leftovers and put them in a sack for "that poor orphan," as she referred to Eva.

Her husband had gone to California to try his luck in the orchards, and Beulah's seven children were farmed out to various relatives. She seemed resigned to the arrangement, even if it meant getting poked by the rat-faced Al Bucklin.

Every morning Beulah accepted deliveries of ice, milk, butter and eggs. Tuesdays, the grocery order would arrive, and she would sign for it and, with Virginia's help, check the items against the order. Thomas Fallows, the butcher, delivered beef, pork and chicken. On occasion, a fisherman would show up at the back door with freshly caught perch and catfish. If the fish met Beulah's standards, she would draw some money out of a mason jar that she kept in the cupboard and pay the fisherman.

On that particular afternoon, the old men were sitting on the front porch after dinner, smoking their pipes and swatting at flies while they talked in lazy, satisfied voices of men whose basic needs have been met. The wind whipped up a bank of gray thunderheads, and it looked like it might be rain-ing to the north. Gilead hadn't seen a drop of rain for more than a month, and the old men, former farmers all, craned their necks at the sky. When a low growl of thunder raked the air, their talk took on the excitement of children at the end of a school day.

"Potato wagon's rollin across the sky," said Elmer Peters. He aimed a long stream of tobacco juice off the porch.

"I reckon we need rain as much as taters," said his neighbor on the porch, a man whose long white beard had earned him the nickname of The Prophet.

"It ain't gonna rain," said Samuel Moore. He thumped his cane on the wooden floor of the porch. "Them damned radio waves and airplanes is messin up the atmosphere. The Lord's tellin us we overstepped our bounds."

The three men studied the sky again.

Elmer Peters had tried his luck in the oilfields on the border before he gave up and came back to Gilead, broke and in poor health. He had traveled farther from home than the other two men, which gave him a certain stature.

"In '32," he said, "them dust storms out in the panhandle was so bad the streetlights come on in the afternoon. You couldn't see your hand in front of your face. That was before the oilfield give out, and I had me a new car, a pretty little Ford, and I kept it parked beside the house. One night a big wind blew up and blasted it with dust for two days. When the storm lifted, my little car was painted on one side and bare on the other."

"If Elmer ever gets to be a bigger liar," said The Prophet, "he'll pop the buttons on his trousers."

"It's God's own truth," Elmer said hotly. He stood from his cane rocker to teach The Prophet a lesson but at that moment fat drops of rain fell from the sky.

They fell like single bullets and pierced the dry ground. Small showers of dust exploded with each drop, and the men watched hungrily like young cowhands at a peep show.

The rain ended quickly, so quickly that the ground under the trees was still dry.

The expression on the men's faces was stoic.

Virginia was in the kitchen, eating sliced peaches from a can. If sex were a fruit, it would be a ripe peach, she thought. She took another bite and felt the juice trickle down the corner of her mouth.

Al Bucklin and Beulah Stivers were upstairs. After the dinner dishes were washed, Beulah had wiped her hands on a dishtowel, took off her apron and said, "Think I'll take me a little rest." Virginia had heard Bucklin's boots clump up the stairs moments later.

Sometimes Virginia remembered Johnny Crow's touch with an intensity that bordered on pain. The first time she saw him was at a dance on the pavilion overlooking the river at Hyde Park in Muskogee. She had been giddy with the feeling of freedom and daring: a schoolteacher sneaking away to a dance! What would people think? Her lips had been bright with Tangee lipstick, and a new bias-cut rayon dress clung to her body.

Johnny Crow was leaning against the railing, a hand-rolled cigarette dangling from his lips. He wore a fringed cowboy shirt, and his jeans were rolled up to reveal boots with four rows of fancy stitching. Not her type at all. But when he looked at her with his smoky dark eyes, she had gone soft inside.

Virginia lifted the peach can to her lips and drained the liquid. She was suddenly aware of someone watching her.

A man stood outside the back door, staring at her through the kitchen screen. He wore a dark fedora perched at a jaunty angle, and his single-breasted jacket was buttoned, even though the just-passed storm had left oppressive humidity in its wake.

He winked at her and said, "I'd like me some of that."

Virginia jumped to her feet and smoothed her skirt as though she had been caught doing something she shouldn't. The peach can clattered to the floor.

"What do you want?"

He looked amused. "I need to see the boss man." He opened the screen door and came into the kitchen. "Mr. Bucklin." The way he drew the name out made it sound like he and Virginia shared some secret knowledge of Al Bucklin.

"Tell the boss man that Frank Pendleton is here to see him."

Up close, he was a big man, bigger than he had looked through the screen door. Virginia backed away to put the table between them. "Mr. Bucklin is busy right now," she said.

"Are you his secretary? You don't look like a secretary." Pendleton took a pack of cigarettes out of his breast pocket and shook one loose. He offered it to Virginia, but she pretended not to notice. He shrugged, lit the cigarette and inhaled deeply.

"Me and your boss have some business, missy," Pendleton said. "You'd best go find him." He sat down and put his feet up on the table.

Bucklin came through the door just then and saved Virginia from the humiliation of following the man's orders. He had caught her off-balance and kept her that way. Whoever this Frank Pendleton was, she didn't like him.

"Mr. Pendleton!" Bucklin sounded nervous. "I hope Virginia is taking care of you."

"She was fixin to make me a tall glass of lemonade," Pendleton said. His eyes narrowed like a cat's when it has a helpless creature under its claws.

Bucklin was still in a fog from his afternoon recreation, and he didn't notice the game being played. "That's a mighty fine idea," he said. "Virginia, bring us both a glass. We'll be in my office."

He led the way, and Pendleton turned to wink at Virginia

on his way out of the kitchen.

When Pendleton came through the kitchen half an hour later, Beulah had left for the post office. Virginia was at the kitchen table mending a towel, and Pendleton plunked his glass down in front of her. Tear-shaped bits of lemon clung to the sides.

"Obliged," Pendleton said. "When I come back next Wednesday, mebbe you can make me some with sizzle."

She looked away.

"You know what I'm talking about," he said. His voice took on a rough edge and he grabbed her arm. "There could be a little something in it for you."

She wrenched loose. "Keep your hands off me."

He laughed. "You're a regular hell-cat. I'm tellin you we could do some business. You like money?"

She looked toward the hall door, but Bucklin wasn't there. "Who doesn't."

"Find out who your boss buys his 'shine from and where they're making it. I'd ruther deal direct."

"How much?" The first part she knew: Slick and J.P. It had to be them. Where they were making it she could only guess.

"Twenty."

"Hundred," she said firmly.

He looked at her with narrowed eyes. "Your eyes are green with greed," he said. "You best be watchin you don't overreach."

"Bucklin won't like being cut out," she said. "I have that to think on."

Pendleton's lips thinned. "Get the goods by Wednesday, and you'll get your Judas money." He doffed his hat to her before disappearing down the steps.

It wasn't two minutes before Bucklin sidled in the kitchen like a co-conspirator.

"What'd that wisenheimer want with you?" he said.

"Mind your own business" Virginia gathered up the mending and put the sewing box back in the cupboard.

"He was in here flapping his gums an awful long time." Bucklin's eyes were bright and suspicious, and Virginia wondered just how much he had heard.

"He wanted what most men want," she said shortly. "What do you think?"

Bucklin grabbed an apple from the bowl on top of the icebox and headed back down the hall, but Virginia's expression was distant and thoughtful. Men were always breaking the law and bending the rules. It seemed to her that women had a natural talent for deception, and if she was willing to use that talent, perhaps she could find her way back to Isabelle.

It was nearly full dark when she walked down the hill toward the narrow bridge by the Old Taney Grove Cemetery. Virginia had been walking this way for weeks, and she no longer thought about her parents each time she passed their graves. Or about her sister who had been laid beside them such a short time ago. Or the stories her father used to tell. Other things pressed on her mind.

On this night, though, a dry rustle in the bushes at the edge of the cemetery arrested her step. She stopped in the middle of the road. There was no traffic, and the only sound in the night was that of peeper frogs. They made a choir of demons, with their loud and insistent disharmonies.

The air smelled of growing things. It was spring, and the wildflowers were struggling to push through the dry ground. She closed her eyes and smelled dust and the dried herbal perfume of the forest.

When she opened her eyes again, she saw a flash of movement beyond the graveyard. Something white glided away from her through the gray columns of trees. It was long and flowing and shaped like a woman.

Virginia stood transfixed, and something went out of her and reached toward the fleeing figure. Something like pity or understanding.

She wasn't afraid. Whether it was mist or a ghost didn't occur to her. She stepped off the road and pushed through the brush, following the figure. It shimmered ahead of her, threading through the trees along the creek bottom. A deer trail paralleled the creek, and Virginia rushed along it, wanting to get closer. She wanted to touch the white mist, to inhale it, to take something from it, she wasn't sure what.

Her pursuit was silent, as though the apparition might disappear if she spoke. Ahead of her, the shape spread, and its wispy threads tangled among the branches of the sycamores that lined the creek.

The brush along the trail tore at Virginia's clothing. The air seemed colder, and she had a sudden memory of the long days in the jail cell during the cold winter just past.

Virginia had never ventured this far up the creek before, not even when she was a child, and in the dark silence, it could have been another country she had entered.

The ground was rocky and uneven. A thorn swiped her face, and she felt blood trickle down her cheek. She stopped and realized then that she was panting.

The luminescence dimmed, and by the time Virginia took a few hesitant steps toward the specter, it had disappeared all together.

She went to the place where the white mist had vanished, and she tried to summon it back. But the night refused to yield its secrets.

"I saw you," Virginia said. "You were here."

Her sign.

11

The spring flowers bloomed with reckless urgency, sending up stalks of yellow, purple and pink a month ahead of their usual schedule. Give us a kiss, Eva thought to the harsh blue sky. Just a little kiss of rain. The daffodils had bloomed in February, only to be struck down by a vicious late freeze. They were followed by tulips and iris. In April, the delicate pink blossoms of wild rose spread their perfume along the fencerows. Eva talked to the sky as she talked to all living things, but she spoke quietly, as though she might wake something that was best left alone.

Eva knew the names of the wildflowers. Her mother had made her memorize them like the books in the Bible: blue-eyed Mary, spiderwort, butterfly weed, shooting star, rose vervain, Queen Anne's lace.

She didn't miss her mother, but she missed the walks they used to share. They would go out behind the smokehouse into the mysterious dim forest and make a game of finding and naming the flowers. Her mother leaned on a cane and carried a little book that told all kinds of things about the forest. She said it was a gift from the daddy Eva had never known. Eva could remember a time when her mother seemed young and slim and pretty, but age had overtaken her, and in the faded housedress that she wore day after day, she looked like one of the Russian peasant women Eva had seen in a March of Time newsreel at the Ritz in Muskogee. Like she carried the weight of the world on her humped-over back.

Once Eva found an orchid in the forest. She didn't know what it was, but she knew she'd never seen anything like it. A fairy flower, its delicate pink mouth hung open and a trio of leaves made star points around it. "Aren't you a pretty," she said to it before calling her mother over to look. Her mother said, "It's a rare gift, girl. Make a wish."

Eva's wish was always the same—that she would escape from this country backwater—escape to a place where people never slept, where she could go to the moving pictures anytime day or night and watch the bigger-than-life figures having bigger-than-life adventures on the screen, escape to a place where you could walk down the street and always hear the sounds of music and laughter. She closed her eyes and wished her familiar wish. Somewhere in the dim woods, a rain crow sounded, and its lonesome cry raised the hair on Eva's neck.

She didn't miss her mother but she missed the rain. When she was small, the rain fell freely and the thunder rumbled, and the rivers and streams overflowed, and the little pool around the spring filled and a rivulet flowed out of it and watercress grew in the cool water. Her mother said she shouldn't eat the cress because the cows drank from the pool, but she loved the tangy flavor. It was like biting into a spring evening.

Some nights she would lie in bed and pretend the sound the wind made through the trees was rain. Eva craved the rolling thunder and torrential rains and lashing lightning bolts. She wanted the sky to come to her. She wanted the sound of thunder to shake the house. She wanted to lie under her quilts while a storm raged outside, leaving her untouched and safe.

She didn't miss her mother. But she missed the certainty with which her mother approached every situation. Right or wrong, Carolina always knew which was which, and that can be a comfort and a thorn to a young woman.

There was no other security. Her aunt had come home like the prodigal son, but there was no forgiving father to kill the fatted calf. And what if he had been here instead of six feet under the red earth down in the Old Taney Grove Cemetery? The woman had lost her husband and the little cousin Eva had seen only once, as though she'd gone to the grocery for cigarettes and forgot to come back. What kind of welcome should she expect?

Her aunt wandered in and out of Eva's life like a ghost. In the three weeks since Virginia Crow had appeared at the kitchen door, she had offered no advice or guidance. She set off to work at that rat-bag hotel before dawn every day except Sunday, and she came home at dusk. She didn't talk; she just sat at the kitchen table and ate the food Eva had prepared with a kind of automatic, machine-like precision. Scoop, chew, swallow, scoop, chew, swallow.

Then she'd go to her room and smoke and fix herself a drink from the bottle she kept hid under the bed—oh, don't think Eva didn't know about that—and stare out the window into the dark as though she were waiting for something.

Eva didn't miss her mother, and she didn't miss the livestock, either.

Except for a few chickens, the farm animals had been sold or butchered. First the spotted milk cow and calf, then the two hogs and finally the horse. She missed the horse, especially in the mornings when she trudged across the dusty fields to Connie Yates's house.

They had a Model T once, but her mother sold it for $85 after the food was gone. Eva still had fifteen of the dollars. She kept them hidden in a tobacco can in the barn. Every once in awhile she would take out the bills, as soft and worn as old linen, and count them. Someday she would take that money and she and Connie Yates would leave this place. They had plans.

Connie Yates was small and compact, and he carried himself with a wrestler's slight swagger, arms swinging in front of him when he walked. His shock of blond hair had a cowlick, just like a little boy, but he knew how to take care of himself.

What first drew Eva to him were the deep, bruised shadows under his eyes, as though untold sorrows haunted him.

He worked afternoons and evenings at Pecky Johnson's garage, pumping gas, repairing tires, tinkering with motors. Mornings he would sleep until Eva came through his kitchen door and fixed him breakfast. He lived in a gray shack a half mile south of Gilead. It slumped beside the dirt road as though it might topple into the ditch. The interior was just as drab. Connie's clothing fell on the floor where he took it off. Cobwebs traced droopy highways along the ceiling and behind the stovepipe. Grime coated the curves and flats of the worn furniture.

After the coffee boiled and the bacon sizzled on the stove, Eva would say, "Breakfast, Connie," and he would groan and roll out of bed, scratch his head, pull on some britches, go out back to do his business, and slowly feel the day separate from the dreams that formed his sleep.

After he had finished his second cup of coffee and smoked the day's first cigarette, then, and only then, was Eva allowed to put a record on the phonograph: Jelly Roll Morton's Red Hot Peppers or Bennie Moten's Kansas City Orchestra. She would dance, her skirt flying above her white knees while she twirled around and kicked her legs high. Connie sat and smoked and watched her.

Eva had never known anyone with a phonograph. Connie had driven his brand new Ford to Tulsa and picked it out of a showroom there. The salesman had talked him into buying the two records, too, telling Connie they were all the rage back

East.

They certainly were the rage with Eva. She played them over and over, and when she tired of dancing, she sat by the phonograph and read the Photoplay magazine with Marlene Dietrich on the cover as though it were some kind of holy scripture. The gift of the magazine had softened her briefly toward Virginia. But Virginia had fallen back into sleepwalking, and the chance for rapport passed.

While Eva read, Connie would clean his guns. His house was sinking into the dirt around it, yet Connie polished and shined his guns. His phonograph, his car, his guns, they fell into a category of their own. They were Connie's treasures that he guarded jealousy, tended to endlessly and watched with tender pride.

He liked to drop hints to Eva about how he'd earned money to buy his car and phonograph—half-told stories about bootlegging and highway robbery. He'd stop midstream and say, "But I ain't s'posed to talk about that." Eva wasn't sure how much to believe, but the car and the music and the guns spoke for themselves.

The handgun was a Smith and Wesson 1917 Army double-action revolver. It had belonged to Connie's father, his one souvenir of the Great War. Connie would polish the brush finish on the barrel and the smooth walnut stock; snap out the three-cartridge, half-moon clip and rub the revolver with a soft cloth. Eva asked him once if she could fire the gun, but he laughed and said, "Ixnay. I wouldn't trust no woman with a gun in her hand. The temptation might be too much to bear."

His other weapon was a shotgun, a Winchester 12-gauge auto-loading shotgun. One day, when Connie was tired of her begging, he handed it to Eva and she nearly dropped it.

"Jesus!" he said. "You trying to kill one of us?"

"I didn't know it weighed a ton."

"Leave it be."

Every so often Eva would hold up a page of her magazine for Connie to look at. "Would you like my hair fixed like that?" she would ask, pointing to the full-page picture of Claudette Colbert.

Connie would like her hair any way she wanted to fix it. His body craved hers, and she knew it.

Sometimes she read articles to him. No matter that the magazine was three years old and in the few days it had been in her possession, she had read it through almost as often as she had played Connie's records.

"Thirty Husbands Taught Her How to Love!" Eva would say in a breathless, starry voice. "Why American Men Make the Best Lovers!"

"Gimme that." Connie grabbed the magazine and thumbed through the pages, his eyes devouring the pictures of thinly clad starlets. He couldn't read the words. That didn't matter, though, when there were so many pictures to look at. "Do this look for me." He pointed to a photo of Loretta Young, with her arms behind her head, her breasts thrust forward and pushing against the tight fabric of her wrap.

Eva gave him her demon child look, drew a deep breath to get in character and did Loretta Young for him.

Connie smiled, his lazy eyes half-closed, and he motioned her closer. "You're a knockout, baby," he said, and he pulled her down onto the bed.

Their ritual didn't vary in substance, only in details. And it always ended the same way. "Connie, you got to take me away from here," Eva would say. "I can't stand it no more."

"Sure. We'll find the bright lights, baby." Connie leaned back and stretched and lit another cigarette. "We just need us a little nest egg first."

His vague assurances weren't enough. It was April, and the

restless perfume of spring was in the air. All nature was on the move, and its primitive impulses stirred Eva, too. She felt it in her heart and in her groin. It was a teasing, rushing pain.

"How's that gonna happen when all you do is lay around and work in that two-bit garage? Don't you love me?" A whine crept into her voice. To ease its effect, she ran her hand up Connie's thigh.

"We just need us a little nest egg," he repeated. "We'll keep our eyes open. Something will come along."

"Things don't just come along. You have to help them." Eva slanted her eyes up toward him. "Do you believe in prayer, Connie?"

"Well. Sure."

"All the trouble and hardships my mama had come from prayer," Eva said. "And all the trouble and hardships my aunt Virginia had come from whisky. That don't leave much in between. I don't know what to believe anymore."

"I'll pray for us then. That we get our nest egg."

"Pray we get it real soon."

He hesitated, and then said, "My aunt Beulah. She works at the hotel with your aunt. She says her boss keeps a sack of money hid away there."

Eva jumped to her feet. "We could be like Bonnie and Clyde. We could take that money."

"They got shot down like dogs."

"Not us. You're gonna teach me how to shoot that big old gun of yours."

Later, when it was time for Connie to go to work, he dropped her off at her house, and she moped through the long afternoon until it was time to fix dinner. Connie would have let her move into his house, but she wasn't ready for that. She wanted to be sure he was the one who would help get her out of this place first. It wouldn't do her any good to jump out of the frying pan only to land in the fire.

Connie was a secret Eva kept from her aunt more out of habit than fear of disapproval. Virginia Crow was a woman who had been around. Eva didn't expect her aunt thought much about her or how she spent her time.

Yet, she had learned that secrets had their uses.

12

A car. The morning after Virginia followed the ghost or whatever it was, she awoke with that one thought in mind. Without transportation, she couldn't find where Slick and J.P. were making their moonshine. It wasn't the kind of thing you could go around asking folks. She needed a car in order to earn that $100 from Frank Pendleton. She made a mental list of the people who might help her. The list had one name, and when Virginia thought his name, it astonished her she hadn't thought it before.

Bill Davis.

Bill Davis had been her father's closest friend. It had been years since Virginia had seen him, but she had no doubt that he would do anything in his power to help his old friend's daughter. If she could find him.

She didn't go to work that day. Instead, she walked a mile to the crossroads and caught a ride with a farmer to Fort Gibson. There, she bought a ticket with her hard-earned pay and boarded the Midland Valley to Fort Smith.

The train rolled past fallow fields and dry creek beds. Virginia clutched her bag, which held a lunch of leftover biscuits and bacon, and a handful of dried apples she had taken from the hotel. After awhile, she relaxed into the soothing motion of the train and watched out the window through half-closed eyes.

The April morning was warm, and the air was hazy from

the black rollers to the west that day after day gouged topsoil from the Oklahoma and Texas panhandles. The horizon faded into the dry land, brown on brown. The branches of the black oaks and hickories hung limp from the drought and the wind.

In Fort Smith, Virginia stood on the wooden platform at the station, getting her bearings. She was suffused with a sudden feeling of freedom and hope that she was taking a step toward reuniting with Isabelle.

If she could get a car, if she could find where Slick and J.P. brewed their whiskey, if she could make some money off Frank Pendleton. Then she might be able to pay Ned Bender to tell her where to find Isabelle. If, if, if.

All those "ifs" made a hard knot in her belly. Every "if" was a siphon that could suck away success. The thought of cutting out Al Bucklin didn't bother her. What he had said about her father being no good made him unredeemable as far as Virginia was concerned. Maybe Finis Watts hadn't lived by the law books, but he'd had his own code of honor that was stricter than anything set down on paper.

A preacher in black paced up and down the platform. He was tall and lean, and his eyes seemed lit by an interior fire. "This know also," he shouted to the passersby and to a small knot of farm folk who had stopped to listen, "that in the last days perilous times shall come. Second Timothy, chapter 3, verse 1."

Virginia stepped around him, but his voice followed her.

"Brothers and sisters, we're living in the final hours, and Jesus is coming to call the faithful home. But before that blessed day, we shall be tested by Satan, and there shall be pestilence and famine. Blessed are ye who walk in his light, but woe to the sinners and blasphemers and all manner of Godless who shun the truth of His Word."

The preacher's hysterical voice faded, and Virginia cut through the railroad yards and past ice plants to Garrison Avenue. The traffic was heavy with Saturday morning bustle. Horse-drawn wagons and shiny automobiles clogged the avenue. The sidewalks were crowded, and Virginia threaded her way through the shoppers to Townley Grocery.

She remembered past trips to this city with her father. Back then, trolley cars had plowed the main street like brightly colored circus wagons. She had been young; Fort Smith had seemed like a big city, and Townley Grocery was a treasure trove of sweet delicacies and magical potions.

It was the closest grocery to the Oklahoma line and thus popular with the Indians who walked or rode across the free bridge once a week to shop. Bill Davis wasn't an Indian, but his wife, Maisie, was, and it was here that Virginia and her father had once come to find him so long ago.

What was it Finis Watts had said about Bill Davis? "He's got mountain sense. He could put out hell with a bucket of water."

Bill Davis had lived with the Watts family one winter, back before he got married. During the short days, Finis and Bill Davis would disappear in the woods behind the hog shed. Araminta told the children that they had a little sawmill set up and that it was too dangerous for younguns to be around, but Charles whispered to Virginia that he had crept up close one day and seen the smoke rolling out of a hole in the ground. "What's that mean?" Virginia had asked. "They're brewin moonshine," Charles said, "but you better keep your trap shut or we'll both catch a whippin."

When Bill Davis wasn't out in the woods, he parked by the stove with his big boots propped against it, smoking a hand-rolled and whittling little animal figures out of pine. He made up names for the children. Virginia was "Sister," Charles was "Big'en" and Carolina was "Puff."

One night Finis put on his storyteller voice and told how Bill Davis had grown up cowboying in western Oklahoma and made some money on the rodeo circuit as a bulldogger. Once, he said, he had seen Bill Davis win a bet by bulldogging a panther and hauling it into the rodeo arena across his saddle. "You should have seen the old boys skedaddle when he set it loose," Finis said. "That was a sight for the ages."

Bill Davis just sat back in his chair by the stove and smiled an enigmatic smile.

Mountain sense? Whatever he had, Virginia needed some right now.

Virginia pushed through the screen door into the grocery. The store was narrow and deep and dim and crowded with shoppers. A barrel of hard candy stood by the counter where the cash register stood. The center of the store was piled with kegs of nails, white blocks of stock salt and bolts of fabric. The general store in Gilead had been getting emptier as the hard times rolled on. This one, though, was a sultan's palace. In the front display window hung a bunch of bananas, as large as an upside-down Christmas tree, and above the butcher's counter draped necklaces of fat sausages. The shelves along the wall were stacked with canned goods and bins full of beans and peas. The sharp perfume of cloves and kerosene spiced the air.

Virginia pulled a grape Nehi out of the pop cooler and took it to the cash register to pay. When the girl gave her a nickel in change, Virginia asked her if she knew Bill Davis.

"I can't call him to mind," she said. "Mebbe Mr. Addison can help you." She used her head to point to the back of the store, where a white-aproned man wielded a meat cleaver.

The apron was blood-stained and torn, but the man wore it with dignity. When Virginia told him who she was looking for, he worked his cigar to the corner of his mouth. "Bill Davis. I ain't seen him in a coon's age. His wife, now she comes in once a month or so with them two little boys, but I ain't seen her of late."

He turned away to help a customer, but Virginia reached across the counter and grabbed his sleeve. "Please, mister, it's real important."

He looked at her hand on his sleeve, and she let go.

"Ask his brother. You can usually find him down to the train depot preachin at any fool who'll stop and lissen."

Virginia remembered walking past the preacher earlier. She didn't want to talk to him. He reminded her of a long parade of past preachers: the holiness preacher who'd come to her jail cell and called her a fallen woman; an endless chain of hellfire and damnation revivalists who used to hold one-week camp meetings in the summers in a field outside Gilead when she was a child. The message was always the same: Mankind had fallen from the grace of God, and punishment would be swift and sure. Maybe they were right, but Virginia felt that the truth was more complicated. That maybe mankind was stumbling around blind, doing its best to get from one day to the next. Why should anyone be punished for that? If God was going to fault men for the failings He had built into them, maybe He wasn't the master architect after all.

And those preachers had plenty of failings of their own. After one of the summer camp meeting services, the preacher, a big man with slicked back black hair, had tried to convince Virginia that she was in need of personal counseling. He had stroked her arm, bare in its summer dress, and she saw the sweat break out on his face and felt the trembling in his fingers.

And the man who had come to her jail cell had reeked of cheap whiskey. How could these lost souls offer her guidance?

She was thinking of these things while she retraced her steps to the train station. The man was still on the platform, shouting out his messages.

"Brothers and sisters," he said, "there's some that say there's no Sunday west of St. Louis and no God west of Fort Smith."

Other than Virginia and the preacher, the depot was almost deserted. A black man leaned on a broom, and a young couple sat on a bench near the ticket window, clutching their bags around them.

The preacher strode up and down the platform, his lanky figure leaning forward as if heading into a wind. He fixed his attention on the boy and girl. "But where can God be found in this land? When our own government tells its farmers to lay aside 20 percent of wheat lands, plow up every third row of corn and shoot every tenth dairy cow, where is God then? 'I will recompense their iniquity and their sin double; because they have defiled my land, they have filled mine inheritance with the carcasses of their detestable and abominable things.' Jeremiah 16:18."

The girl's eyes widened, and the boy moved as though to shield her.

Virginia stepped between the couple and the preacher. "Mister," she said. "I need to talk to you. I heard you're the brother of Bill Davis."

The light seemed to go out of the man's eyes, and he stood a minute as though he was a windup toy that had run down. Then he walked to the end of the platform, hurried down the wooden steps and disappeared around the end of the building. Virginia stood a moment and then followed.

She rounded the corner just in time to see him turn down a narrow alley. The buildings were tall and empty, with windows broken and weeds growing against the walls. The light was dim in the alley in the afternoon sun, and Virginia didn't see him. The preacher reached out a long arm from the shadows and jerked her close.

"They sent a woman to do a man's job. That's the way of it now." His hands were rough and strong. Her arms hurt where his fingers dug into her, but she didn't struggle. She had learned in the prison not to struggle. Some lessons stuck with you.

"Mister, I'm a friend of your brother's. I need to find him." She kept her voice low and level.

He pushed her away, and she fell to the ground. A jagged chunk of glass pierced her hand. She huddled against the rough wall, holding her hand to her mouth.

The preacher paced back and forth, much like he had on the depot platform, but this time his message was more personal.

"In '33, they tractored out our neighbor. Clive Griffith was a good man, a hard worker, and he had eight children and another on the way. But that didn't stop the bankers. They foreclosed on his loan and gave him 24 hours to get off the land he was born on. He went in front of the judge and the judge said son it's the law and he couldn't find no help. Clive Griffith wasn't the first good man the banker and the judge had done that way. Some rob a man with a six gun, some with a fountain pen. That's what they say.

"William, he couldn't take it no more. Him and some of the others got together and they went to the judge's house that night and they pulled him out of bed and put a blindfold on him. They took him out to the courtyard and they threw a rope over a big cottonwood branch.

"Some of the men had bandannas over their faces and one of them said judge do you swear you won't sign no more mortgage foreclosures and he said I won't swear no such thing. Three times they asked it and they put the noose around his neck and still he wouldn't swear.

"They kicked him and they ground dirt into his clothes and they told him to get down on his knees and pray. But they weren't killers, they was just farmers and family men and they wanted to keep their homes. They finally left the judge laying on the ground under the cottonwood tree.

"He named William as one of his attackers and they swore

out a warrant and the bankers posted a reward. I reckon that's what you're after."

He fixed his terrible eyes on Virginia and said. "William is a good man. He has a heart as soft as butter. That was his downfall. I pray every night for the Lord to bring him back into His fold."

Virginia rose to her feet. "I need to find him. It's nothing to do with any reward."

"He's a will-o'-the-wisp. I never know from one hour to the next when I'll see him."

He looked away from Virginia when he said the last, and she felt a small ember of hope. Lying didn't come easy to the preacher. "If you see him or if you see Maisie, would you tell them that the daughter of Finis Watts needs his help? Tell him Sister was asking after him."

"Finis Watts, eh? I heard the Lord called that old horse trader home."

"Just tell Bill Davis for me. Please." She turned away and hurried back toward the platform.

Her train wasn't due for another hour, and she wrapped her bloody hand in a handkerchief and wandered along Garrison Avenue, searching the faces of the shoppers for those of Maisie and Bill Davis. She looked in the shop windows at dresses she couldn't afford and watched the stylish families parade up and down the street, the children dripping flavored ices and the fathers smoking long cigars while the mothers kept them bunched with the efficiency of a good cow pony. She tried to think of the children as another species. Small fuzzy animals that trailed at the heels of their owners or ran wild in packs. Nothing to do with her and Isabelle.

13

When Eva thought about her grandfather, she remembered the smell of his Briggs pipe tobacco. He would fish the drawstring bag out of the pocket of his bib overalls and spill tobacco into his pipe bowl. The aroma was exotic to Eva, as if it had floated in from Timbuktu, wherever that was. Somewhere near the ends of the earth. Then he would tamp it down, strike a kitchen match against his thumbnail and draw gently on the pipe until smoke threaded out the bowl. The match flared with sulfur when lit, and those two odors, sulfur and tobacco, were linked forever in Eva's mind with Finis Watts.

He was a man who disliked solitude, and when his running buddies were unavailable, he would take Eva with him on his rounds. The first time, she was eight years old. Her mother and grandmother were canning apples and they didn't want Eva underfoot, so they made Finis take her. He didn't mind and Eva didn't mind, and it worked out well.

Finis had deliveries to make. "You're ridin shotgun," Finis told Eva. "Like on an old West stagecoach. Your job is to watch out for the bandits." She felt a thrill deep inside that he would entrust her such an exciting job. The hound dog jumped in the Model T first, and Eva crowded in beside him, jabbing him a bit with her elbow to shove him over. The dog filled the space with a deep, musky aroma, as though he carried the odor of the forest.

Finis made her lift her feet to make room for a wooden

box filled with gallon jugs of moonshine. Eva had never tasted any, she knew it was for grownups, but she wondered if it tasted like lemonade, and if it did, why she couldn't have any.

Eva watched for bandits while as they drove up and down the red dirt roads, roads that were sometimes no more than wagon tracks. They stopped now and then at a farmer's barn or a country store and once at a flour mill, and Finis made her stay in the truck while he conducted his business. The jugs disappeared one by one.

Finis told Eva stories about the people he did business with. There was old Mrs. Witherspoon, who needed a jug each month to take the edge off her rheumatism and the Lessleys, whose cousin was a notorious bank robber. "I know Mamie Floyd," Finis said, pulling on his pipe while he drove the car with one hand. "She puts too much stock in that boy of hers. Charles Arthur Floyd's no killer, but he's sure as shootin a thief."

Eva stayed in the car like Finis told her to and she tried not to act bored, or she'd have to go home and work in the kitchen with her mother and grandmother. One day, though, the deliveries stretched out. Something unusual was happening, and Finis talked at length to the men at each stop. Then he drove to the flour mill in a murderous silence.

The mill was deep in the country along a clear-running stream, and other than the mill-owner's house and outbuildings, no other habitations were visible.

"You stay here," Finis told Eva when he parked the car out front. He didn't have to tell her to stay put. She had been doing that for months now, and it stirred her curiosity that he would say it. Then he pulled out a crowbar from under the driver's seat and took long steps across the bare yard and into the mill.

After a few minutes, Eva slipped out of the car and pushed the dog back inside. Red whined, but she left him there, and she crept up alongside the rough wooden wall of the mill and peered in a window.

The window was dirty, the light inside dim. Eva could just make out the machinery, caked in gray wheat dust, and the wooden tables piled high with sacks of flour. The mill owner was on his knees and Finis towered over him, holding the crowbar up like the sword of God. Eva couldn't hear what the man said, but she heard her grandfather's voice. "I warned you before about poaching on my territory."

"I'm sorry, Doc. Don't…"

Finis smashed the bar across his arm, and the man's words were cut off with a scream. Eva thought she heard the bone snap. At that moment, the car horn honked, a silly little toot that made Eva jump. The mill owner writhed on the floor, hugging his arm, and Finis turned toward the door. Eva ran back to the car and was sitting beside the dog when Finis came outside.

She couldn't bear the look on his face. It was fierce and black, as though he had reached down into hell and pulled something out. So when Finis opened the driver's door and said in a cold voice, "Who honked that horn?" Eva was looking at the floor.

"Red did it, grandpa," she said. The dog wagged his tail, happy to see his master.

The old man's face softened, and he shoved the crowbar back under the seat. "He used to do that when I took too long. That was before I had you riding shotgun. He'd honk the horn for me if he thought I took too long conductin my business."

He started the car, and they took off down the road. After awhile, Finis whistled a tune that Eva had heard him play on the fiddle.

She had that feeling now, of trailing along after her grandfather. Connie Yates led the way. They were at the back of the Gilead Hotel, and Connie wore his father's Smith and Wesson revolver strapped around his waist and carried the 12-gauge with both hands. He looked like a dangerous man.

"I could love you right this minute," Eva said. "You're my desperado."

"There'll be time for that later," Connie said, frowning. "I gotta keep my eye on the prize." He hitched his pants up because the heavy revolver made them sag.

He hadn't wanted her along, of course, but she had pouted and cried, and finally he said she could be lookout while he went into Al Bucklin's office where his aunt Beulah said the old man kept his money.

Before he went through the back door, he pulled a bandanna over his face, and Eva giggled, because he looked like one of the old-time train robbers in a movie. Then he clapped a Stetson on his head and went through the door.

My own Jesse James, thought Eva. My own Clyde Barrow.

What they were doing didn't seem real to Eva. It was a scene from a movie, and she was the female lead. A screwball comedy, perhaps, with Jean Harlow. In the end, everyone would be happy, and the woman would discover that she had a rich uncle or something.

The building seemed deserted: Al Bucklin and Beulah were upstairs, and the old men were on the front porch, where they spent most of their days. Matt the bellhop was at the front desk, polishing the dark walnut panels as though the dust wouldn't settle right back down on it.

Connie stuck his head back out the door. "There ain't no one here," he whispered. "Come on in the kitchen and keep a lookout."

If anyone came in, Eva was supposed to say she was looking for her aunt. She was to say it in a loud voice so Connie could hear her back in the office and get the hell out. All Eva knew was Virginia had disappeared early that morning, and she hadn't gone to work. It was as though she knew something was up and she didn't want to be in the middle of it. That woman was smart like a fox.

The windows were closed, and in the kitchen it was quiet and solemn. A basket of apples stood on the counter, and a blackberry cobbler cooled above the water reservoir on the cookstove.

Connie signaled to Eva to stay put, and he cautiously peered down the hallway. Seeing no one, he hefted his shotgun, scooted into Al Bucklin's office and pulled the door shut.

The office was cramped and dark, but Connie was afraid to turn on the electric light. He laid the shotgun on top of the big desk and started going through the drawers. Then he came to the locked drawer.

"That goddamned coonsucker," he said. "Summabitch."

He pulled out his Old Timer pocketknife and tried to pick the lock. When that didn't work, he used his knife to splinter out the wood around the lock. It took longer than he wanted, and he kept looking over his shoulder and listening for footsteps.

The hotel dwelled in a church-like calm.

On the front porch, Samuel Moore slept, his head lolling back like a rag doll's, and his wispy white beard fluttering in the breeze. Elmer Peters was telling the Prophet about a run-in he'd had with some hot oil runners at Seminole. "When Governor Murray shut down production in '31," he said, "some of them old boys was so mad they couldn't see straight. They took to hauling oil on the sly like it was black moonshine or somethin. I was some kind of innocent going into that town, a reg'lar Pilgrim's Progress, just looking for any kind of work to keep my belly from sayin' howdy to my backbone.

"I tell you now, that town was wide open." Peters looked

over at the Prophet to see if he needed to spice up his story to hold his interest. The Prophet's eyes were following the figure of Banker Jensen's wife as she left the general store and headed down the street toward her home. Probably spending some of that money the banker had socked away before he declared his bank bust, the Prophet thought.

"There was a part of town they called Bishop's Alley," Peters said, "and any time, night or day, there was pickpockets and dope peddlers and floozies on the street."

The Prophet tore his eyes away from the woman and looked at Peters.

At that moment, from inside the hotel, a shotgun exploded.

Connie had come close to pulling out the locked drawer. He thought about his aunt's tales of a bag of money in the desk and how easy she said it would be to walk in and take the money. "That lying bitch. I'll kill her," he said, and he gave the drawer pull a vicious yank. The shotgun clattered to the floor and went off, turning a chunk of baseboard into splinters.

Overhead, feet hit the floor, and Connie heard someone start down the stairs.

Connie was rooted in place, and when Eva ran through the door, he was standing by the desk with the drawer pull in his hand. The drawer was still in the desk.

"We gotta git," Eva said. Her face was flushed, and she grabbed his arm and yanked him forward. Then she saw the shotgun on the floor. She leaned over and scooped it up, and together the two ran out of the room and down the hallway. Eva burst through the kitchen and out the back door, but something compelled Connie to stop in the kitchen and look around.

"I ain't leaving without nothin," he muttered, and he grabbed the blackberry cobbler from the stove.

At that moment, the Prophet and Elmer Peters popped

through the door into the kitchen, and behind them, Al Bucklin was yelling for Beulah to call the sheriff'.

Connie drew his revolver and fired wildly. The bullet shattered a crock of buttermilk and showered the men with the tangy white fluid.

Connie hurled the cobbler toward them and ran out the back door.

The Prophet licked blackberry cobbler off his hand and said, "Now that was a waste of good pie."

Connie had parked the Ford in the alley behind the True Followers of Christ the Redeemer Church, where a hedge of Osage orange hid it. By the time he reached the car, Eva was already inside, holding the shotgun at ready as though she knew how to use it.

Connie jumped in the driver's side and started the car. He tore the bandanna off his face and shoved the revolver toward Eva.

"Take care of this." His voice was tight with strain.

"What on God's green earth was all that?" She grabbed the gun and laid it on the seat beside her.

He didn't look at her. "Shut up. Just shut up."

"How come the shotgun to go off?"

Connie eased the Ford into the street. His hands were shaking. He had broken the law before, but he had never come face-to-face with the consequences. He thought he might be sick.

Connie pointed the car in the direction of his house. When Eva twisted around to look back, she could see Al Bucklin running down the middle of the road. His shirt tail was flapping in the breeze, and he hadn't put on a hat.

"You can't go to your house," Eva said. "If they got a good look at you, they'll be coming for you."

"We were kinda countin on that money—which we ain't got—to be our ticket out of here," Connie said. "We don't have hardly enough gas to make the county line; they'll pick us up on a vag charge." He wanted to cry and he wanted to choke his aunt who had made it all sound so easy to get that bag of money out of Al Bucklin's desk.

"Did they see you?" Eva thought of the $15 she had socked away in the tobacco can in the barn. It wouldn't get them far.

"Them two old men who live there, they got a look at me, but my face was covered."

"I heard your gun go off, Connie. Did you kill someone?" Eva placed the shotgun on the floorboard and picked up the revolver as though it were a sacrament. Her eyes were huge.

"I didn't kill no one. I didn't even hit them old boys," he said. "I just wanted to keep 'em off me."

By now they were in the country, and Al Bucklin's running figure had disappeared. Connie still drove as though pursued, though, and the car bumped over the ruts in the road and spewed out a cloud of dust.

"Slow down, Connie Yates!" Eva's voice was commanding, and Connie naturally obeyed as though she were his mother. "There's no need to panic. I'll get word to your boss that you're sick, and you lay low for awhile till we know if they're looking for you."

"Lay low. And just wait for 'em to come put me in jail?"

Eva spoke slowly, working out the details just ahead of her words. "We'll put the car in the barn at my place. You can hide there, too. Up in the hayloft. It's plenty comfortable there, and I'll bring you blankets and see you get fed. If no one's looking for you, then you can just go on home in a day or two with no one the wiser. If they are looking for you, then we'll have to deal with it."

"Hide out at your place. Your aunt won't like that."

"She's got her own problems. She'll never know."

14

The two men boarded the train at Muldrow and took the seat in front of Virginia. She had been half asleep, lulled by the rhythmic clacking of the wheels on the rails. She opened her eyes briefly. Laws. She could tell a lawman from his back. From the set of his shoulders, from the look of his neck, as thick and straight as a hickory log. She closed her eyes again, but she stayed alert.

The men sat in silence until Wild Horse Mountain came into view south of Sallisaw. To the north, Brushy Mountain and the Cookson Hills rose above the river valley. The train rattled along the rails between the hills, and one of the men said, "I ever tell you I was out there at the Akins Cemetery the day they buried Pretty Boy?"

The other man grunted. "That musta been some kind of a circus."

"They flocked in like buzzards after a gut wagon. Some of 'em camped in the graveyard the night before. Grannies and little kids and moms and pops with their picnic baskets, sitting on the gravestones eating fried chicken. It was hot for October. Women fainted, men got drunk and started fights. We had two dozen special guards, but it wasn't even enough to deal with the traffic. What's the world comin to when they honor a bank robber thataway?"

Virginia opened her eyes and looked out the window. Akins was just a few miles to the north, but the thick growth of black jack oak and hickory shielded the view of the town where Pretty Boy Floyd was buried. She closed her eyes again and pretended to sleep.

"He wasn't even a good bank robber. Never wore a disguise. Never thought about how to get away. Just went in the bank and announced his intentions."

"Not like Harvey Bailey," the other man agreed. "Now he figured out how to run them cat roads. That's what they call 'em. Cat roads. Roads so narrow and twisty only a wildcat can run 'em at night. Spent days before a job measuring distances and figuring out his escape routes.

"They caught up with him though. He was shipped off to that new island prison. Alcatraz. He ain't gonna waltz away from that one."

The words washed over Virginia. While the Laws talked of burials and prisons, she deciphered the code. Banks. Disguises. Cat roads.

An idea was germinating in her head, an idea so reckless and daring that she tried to shut it out. It found a little corner, though, where it wasn't disturbed, and the idea began growing.

All it took to rob a bank was determination and planning. Most robbers she had heard about, including Pretty Boy Floyd, had plenty of guts, but they didn't play it smart. Maybe if they had, they'd still be alive. And rich. If she was ever going to raise the money to find her Isabelle and start their new life, maybe she had found an answer.

Robbing banks wasn't right. She knew that. But the legal doors had closed. All she knew about right was that she had a right to her own child. Whatever it took.

When the train pulled into Fort Gibson, it was late afternoon. Virginia caught a ride in a Model T whose top had been sawed in half to make a flat bed behind the cab. It jostled over the bumps in the dusty road, and in the front rode the farmer, his wife and baby, and an ancient, crone-like woman who seemed to be the matriarch of the clan. Virginia shared the space on the flat bed with three barefooted boys. They crowded together to make room and peeked shy smiles at her.

The wind had picked up and the sun disappeared behind a bank of black clouds to the west. "Reckon it'll come a black roller?" said the older of the boys, looking at the clouds.

The two younger boys said nothing, and they all looked at Virginia as though she might know what the sky was going to do.

"Reckon," she said, and then she turned away from them and stared at the drought-ravaged landscape. It wasn't the thin grass or the droopy-leafed oak trees on the barren hillsides she studied. She kept hearing the voices of the two men on the train. She was coming home with a brand-new plan.

Banks. Disguises. Cat roads.

15

"Tell me what it's like to live in the city," Eva said.

She sat at the kitchen table with her chin in her hands and she looked at Virginia as though she were watching for pearls to fall from her lips.

Virginia pushed aside her half-consumed plate of beans and biscuits and lit a cigarette. She didn't know what to make of Eva. The girl had been fluttering with suppressed energy ever since Virginia had returned from Fort Smith. She was usually so sullen that they could go for days without exchanging a dozen words.

Virginia looked at her niece, who was looking out the window again. She'd taken a position in the kitchen where she could see any passing car, and every so often, she would lift the curtain back and look out into the darkening night.

"It's nothing special to live in the city," Virginia said. "Just more people closer together. That's all."

"But there's theaters and music and shops," Eva said. "I want to go to Hollywood and see them movie stars in their big cars and their fancy clothes." One hand crept toward the curtain again, but she made it fall back in her lap. Her heart-shaped face was tight, and her lower lip was red from her biting it.

"What is wrong with you? You've been fussing all evening. If your mama was here she'd give you a dose of castor oil."

"I got to get out of this dump," Eva said. "I just can't hardly stand it."

"What would you do in the city? How would you get by?"

"There's plenty of work for an enterprising girl."

Virginia's voice was harsh with exhaustion. "Sure. You could sell waltzes at a dancehall for twenty-five cents. The manager would let you keep a dime. When you got tired of that, you'd find there's more money to be made in the brothels."

Eva's face flushed. "Stop it. You're just sour on it because it didn't work out for you. I'd not make the same mistakes. If I had a husband and baby, I wouldn't let them take me away to jail and come home with nothin!"

Virginia slapped her. "You just be quiet about my baby," she said.

Eva put her hand to her cheek and sat at the table. "I didn't mean nothin by it."

They sat in uneasy silence, and after a minute, they heard a car motor. Eva looked out the window again and said, "It's the Laws. They're comin."

Virginia went to the window and stood behind her niece. "What are they doing here?"

"I don't know."

"You're a liar."

"I tell you I don't know."

The car, a black Plymouth, drove around back of the house and parked by the well. Two men, one tall and lanky, and the other short and round, emerged.

"I know that man," Virginia said. "The tall one. I didn't know he was a copper."

She was talking to herself. Eva had disappeared.

The two men walked around the house and knocked on the front door. The old hound stalked out on stiff legs to sniff them, and then he returned to his place under the porch.

Virginia removed her apron and smoothed the front of her dress. Her heart was pounding, and she racked her brain for any hint of what the law might want with her. Had she done anything wrong? She didn't think so. Not yet, anyway. Could they have news of Isabelle? Hardly likely. She was grasping at straws. She told herself she had nothing to fear, but as she opened the door, her face was clammy.

The two men looked at Virginia and removed their hats. The wind, which had picked up its tempo since sunset, ruffled the tall man's hair. The short man didn't have any hair to ruffle.

"I'm Sheriff Ray Callahan," the tall man said. "This is my deputy, Cletus Baker. We need to ask a few questions, Mrs. Crow."

"Your mama doesn't cut your hair anymore, Ray," Virginia said. "Looks better."

Callahan self-consciously ran his fingers through his hair. He and his four brothers, Roland, Russell, Robert and one whose name she couldn't remember other than that it began with an R, had been objects of mirth back when they went to school with Virginia and Carolina and Charles. The Callahan's mother would put a bowl over their heads and cut off anything that stuck out underneath. Even though his hair had looked funny, Virginia remembered having a crush on him when he was in high school. Ray Callahan was smart, and she could tell he was going somewhere. Now he was the county sheriff. Maybe that's what happened when you spent your childhood with other children poking fun at you.

Virginia stepped aside and led them into the parlor. They stood awkwardly in the middle of the floor until Virginia sat down and waved them into chairs. The two men chose ladder-back chairs, and they perched stiffly on the edges. Virginia took out a cigarette, and Callahan stood as though to light it for her, but she coolly struck a match and held it to the tip of the cigarette. It was a coolness she didn't feel inside. Inside, it felt like brewing disaster.

"What can I do for you boys?"

"There was a strong-arm robbery at the hotel today," Callahan said, "and you didn't show up for work."

Virginia tried to hide her surprise. "So?"

"Looks a mite suspicious."

"It's my right to take a day off work. If Al Bucklin doesn't like it, he can find another woman to sweep up after him."

"You have a history," the deputy said.

Virginia's eyes narrowed, and she blew out a slow stream of smoke.

Even though the deputy was short and round and bald, he had a sharp edge to him. "You were a schoolteacher," he said. "Went to the Normal School up at Tahlequah and came back to teach near here at the Honey Springs School. Then you met Johnny Crow, and you threw it all away on a common criminal."

While Callahan stood by, the deputy's voice continued, sonorous and measured, like a judge handing down sentence. "You married Johnny Crow and moved to Oklahoma City, where he engaged in various criminal activities. September 1933 you were with your husband in Kansas City. He was running a load of moonshine and weapons. When the cops stopped your husband, he opened fire and shot one of them. You fled, but the cops picked you up the next day. The cop your husband shot died, and the state hanged Johnny Crow. When you were released from jail, you returned to Oklahoma City to pick up your daughter, but she had disappeared."

"My life is none of your business," Virginia said. She felt like something was squeezing her until she could hardly breathe.

"You came back here, and next thing we hear, you're burying your sister."

"It's the same old copper trick," Virginia said. "You're supposed to make me mad, and then I'll say something that tips you off. Or maybe I'm supposed to cry. It won't work this time because I don't even know what you're talking about. I wasn't at the hotel today, and this is the first I heard about any robbery."

The two men exchanged glances. "There's a girl lives here, too," Callahan said. "Your niece? Where's she?"

Virginia hesitated. Eva's edginess suddenly made sense. The girl knew something. "She's sick in bed. I've been nursing her today."

"We need to talk to her."

"She's sick, I tell you. She finally went to sleep just before you came. I won't have you bothering her while she's poorly."

Callahan uncrossed his long legs and leaned toward her. "Do you know a boy named Connie Yates?"

"No."

"Does your niece know him?"

"When she feels better, I'll ask."

"Do you keep a gun in the house?"

Virginia drew a deep breath. "My father's shotgun."

"Has it been fired recently?"

Virginia stood up and headed toward her bedroom. "That's for you experts to say."

With every word, with every movement, she thought, they were violating her. Throwing out pieces of her life to be examined like unwashed garments. Sure, they were acting as respectful as an undertaker at a wake, but behind the polite mask, they were toting their figures, measuring the body. If she had been under the illusion that she would be treated as an ordinary human being after her release from prison, those thoughts were now laid to rest. Her one place of safety - the house where she had been born - was not a sanctuary. They could come whenever they pleased and reduce her to nothing.

Callahan followed her to the bedroom and stood in the doorway while she opened the cedar chest. She kept her movements deliberate and slow. "It's in here," she said, backing away from the chest. No need to touch the gun and have some half-cocked Laws shoot her.

"What happened to your hand?" The sheriff took her hand and inspected the bloody bandage Virginia had applied after Bill Davis' brother had pushed her onto the broken glass.

She snatched her hand away. "I was peeling potatoes. Anyway, it's none of your business."

Callahan turned away. He seemed suddenly awkward in the bedroom, as though he was embarrassed by what he was doing. In the dim light, the room looked worn and tawdry - the paper peeling on the wall, spider webs in the corners, the iron bed carelessly made and Virginia's nightgown tossed over the quilt.

He removed Finis Watts's neatly folded second-best suit from the trunk and lifted out the gun and sniffed it. Then he replaced the gun and the suit and closed the lid of the cedar chest.

"Thank you," he said.

"I'd say you're welcome, but you're not."

"Unsettled times," Callahan said.

Their eyes briefly met.

Anger surged through Virginia, and she stepped so close he was forced to look at her. "It will never be over," she said. "No matter what I do for the rest of my life, I will be branded as the schoolteacher who made a poor choice in a husband and went to jail and lost her baby. Just another cheap tale in a women's confession magazine."

"It ain't like that," the sheriff said. He looked like he wanted it to be true.

But they both knew it wasn't.

After the two men left, Virginia went to her room and poured herself a drink. Then she went in search of her niece.

Eva lay in her bed in the dark.

"Are you awake?"

She rolled over and murmured something.

"The Laws said the hotel was robbed today," Virginia said. "They were asking after a boy by the name of Connie Yates."

From the bed, silence.

"Do you know him?" Virginia had a sudden flashback to similar times with her mother when Virginia was a teenager. The accusing questions, the sullen silence, it all had an uneasy familiarity. Even the light from the hallway silhouetting her in the doorway. It had all been done before.

"I know who he is," Eva said. "It's hard not to know who everyone is in this little burg."

"The Laws seem to think you might know him in a special way."

Eva sat up in bed and looked at her aunt. "I heard you tell them I was sick in bed. That was smart thinking. Thank you."

Virginia could tell she wasn't going to get more out of her niece. For tonight, she'd have to settle for gratitude. "You're welcome," she said, closing the door.

Back in her own room, Virginia placed her parents' belongings back in the cedar chest. On top, she laid the half-finished baby blanket she had found the first time she went through the chest. Isabelle's blanket.

She buried her face in the soft yarn, and then she laid the blanket in her lap and studied it. A simple garter stitch. Her mother, Araminta, had taught her how to knit. She had the sudden thought to complete the blanket for the day when she found Isabelle. She closed the lid of the chest and set the unfinished blanket on top. She could never give up hope. The absence of hope would mean the absence of life.

16

That night, Virginia dreamed of Isabelle. The branches of the elm tree, pushed by the wind, made a scratching sound against the wall of the house, and the sound incorporated itself into her dream as the old dog scratching at the door to get in the house. Except the dog was young, and his coat was shining and lustrous.

A man stood behind her with his hands on her shoulders, laughing at the pleading dog. "Let him in," he said. She turned and saw the sheriff, Ray Callahan, and then they were on the bed, and she felt the heat rising in her, but a child was crying in the other room, and Virginia pushed herself away from the man and ran down a maze of dark halls and the child's cries never seemed any closer. She recognized the voice though. Isabelle was nearby, and her heart raced with a wild joy.

Finally, when she thought she couldn't stand it anymore, she burst through a door. On the other side, Isabelle lay in a crib. She was waking from a nap, and Virginia leaned over her, smelling her sweet baby odor. She brushed back the damp curls from Isabelle's forehead and picked her up. She wanted to feel her little girl's arms around her neck, but Isabelle began crying in terror and struggling to escape the stranger who held her.

Her mother. The stranger.

Virginia awoke in the dark room, her face wet with tears.

A shadow moved in the darkness. "Are you sick?" Eva's voice

was disembodied in the night. "You were making a noise."

"She didn't know me." Virginia was still half in the dream, and she felt a terrible weight pressing down on her.

"Who?" Eva's hand cupped her forehead as though checking for a fever.

"Go away. Just go away." Virginia half-fell out of the bed and pushed Eva from the room. She closed the door and then with shaking fingers lit a cigarette. The tears kept welling from her eyes as though a river of grief had escaped the dam, and there was no stopping them.

She sat on the edge of the bed and stared sightlessly through the fluttering curtains into the night. At one time, the thought came to her, must our lives be measured in losses?

The wind blew with an evil vengeance. Ever since the gray and pallid sunset, its fury had grown, and it whistled around the corners of the house and through the cracks in the walls. The air was warm and dense—tornado weather —but there was no moisture in it. The wind pushed dust ahead of it, and she remembered a dust storm in Oklahoma City just after Isabelle was born. Johnny had hung damp sheets over the windows to keep out the worst of the dust, but from the room above them, they could hear old Mrs. Thompson coughing through the night. The three of them, Virginia and Johnny and Isabelle, clung together on the bed like survivors on a lifeboat while the wind howled a refrain of rage and shook the building.

They had made it through that night. But now it seemed that the storm had been warning of disasters yet to unfold.

Morning finally came. Virginia sat on the edge of bed, Isabelle's picture in her hand. The edges were getting worn and dirty, and Virginia thought she should wrap it in cellophane.

In the photo, Isabelle's eyes held a mischievous glint, hint-ing at her headstrong personality. "That girl knows what she wants," Johnny used to say. And it was true. Isabelle learned to grasp objects early on, younger than most babies, Virginia thought, and whenever she was offered anything, a soda cracker, a toy, she would snatch it with greedy hands as though the offer might be rescinded. Virginia's hand unconsciously strayed toward her ear, where Isabelle had once grabbed an earring and nearly tore off Virginia's lobe.

Grit had settled on Virginia's face. Her eyes were bloodshot and raw. She put away the photo and waited.

When Virginia had asked Eva about Connie Yates the night before, the girl had avoided her question. If Virginia had learned anything from her days as a teacher, it was to recognize when a child was lying.

The wind hadn't let up, and in the gray light of morning, the dust in the air formed a filmy curtain that obscured the world like a painting that has hung in a smoky hall. Through the veil of dust, she saw Eva leave the house and lean into the wind. She held something close to her body under an old coat, and she carried it into the barn.

Virginia followed. Outside, the wind blasted her with dust. It was a hungry, angry beast, picking up bites of the earth and flinging it at everything in its path. Virginia ran across the yard and into the shelter of the barn. She slipped through the side door that opened into the corn crib, the secure room where Eva had stowed her mother's body.

It was calm inside the solid barn, but the wind battered the old building and made the rafters creak and groan like a ship's timbers in a storm at sea.

She opened the door that led from the corn crib to the wide passage where her father used to keep the wagon and later, the Model T. Virginia expected the space to be empty, but another vehicle stood in the old car's place.

Her eyes widened. She recognized the model, a nice little

two-door Ford, but she was sure she had never seen it before. When was the last time she had been in the barn? A week or so ago when she had caught one of the hens for Eva to cook? The remaining hens - all nine of them - were perched in a row on a rafter above the car, sad and drooping and unwilling to go out and scratch for bugs in the midst of a windstorm.

She heard voices on the other side of the car.

"I'm goin back to that hotel, and I'm goin to shoot the lock right off of that old man's desk this time. When I get that money, I'll be long gone." The aggrieved voice was male. Virginia edged around the car to get a view, but the speaker was inside one of the horse stalls.

Eva's voice, sarcastic: "That'll be the day." And then conciliatory, as though she was humoring a child: "You'd best just eat these biscuits and bacon and settle in for the day. You don't want to drive your car in this dust storm anyways. It'll do somethin bad to the motor."

The voices went on in a softer hum, but Virginia had turned her attention to the car and was no longer listening. She gently opened the passenger door and slid in. The interior smelled of tobacco and motor oil, but it was clean.

She pulled some papers out of the glove box and studied them, and as she was replacing them, felt a flat flask in the back of the compartment. She uncorked it and sniffed.

Virginia Crow smiled. She knew that smell. Recognized the sharp odor of J.P. and Slick's brew. Suddenly, the boy on the other side of the stall, who had been a problem to solve, was an asset. He might lead her to J.P. and Slick.

She put the flask in her pocket, stepped out of the Ford and went around the back of it and entered the stall.

Connie and Eva sat side by side, their backs against the wall, and when Virginia rounded the corner, they both jumped.

Connie grabbed his revolver and pointed it at Virginia. His hands shook.

"Connie Yates, don't you point that thing at me," Virginia said in her official teacher's voice.

Connie's hand fell to his side, but he held onto the gun.

"I don't know you," he said.

"We're fixin to get acquainted," Virginia said.

Eva had slid away from Connie. She remained on the floor and watched Virginia.

"You're a little hotel-robbing punk," Virginia said, "but you take good care of your car. Work at a garage, don't you? Thought you could make some money by breaking into Al Bucklin's office. Where'd you get that idea? You must be one of Beulah Stivers' passel of relations. But the most interesting thing about you is this." She pulled the flask out of her pocket and held it high in the dim light. "I know who makes this poison, and if you buy it direct from them, from Slick and J.P., then maybe we don't have to let Sheriff Ray Callahan know you're hiding in the barn like a common criminal."

"Jeeze. Where'd you promote all that?" Connie looked at Eva. "I thought you were gonna keep your trap shut."

Eva shrugged, elaborately innocent. "She didn't hear it from me. I didn't know the half of it."

Virginia directed her attention at Connie. "The moonshine. Where'd you come by it?"

Connie's blond cowlick was standing straight up, and a piece of hay stuck out of it. "There's a couple of old boys out east of the Verdigris River Bridge. Back in the hills there. I bought it from them."

"Did you get introduced?"

"What you called them before. Slick and J.P."

Virginia smiled. "Well, Connie Yates, you're in business with me now. I need me a driver." She saluted Connie with the flask and took a sip.

The wind died at dusk and left behind a fine sifting of gray inside the house. Even behind the cupboard doors, the plates and cups had collected a coat of dust and had to be wiped before they could eat. Connie had been allowed in the house, where he would sleep on a pallet in the front room. It was agreed that he and Virginia would take his car and leave at first light to go to the place where Slick and J.P. brewed their moonshine.

Over a dinner of chicken and dumplings, Connie opened up. "J.P.'s my cousin on my mother's side," he confided. "He's older'n me, but we always did get on."

Eva flounced around the kitchen like a little girl whose play pretties had been put on a shelf beyond her reach.

"You're driving me to distraction," Virginia finally told her. "Be still for a minute."

Eva's eyes slanted and her hands clenched. "Be still so you and Connie can hatch your plans? I notice I ain't being brought in. If it wasn't for me yesterday ..." Her mouth suddenly snapped shut, and she thrust a load of plates into soapy dishwater.

Virginia went out to the front porch and sat and smoked, and the old dog came out from under the porch and sat beside her and thumped his tail. She absently patted his head while two voices inside the house rose and fell in anger.

"Young love," she said to the dog. "Ha."

First thing after breakfast, Virginia and Connie drove west on the county road toward Muskogee. Eva, sulking in her room, didn't put in an appearance.

Even though it was early, the air was warm and humid. The oak trees that covered the steep-sided hills were fully leafed out, and their greenery created a false sense of flourishing nature. However, the bushes along the fencerows were frosted with dust, and the colorful flags of the wildflowers faded. The cows in the fields grazed the scanty grass with a sort of desperation, the scaffold of their ribs showing.

They stopped at a Conoco in Muskogee and used the last of Virginia's money to buy gas and cigarettes. A stack of newspapers lay by the door, and she read the headlines. "Exodus From Western Part of Oklahoma Underway as Crops Hopelessly Lost" and "Worst Dust Storm Comes on Heels of Prayer for Rain." She laughed at the second one, a short, humorless bark. A new agnostic is born, she thought.

Connie heard Virginia laugh and looked at her. His eyes were eager for approval, like those of the hound who lived under the porch.

They crossed the Arkansas River at Muskogee. The water lay far below them, a cinnamon-colored, sluggish stream. A flock of crows pecked at the rocks along the water's edge, and their black coats glistened in the morning sun.

A few miles farther on, the road rose into the hills. It grew twisty and cratered with potholes. Connie gripped the wheel tightly with both hands and guided the little car up and down the hills. They saw no other travelers. The only animals were scrawny goats, with brown-spotted hides, who had worn paths across the barren sides of the steep hills.

They had passed the last farmhouse a mile back when Connie turned onto a single-track lane. The way was paved with leaf debris.

"What's this?" Virginia said.

"Logging trail."

The two had hardly exchanged ten words since they left the house, and now their conversation had the rhythm of code.

"Not for bootleggers."

"You'll see."

The trail wound steeply up the hill, and branches overhung the road, forming a leafy tunnel. The tips reached out and brushed the doors.

Connie finally pulled the car into a thick growth of cedars and shut off the engine.

"Follow me," he said.

Virginia shadowed him along a wild animal trail until they came to a rocky overlook. Connie signaled her to drop down, and together they inched to the edge of the bluff. She tried not to think about ticks and chiggers and other biting things.

Below them, half-hidden in the trees, stood a ramshackle cabin. Smoke feathered from the stone chimney. Behind the cabin, stood an equally decrepit barn. There were no signs of life outside the buildings, but a pickup was parked near the door.

Connie grunted and led the way back to the car.

"What was that about?"

Connie flexed his long arms and popped his knuckles. "I ain't goin down there unless they're home. That J.P. don't trust no one. When they're not there to guard the place, he's got the place booby trapped a hundred different ways."

"Well, can you tie that? You're a sneaky sort to know the lay of the land like you do."

"My daddy didn't raise no fools." Connie rode the clutch and let the car coast back down the hill.

Once they got back on the county road, the twists and turns took a good while to get them to the rough road leading to the cabin. A distance from the house, Connie stopped the car and honked the horn.

A man came out on the porch with a rifle held loosely in his hands. His suspenders were down and his feet bare. A week's growth of beard grayed his chin.

"Slick," Virginia said.

Connie glanced at her. "These are rough honyockers," he

said. "Want I should talk to him?"

"Stay here," Virginia said. She stepped out of the car and started for the porch. She marched with strength and purpose, like a war widow in an Armistice Day parade. She pushed away the fear and reminded herself of her purpose. For Isabelle. Those two words gave her strength.

At the sound of the car door opening, Slick had lifted his rifle, but when he saw it was a woman who walked toward him, he lowered it again and snapped his suspenders over his shoulders.

When Virginia drew closer, his face lightened in recognition, and he forced a smile. He didn't look happy to see her.

"Why, Mrs. Crow," he said.

"Slick."

"You do us right proud to come all this way."

"Where's J.P.?"

Virginia heard a rustle in the bushes at the side of the house, and Slick's eyes strayed toward it.

She casually moved to the other side of Slick so his body was between her and the hidden man.

"How is Johnny?" The strain was evident in Slick's voice. He peered at the car and beyond as though a whole tommygun-toting gang might be creeping up on the house.

"Haven't you heard? They hanged him. You cost me my husband and eighteen months of my life." Virginia would have added, "and one stolen child," but she didn't trust her voice.

"They had us dead to rights," Slick said. He sounded more confident; the moment had passed when she might have signaled someone to cut him down.

"There's always choices, Slick. You made yours."

"I didn't mean for no one to get hurt. It was just bidness."

They were engaged in a complicated dance, each trying to appear natural as they maneuvered to keep the other between them and a real or imagined foe.

Virginia finally had enough. "Come on out, J.P.," she said. "We have business to discuss."

J.P. emerged from the bushes, wearing a shamed-face smile. He was attractive in a dirty, unshaven sort of way. Tall and thin, he walked with a simian grace similar to Connie's.

"Howdy, Mrs. Crow," he said. He jutted his chin toward the car. "Who all you got with you?"

Virginia signaled to Connie to join them.

When J.P. recognized his cousin, he said something under his breath, but he reached out his hand to shake Connie's.

"Let's get down to business," Virginia said.

17

On Wednesday, Virginia and Connie parked the car in the alley behind the True Followers of Christ the Redeemer Church where Connie and Eva had parked a few days earlier. Virginia peered through the hedge of Osage orange to get a view of the back of the hotel. When Frank Pendleton showed up, she planned to stop him before he went inside. Connie's instructions were to leave when Pendleton came and to wait on the rocky bluff above Slick and J.P.'s cabin. With the way the dust billowed up on the back roads behind cars like looming thunderheads, Connie would be spotted if he tried to follow. It was best to be there first.

Connie was to keep watch on the bluff in case something went wrong. Virginia didn't have much faith he would be effective, and she had taken his guns and ammunition and secured them in her room because she didn't want to become an accidental target. Even so, it was comforting to have some kind of backup.

The idea of being at the end of beyond with a rough crowd like Pendleton and the two moonshiners tied Virginia's insides up in knots, but she had to see it through. She had come to believe that it was the best way to raise the money to pay Ned Bender to tell her where to find Isabelle. The thought of her daughter gave her courage. She could do this for Isabelle.

The temperature was dropping, and a sharp wind suspired through the Osage orange and whipped up old leaves and paper scraps. Virginia shivered in her thin cotton dress.

By the time she saw an unfamiliar car drive behind the hotel, she was cold to the point where the pain was abstract, pushed deep into a corner of her mind. Virginia waited until she was sure Pendleton was the driver and that he was alone, then she signaled to Connie. Connie nodded, and Virginia stepped out from behind the hedge and went to meet the bootlegger.

He laughed when he saw her, and his sharp eyes narrowed.

"Do we have a deal then?" Virginia said.

"Lead me to it, baby doll."

He opened the passenger door for her, and she slid in, darting her eyes over to the hotel to see if anyone saw her. But the weather had driven the residents to the lobby, where Al Bucklin had a coal fire, and Virginia saw no one at the windows.

She lit a cigarette and leaned back in the car seat as though she had no concerns. Inside, though, her guts were twisting.

Pendleton started the car. "Which way, Lady Lindy? You're my navigator."

She didn't correct him, although for a fleeting moment, she was tempted. Amelia Earhart wasn't a navigator, she was an aviatrix. She didn't sit on the passenger side for anyone. But there was no point in contributing to the education of a man like Frank Pendleton.

They pulled onto Main Street, and Virginia pointed with her cigarette to the west down the graveled roadway. "I need the money before we go any further," she said.

"You'll get your money when I see those boys that make the woods whiskey." In profile, Pendleton's face was hatchet-sharp.

"You can drop me off right here then."

They were past the outskirts of town, and now that Virginia had started to thaw out, she was shivering uncontrollably - it was part cold, part fear, part excitement.

Pendleton slammed on the brakes and stopped in the middle of the road. "Let's get this straight, baby doll," he said, his voice ugly. "I'm calling the shots. You'll get paid when I say so."

She was silent for a minute, weighing the options, shivering on her side of the car, and he pulled off his jacket and gave it to her. "Warm up some," he said. "You're too cold to think."

After a moment, she put on the jacket. It was still warm from his body, and it smelled of tobacco and something dark and musky like wild animal. She had almost forgotten the smell of a man.

A car edged past them, tooting its horn, and Pendleton cursed. "I don't like to hit a woman," he said, "but that don't mean I won't."

"I've been hit before. Just give me the money."

He cursed again. "Half now. Half after."

She didn't like it, but it was better than she'd hoped. "Just don't think you can chisel me out of the 'later' part."

He pulled a money clip out of his pocket and peeled off some bills. He watched while she tucked them down the front of her dress. Then he laughed. It was a short, hungry laugh, and it hinted at later plans.

I'll have to deal with this one before it's over, she thought.

In silence, they traced the path Connie had driven two days earlier, and Virginia hoped that the column of dust that rose far ahead of them was made by Connie's car. But the column headed north, and they cut back into the hills.

When they got to the turnoff, Virginia said, "They're expecting us, but that don't mean we're entirely welcome."

"They'll be proud to see us," Pendleton said. He pulled a gun out from under the seat and laid it between them. Virginia didn't know what kind it was, but the barrel was long and lethal-looking.

"Just stay on the road, such as it is," she said.

"Such as it is."

Smoke threaded from the cabin in the clearing. An old pickup stood in front of the barn. Virginia wasn't sure if her uneasiness was a premonition of trouble or a realization that she already was in trouble.

Pendleton stopped the car beside the pickup and honked his horn. It sounded silly and insignificant. An echo came back from the bluff. Virginia hoped Connie was watching from above.

Slick stepped out on the porch, and dipped his head in acknowledgement. There was no sign of J.P.

"You stay here," Pendleton said, "while I tend to my business." He started for the house, carrying the gun loosely in one hand. The muzzle was pointed toward the rocky ground.

Slick pulled at the hair on his chin and watched him come. A rifle leaned against the cabin wall.

"Dammit. Dammit all to hell," Virginia said. This was what she hated about the whole business of moonshining. The distrust, the danger, the dance of striking a deal. Too many things could go wrong. One false move or a word misconstrued, and the next thing you knew, guns were blazing.

She jerked as if waking from a dream and watched Pendleton cross the final distance. This was one of those moments. She was suddenly as certain of it as she was certain the wind would blow. She eased the car door open and leaned out, preparing to duck into the woods.

An explosion sounded from behind her, and a blossom of red appeared on Slick's chest. He staggered backwards. Pendleton dived to the side, and came up shooting wildly back in her direction. Someone was shouting a name, but it was no name known to her.

Virginia ran for the line of trees. From the shelter of a thick hickory, she saw Slick on the floor of the porch, trying to rise on one elbow. Another shot sounded, and the top of his head disappeared into a thousand bits of flesh and bone.

The shots continued like a turkey shoot gone mad. Virginia scrambled through the brush toward the bluff. A deep runnel cut by eons of rainstorms led up one side of the rocky face, and she followed it.

The hillside rose almost vertically, and she pulled at tree trunks to hoist herself up foot by foot. Her shoe slipped on loose chert, and she felt something tear the soft flesh of her leg. The gunshots and the shouting intensified, and then ceased.

All Virginia could hear then was the ragged gasping of her breath.

She reached the top of the bluff, rolled onto the flat ground, looked at who waited there and cursed.

18

Eva couldn't believe that she had once admired her aunt. Just because she had breezed into Eva's life smelling of distant places and tragedy didn't mean she was anyone special.

And just because she told Eva she saw a ghost at the Old Taney Grove Cemetery didn't make her anyone special either. Virginia had told Eva the story—how Finis had told it and how she had seen the ghost with her own eyes and even followed it along the creek.

Eva believed in ghosts and such. She had seen the ghost of her own mama after she had dragged her body to the corn crib. It had been the middle of a moonlit night, and a sound had awakened Eva. The sound was like a mouse scratching in the wall. Clothed only in a ragged nightgown that had grown too small, she rose from her bed and followed the noise.

The noise seemed to keep moving away, and Eva followed it through the kitchen and out the back yard toward the corn crib where her mother lay. A white cloud floated there beside the barn, and Eva ran toward it with outstretched hands, but the hound ruined it all. He ran up beside her, barking. The apparition disappeared, and Eva was left alone, shivering in the dark.

After Virginia told her the story, Eva wondered if the ghost had been her mother or the other mother, the one who had killed her own son.

Eva was sometimes a ghost. She haunted the deep corners of the house. She overheard Virginia and Connie hatching their plans to cut old Mr. Bucklin out of his middleman role, and she burned with anger the she, too, was being cut out. After the house was dark and silent, she crept to the pallet where Connie slept in the front room.

There was still a fine shiver of dust on everything from the storm, and she felt it settle between her toes like talcum powder.

A thin shaft of moonlight poured through the window, and by its light, Eva skirted around the big chair and the desk to Connie's pile of blankets. She knelt beside him, as serene and graceful as a dancer, and placed her hand over his mouth.

He bucked in alarm, and she put her mouth next to his ear.

"Shhh. It's just me. Hush now."

Connie tried to say something, but Eva's hand was firm on his mouth.

"Shhh. We don't want her to hear."

Connie pulled her hand away. "Go away before she finds you here."

Eva laughed, a tiny, tinkling sound that masked her jealousy. She slid her hand under the quilt and onto his bare, warm skin. "Tomorrow," she whispered, "come back and get me when she sends you ahead. Promise me now."

Eva left, and her touch was a lingering burn on Connie's skin.

Now, the next day, she paced the empty house like a caged animal waiting for Connie to come for her. The day had turned cloudy and cold, and Eva kept looking out the window for signs of rain, for signals of change, for anything.

She paced through the small house while she waited, holding her chin high as though she balanced a book on her head. Seven steps across the front room, through the door into Virginia's room, seven steps, tag the window, back through the door and then into her own room, tag another window, out the door and into the kitchen where the route began anew.

It was a game to pass the time, she told herself, but she couldn't stop until she had walked the route 15 times, her exact age.

She drank water from the dipper in the kitchen, and then she began searching for the weapons Virginia had hidden from Connie, as if he couldn't be trusted with them. On this issue, Eva didn't differ sharply from her aunt. She had seen firsthand what Connie did when rattled. Connie had been subdued since that day in Al Bucklin's office, as though he had learned something surprising about himself.

Eva, however, was a different story, she told herself. She was calm and cool, and she should be the one in charge of Connie's guns. Eva went to Virginia's room and searched the musty wardrobe. Nothing there but shoes moldering in the bottom, a fine coat of green dusting the leather, shapeless dresses and coats hanging from the rod, a stack of unfashionable hats on the top shelf. She turned her attention to the trunk.

Inside the trunk was a half-knitted baby blanket. Eva set aside the bundle of yarn and blanket, along with her grandpa's suit and her grandma's wedding dress. Below was the one shotgun she already knew about - Finis's old bird gun, which she laid on top of his suit. It wasn't until she neared the bottom of the trunk that she felt solid metal. She pulled out the heavy Winchester 12-gauge and the Smith and Wesson revolver and ran her hands over the finish. The metal felt sensuous and smooth.

Eva smiled a secret smile and replaced the clothing in the trunk. The guns she took to her room.

From the drawer in the bottom of her wardrobe, Eva pulled out the few items she had taken from her mother's room after her death: a rhinestone dress clip, a fox collar, a scrapbook, an envelope filled with tatted collars and a bottle of Evening in Paris perfume. She dabbed the perfume behind her ears and fastened the fox collar around her neck with the dress clip.

She looked in the mirror and frowned. Something was missing. She looked incomplete. She went to her aunt's room and found some Tangee lipstick to add color to her face. Satisfied, she began pacing again.

When Connie finally pulled up to the house, Eva waited for him to come inside. She boosted herself on top of the kitchen table and struck a pose - her legs crossed and dress hiked and the revolver clutched in her hands - so that when Connie came through the door, he stopped short and stared.

"What are you doing?"

"I'm your little gun moll." She lifted the gun and blew an imaginary wisp of smoke from the barrel.

"Your aunt put those guns away."

Eva's eyes narrowed. "Are you for us or for her?"

"Us, baby." His face squinted, and with his long swinging arms and squinty face, he reminded Eva of the sad little monkey she had seen once when a band of gypsies had come through with their circus. One thing was sure, when she had some money, she was going to find a man who didn't have to use his face to think.

"Let's go, cowboy," she said, and she lifted the shotgun from behind the door and led the way to the car.

She was silent during the drive, and when they came to the end of the logging road, she followed Connie to the overlook. He carried the shotgun, but she held onto the revolver. She felt she had earned the right.

They weren't in position when the shooting began. Eva had just a second to wonder what the sound was when the next shot exploded and then more, one coming on the heels of another, like popcorn on a hot fire. Connie grabbed her arm and pulled her down, and together they peered over the rock ledge to the scene below.

Slick's body lay in a pool of blood on the porch, and Virginia was sprinting for the base of the bluff below them. Two cars blocked the road: the Packard Virginia had just exited, and behind it, a glossy Pierce-Arrow that Connie recognized.

"Christ almighty," he said. "It's Al Bucklin. He's gone berserk."

Al Bucklin, shielded by the heavy body of the car, took aim at Pendleton, who ducked around the end of the cabin.

"Where's J.P.?" The barrel of Connie's shotgun followed his line of sight as he searched for his cousin.

It was at that moment that Virginia hoisted herself over the last rocky overhang to gain the top of the bluff. Connie leveled the shotgun toward her and tightened his finger on the trigger.

Eva slapped down the barrel, and Connie looked at her wonderingly, as though surprised to find her there. A gust of wind shook the leaves over their heads and made a sound like ghosts rushing through the forest. Eva was suddenly aware of the cold.

She held onto the barrel while Virginia lay on the bluff's edge and cursed.

"You're about as useless as brains in a preacher's head," Eva said to Connie. "Just what were you fixin to kill?"

Connie wrenched the gun away and aimed it down in the hollow again, where Al Bucklin was reloading his gun.

"I could get that old boy right now."

"Don't be stupid," Eva said. She'd never seen anything like the scene played out below, and a current of excitement vibrated through her.

"You'd tell the Devil how to run hell." Connie tried to think back to the moment when he had lost the upper hand with Eva, but it all seemed like murky water with little dark creatures darting in and out of view.

Virginia sat up and examined the gash on her leg. It was bleeding freely, but she ignored it and crawled across the rock next to Eva and Connie.

"What in God's name is going on?" Her voice was low and dangerous, on the verge of losing control.

"It's Al Bucklin," Connie pointed to the man, who had finished reloading and was creeping alongside his car. He made a sudden quick move and was inside Pendleton's Packard.

"He must have followed us." Virginia bent a small sapling and looked through the leaves so her face would be shielded from anyone who looked up from below. "What happened to J.P. and Frank Pendleton?"

"I never seen J.P. The other man ran around the end of the house. I ain't seen him since."

Virginia's eyes raked the little valley. Bucklin started the Packard and aimed it toward the house. He stepped on the gas, and when the car had bumped across the grass and was almost against the porch, Bucklin bailed out and rolled into the shelter of the pickup.

The car hit the porch with a splintering crash, and Slick's body jumped as though he had been jolted back to life.

Pendleton ran from behind the house and fired at Bucklin. Bucklin fired back, but he was open to the other man, and Pendleton kept firing. The sound of the guns echoed in the valley, and even after Bucklin lay still on the ground, Pendleton walked toward him, firing into his body until the gun was empty. The sudden silence was shocking.

From above, Eva and Connie and Virginia seemed pinned to the ground by a force greater than gravity. The cold wind blew on their backs, and they didn't notice their shivering.

Pendleton reloaded his revolver with deliberation. Each bullet fell home in its chamber with a soft snick, and he snapped the cylinder into place. Then he turned in a careful

360-degree circle and bored through the thick brush with his eyes. But he didn't look up. It was as though all memory of Virginia had evaporated. Or perhaps he only worried about the danger the second moonshiner might pose.

Satisfied, Pendleton examined the damage to the Packard, then dragged Al Bucklin's body to the Pierce Arrow and hoisted him into the driver's seat. He went to the cabin, stepped over Slick's body and disappeared for a time inside the house.

On the bluff above, the watchers waited. Virginia tried to think but her mind stretched and wobbled as though she was drunk. It seemed dangerous to leave and dangerous to stay. Either way they might be discovered. Given the choices, it was easier not to make one. They stayed. They didn't speak. They were like mice on the rocky bluff, hoping that by their stillness, the hawk wouldn't spot them.

When Pendleton reappeared on the cabin porch, he carried a gallon jug in one hand. It was full of a clear liquid. Most of it he poured on the dead man's body and his car. The last little bit he drank.

He pulled out a match and lit the liquid, which burned with an almost invisible blue flame that licked away at Al Bucklin's clothing and the upholstery in the car until black smoke billowed out. Pendleton's face was impassive as he watched the fire take hold.

He went back inside the house, and when he emerged again, flames licked at the windows. By the time Pendleton drove away in his car, flames were shooting through the cabin's roof. The smoke swirled in the air and covered the valley in a toxic film.

Even after Pendleton had gone, Virginia and Eva and Connie waited atop the bluff. They didn't know for what. Then J.P. materialized from the thick black haze out of the dark mouth of the barn. His face wore a terrible blankness. For a time, he watched the fire eat at the cabin and Al Bucklin's car, and then he held his squirrel gun over his head like a declaration of war.

"Virginia Crow," he yelled, "this is on your head."

19

"It made hell look like a lightnin bug!" Connie was lightheaded with the novelty of bearing witness to blood and fire, and he bounced back and forth between Virginia and Eva, replaying the day's events.

Virginia tried to ignore him. Perhaps, she thought, in Connie's eyes the violence he had seen was no more real than the sideshows at a circus. In her memory, though, blood roses bloomed in an endless loop. She wanted to start the day over. She had set something in motion that had spun out of control. Blood was on her hands.

Only Eva seemed calm. "I was there," she said to her aunt. "You can't leave me out now." She had relinquished the guns to Virginia, but she held onto the power they had bestowed.

They were back at the house in the kitchen, and the wind whispered a mournful tune around the edges of the rooms. Even though the sun shone, it seemed that spring had made way for a more wintry time.

Virginia built a small fire in the stove to make coffee, and she sipped the strong and bitter brew and smoked cigarettes, one after another. She finally left the house altogether to rid herself of Connie and Eva. She had to think, and they were like flies buzzing around her head.

She still wore Frank Pendleton's jacket, and as she took off down the road at a brisk pace, she drew it close around her. The old dog crawled out from under the porch and limped after her. Together they walked down the hill to the cemetery, and Virginia drew open the iron gate and entered.

Under the trees, the grass was sparse, gathered in droughty clumps. It grew thicker and greener along the dry creek, as though it found some memory of water there.

The pale sun created a mosaic of shadow and light on the graves of Virginia's parents. She stood between their headstones and read the inscriptions as if seeing them for the first time: Araminta Watts, March 1, 1932; Finis Watts, March 18, 1932. The dog waited patiently beside her. Virginia's parents had been good, hard-working people, and now they were crumbling back into the earth.

Virginia didn't admit it even to herself, but she was hoping the ghost would appear, or the apparition, or the moving mist or whatever it was she had seen before. Her sign. Did people really have spirits that lingered after they died? Would the spirits of Slick and Al Bucklin haunt the spots where they had fallen? What about Johnny Crow? Where had his spirit gone?

She stood for a long time, and once, she sensed movement from the corner of her eye. Something white. But when she turned her head, nothing was there. Only the wind blowing the branches of the trees.

She had to think. She had decisions to make, but the world was whirling through space at a faster pace than it had that morning.

At least it was quiet here in the cemetery. On other days, in other years, she would have been surrounded by sound. Redbirds chirping with a violent insistence, crickets sawing in the grass, crows calling out their dominance.

Usually in the spring, birds would flood through on their northward migration: great flocks of cedar waxwings, wearing bandit-like masks; wedges of Canada geese, flying high overhead and sounding a cry like freedom unbound. Virginia couldn't remember hearing the voices of the birds this year.

In this dry season, even the birds knew to flee. It was another sign, she thought, that the world was plunging into chaos, and the things she once thought she knew no longer held true.

She sat down and leaned against her father's headstone. The dog circled twice and curled onto a hammock of grass nearby. After awhile Virginia's eyes closed; she may have dozed off.

She had a half dream, half memory of a day three years earlier. It had been spring then, too, but the day had been warm and moist. It promised better things, and Virginia had been waiting for Johnny to come back to their room at the boarding house. He had gone out earlier to collect a debt, and he said they would have a night on the town when he returned.

Virginia hadn't told him when he left that they had something special to celebrate, something both had given up dreaming of, but it was true, she was sure. They were going to have a child.

When he finally came in, the light had long vanished from the sky, and Virginia sat at the kitchen table as she had so many nights, smoking cigarettes and wondering why she waited for him.

He half-fell through the door and slid to the floor, his face a mass of bruises and blood.

"Johnny! What happened?" Virginia knelt beside him and pressed a clean handkerchief to the blood trickling from a cut on his scalp. The hope was draining from her even as she tended to him.

"S'nothin," he said. "Don't matter none." He smelled like cheap applejack.

"Did you get the money?" It may have been the wrong time to ask about the money, but they needed it. Times were tough.

A crooked smile crossed his face, and she saw that a tooth was missing. He wouldn't be her handsome Johnny anymore.

"I got it. I had it. I was up. And then, just one little roll of the dice, baby. You know how that goes."

It was that moment, so clearly defined, when her last illusions vanished about the life they might have shared. Johnny Crow was not to be relied on. When he had money, he would try the sucker's way of doubling it. She should have known that since June 12, 1930, when he lost the rent money on the Max Schmelling-Jack Sharkey heavyweight boxing title. She blamed herself for not learning her lesson then, but it was now branded on her heart. If Virginia were to have comfort and security for their child, it would be up to her to provide it.

A change in the light above made her stir. The sun shone from behind and created a radiance around the figure.

"They said you was lookin for me, Sister."

Virginia sprang to her feet and backed off before his words registered. "Bill Davis!"

Relief, as unexpected and strong as a flood, swept through her at the sight of the older man. After the events of the day, his appearance seemed like a miracle.

The dog wagged his tail and walked with stiff legs to the man.

Bill Davis squatted down and petted the dog's head. "Is this your Pa's old dog Red? Well, I'll be; I think he remembers me. He must be older than a coon's age. He always could scare up more squirrels than a feller could eat for supper."

"Now he spends his days under the porch."

"He's earned a rest."

The man stood again and looked at the gravestones. "Your pa, too, I reckon. Doc earned his rest." He took off his straw hat and bowed his head in front of the gravestones.

Bill Davis was tall and spare, and the years rested lightly

on him. A little older and more stooped, perhaps. His sandy hair was going gray, and his thin face was polished leather.

They walked together up the hill.

Virginia spoke. "After you hear what I have to tell, you'll be wanting to be on your way."

Bill Davis cocked his head and looked at her.

She rushed through the story of the day's events, neither embellishing nor making it less than it was. The telling lasted longer than the road, and they stopped shy of the house, the two of them standing in the road talking about betrayal and murder.

"This Pendleton," Bill Davis said, "he know where you live?"

"No. I don't know. Anybody could tell him."

"He's probably gone to ground. Lyin low till he knows if the Laws are lookin for him. But mebbe not. If you needed help before, you need it more now. A woman shouldn't be alone with a man like that on the loose." He looked down the hill at the cemetery they had just left. "Your pa helped me through hard times a'plenty, and I made a promise to him, Sister. That I'd always watch after his children as my own."

Virginia felt free of Pendleton now that she had told Bill Davis the story. Her thoughts turned to another direction, to the plan that had been hatching ever since she heard the Laws talking on the train ride from Fort Smith.

"Your brother, the preacher in Fort Smith, he told me you had a run-in with a judge."

Bill Davis's face darkened. "That belly-crawlin snake had no right to call himself a judge. He was in cahoots with the banker, and they was runnin all the little farmers and share-croppers out of business."

"You don't care much for bankers and judges, do you?"

"You got that right."

"I've been workin on an idea." Virginia pressed the valley between her breasts where she had stashed the small wad of bills she had finagled from Pendleton earlier in the day. "But you'll probably want a bite to eat before we get into that."

"Did you learn to cook like your ma? She used to make biscuits that would float off the plate."

"I do believe you're hungry," Virginia said.

The evening turned into a celebration of sorts. Virginia killed and plucked two of the remaining hens while Eva peeled potatoes and fed chunks of seasoned oak into the cookstove. From the back of the house came the reassuring thunk of an ax splitting logs into smaller pieces. Bill Davis wielded the ax; Connie Yates carried huge armloads of wood into the kitchen until Virginia told him to stop.

For dinner, they had fried chicken and potatoes, biscuits and gravy, canned peaches and a steaming pot of coffee. It reminded Virginia of long ago Thanksgiving feasts, back when times weren't so hard, and everyone sat around the table smiling and chattering, their bellies filled to bursting and their hearts never suspecting what lay ahead.

Bill Davis didn't waste any time coming up with a nickname for Eva. He had brought with him a half dozen lemons, offered as casually as if he had gathered them from a fencerow, and Eva made a pitcher of lemonade.

When she gave him a tall glass, he said, "Lemonade, made in the shade, by an old maid, stirred with a rusty spade."

Eva gave him a poisonous glare, and he continued, "I used to know an old maid named Esther Dunbar, could turn a man to stone with one look." As far as Bill Davis was concerned, Esther was Eva's name thereafter, and there was nothing she could do about it.

The house was too small for four people, even though there had been five who lived there when Virginia was a child. Somehow the house had grown smaller. After they had finished eating and the dishes were washed, Eva and Connie put on coats and went outside. It was after sunset, and there was no place to go except maybe the barn. It wasn't any of Virginia's concern where they went or what they did, she thought, so long as it didn't interfere with her plans.

And she had plans. Big ones. The sudden appearance of Bill Davis had diminished the horror of what she had seen earlier in the day. The gunfire, the blood, the fire: that was behind her. She was infused with hope and optimism that she could make everything right again.

The gash in her leg was wrapped with a bandage she had fashioned with strips torn from a raggedy bedsheet, and Virginia was hardly aware of the ache.

She and Bill Davis sat at the kitchen table, sipping the last of the moonshine she had confiscated from Connie Yates's glove compartment. She made a silent toast to Slick and J.P. and even to that bastard Al Bucklin.

The light subtly shifted, and it was as dark outside as it was in. Virginia lit the kerosene lamp and set it on the table. It was harder than she had expected to just come out with what she wanted from Bill Davis, and she filled the gap with small talk.

"Doesn't seem like folks make good sippin whiskey anymore."

Bill Davis held his glass up to the light and inspected the color. "Your pa didn't make brush arbor whiskey," he said. "His was premium applejack: crystal clear, water white, simon pure, double run and three times twisted."

His reverence made Virginia laugh. "He never let me taste it."

"Doc was a righteous man."

She turned toward him. "You're a wanted man in some places."

Bill Davis leaned back in his chair and stared into the distance. "Well, Sister, I've been just another hungry man on the road. That don't attract no attention these days. We're as common as thistles.

"I was offered a job in the zinc mines up to Joplin. I don't want no such job as that. I'd rather be in hell with my back broke." He gave her a comical look. "I ended up out by Garden City working a farm for some old feller. Worked for chips and grindstones. Never did see a red cent. About that time the wind started blowing out of Nebrasky without a button-push to stop it. Then the hoppers come. Wasn't a green stick left on that place.

"It was time to see to my family anyways. You probably don't know I got a wife, Maisie. She's a Cherokee. A good woman. And two little fellers, Rowdy and Big Tater. They're up by Tahlequah with her folks right now until I can get us a place and settle back down. I just need a little grubstake. I ain't going back till I can do right by my family."

They sat in silence for a moment, thinking about the weight of family and their respective responsibilities. To Virginia, it was a straight and simple proposition. Her daughter, Isabelle, was her flesh and blood, born in pain and then torn from her. There was no question what had to be done.

A sudden breeze made the kerosene light flicker, and the play of shadows on their faces at the table reminded Virginia of hunters around a night fire.

Bill Davis's voice broke into the silence. "You met my brother, Leon, at the train station in Fort Smith. He got word to Maisie you was lookin for me."

He looked at her expectantly. The moonshine had loosened his tongue and provided the opening. Virginia chose her words carefully.

"I've been a month out of prison. I made a mistake, and I paid for it. They took more than a year of my life. The State of Missouri took my husband. But that's the least of it. My child was stolen from me, and I aim to get her back."

Bill Davis put one big hand over hers on the table and waited.

"I need money, and I need it now. I heard these lawmen talking on the train from Fort Smith about bank robbers, and it set me to thinking. If a person planned it right, it wouldn't be much of a risk. Wear disguises, plan a getaway, then count the money."

Virginia looked Bill Davis square in the face. "You may think I'm a bad woman, but I'm in a place outside of bad and good."

"Sometimes the law can't be follered," he said. "Sometimes you got to sift the law."

She took a deep breath. "Yes."

20

If Eva had her way, they'd enter the bank dressed in long strapless gowns like Hollywood movie stars and with guns blazing. Put on a show, that's what people wanted. The backward townsfolk would talk about it for years to come. Maybe somebody would write a song about them or even make a movie. But her aunt was in charge of the planning, with the help of that annoying Bill Davis, and no one listened to Eva.

She sat in the back seat of the Ford and fumed. The wool suit made her itch, which was bad enough, but even worse, she carried a gun without bullets. What on God's green earth was her aunt thinking? It would be her chance to prove she was an actress, Virginia had said when Eva complained about the unloaded gun. "You'll have to scare them with your acting," she said, smiling.

Virginia was smiling too much these days, Eva thought. Ever since Bill Davis had shown up a few days ago, her aunt had acted as though all their problems were solved. The Laws hadn't been back to the house. That was about the only good thing.

Eva had gone into Gilead to catch wind of the gossip at the general store, and all the talk was about Al Bucklin and the fire. Beulah Stivers was keeping the hotel open, and one of her girls had returned from her uncle's house to help out. Nothing like this had ever happened to one of Gilead's own. Everybody seemed to agree that big city bootleggers were responsible. Probably from Tulsa, some said. Others blamed the rumrunners out of Oklahoma City.

The Laws had their hands too full to be bothering Connie Yates about a botched hotel robbery.

Eva leaned back into the seat and closed her eyes. Whenever she felt put upon or passed over by the others in the car, she escaped into a memory of the shooting and the fire and Frank Pendleton. Seen from the bluff top, the events of that day had seemed less than real - kind of like a gangster movie she had sneaked off to see with her friend Dodie Ashton. Eva remembered the hard expression on the man's face as he set the car afire with Al Bucklin's body in it. She was drawn to him, and she feared him. Her heart skipped a beat every time she thought about that day.

Virginia had never said his name, of course, but Eva was wearing his jacket, and Frank Pendleton's name was inked into the lining, along with the tailor's name: Ralston Brothers, Tulsa, Oklahoma. She thought she could find him if she wanted. She wouldn't be wearing his jacket then, of course. She'd be outfitted in some tight-fitting, slinky gown, and he'd see her and the eyes would pop out of his head. Then he'd do something gentlemanly, like invite her for a drink. He'd say, "I never seen any girl as pretty as you." Or he might say, "Your eyes shine brighter than the stars at night."

Eva smiled, and went on dreaming.

The car crested a hill, and a little town lay in the valley below. Paradise, Arkansas. Bill Davis's hometown. Connie pulled the car over and the four of them, Virginia, Bill Davis, Eva and Connie, got out.

Below them, a white church steeple rose out of the trees. Bill Davis pointed to a distant spot. "My place was west of town." His voice was matter-of-fact, as though he were talking about someone he knew. He raised his hand to trace the line from the tip of the steeple to the thick growth of trees along the river. "Now just down the way from there, headed out towards the river is the bank."

"Where's the sheriff's office and the hotel?" Virginia shifted from foot to foot. She felt as nervous as a spider on a hot skillet. Their plan suddenly seemed insane.

Connie was silent, glancing back and forth from Bill Davis and Virginia to the town below.

Eva sniffed. Was she the only one who had any guts?

Bill Davis picked up a stick and sketched their positions in the dirt and once again explained what would happen. After everyone had a chance to study it, he scuffed it out. He wore boots and a wide-brimmed hat, looking every bit the cowboy.

"We shouldn't be out in the open here for anybody to view," Virginia said. "They might recognize you."

"That's so, Sister," he said, and he led the way back to the car.

One thing was sure, no one would recognize Virginia or Eva. Virginia wore her father's second-best suit, taken from the cedar chest. With Finis's hat on her head and a straggly mustache she had crafted from the hair on the coonskin that had been hanging forever on the outside wall of the house, she looked like some down-on-his-luck hobo.

Eva was supposed to be her youthful male accomplice. That's how they imagined the newspapers reporting it: "An older man and a youthful male accomplice robbed the Paradise County Farmers Mercantile Bank today. They escaped with an undisclosed amount of cash."

Eva liked to think about the cash. Piles and piles of money. That's the only way she would agree to wear men's clothing. In addition to Frank Pendleton's jacket, she had on a pair of Sunday pants Connie had outgrown. Her hair was tucked under a cap.

Coming up with two pairs of men's shoes had been a challenge. Virginia had made do with a pair of Connie's shoes after she stuffed newspaper into the toes. Eva's tiny feet, though, posed a more difficult task.

Bill Davis had spent an evening with knife and awl, taking apart a pair of Finis's old shoes, oiling the leather to make it soft and pliable, then cutting down each piece and sewing them back into a shoe shape. With a liberal application of shoe black, the result passed inspection.

Once the leather had dried, the shoes were stiff and uncomfortable, and Eva had taken them off for the trip to Paradise. Now it was time to put them back on.

They drove down the main street and tried not to look like ogling tourists while Bill Davis pointed out the important landmarks: the bank, the sheriff's office, and then at the end of the street near the train depot, the hotel. It was Friday noon, and the little town looked busy and prosperous. Women bustled in and out of shops; a line of trucks waited to be loaded in front of the feedstore; children ran and screamed on the school playground.

Busy was good. They were counting on maximum confusion.

On the outskirts of town, a bridge crossed the river. The water ran brown and sluggish underneath. On the other side was a small roadside park with a grassy area that was growing weeds.

Bill Davis nodded his head, and Virginia said, "That's it."

Connie drove on a quarter mile or so on the improved road as he had been instructed, and pulled into a quiet country lane. He turned the car around and let Bill Davis out. The man faded into a line of trees that fronted a pasture. In the distance, Eva could see the flat roofline of a stable. A dozen mares and their foals grazed in the pasture. The stallion had his own paddock.

Eva let out a breath she hadn't realized she'd been holding.

"He'd better be a real cowboy," she said.

Connie's eyes darted toward Virginia.

Virginia told the story again like a liturgy. "Once he bulldogged a panther and hauled it into a rodeo arena over his saddle. I reckon he's up for this."

As she listened to her aunt, Eva wondered how much others had embellished the story over the years. Maybe it was the neighbor's tomcat he had bulldogged. Or a flea-bitten, hungry coyote. Some sorry critter like that.

Connie pulled the car into the roadside park, and they unloaded a picnic hamper and spread a quilt. The quilt lay the weeds down in front of it, creating a green-fringed border.

Something had died nearby, and the air was filled with a heavy, sulphurous stench.

If any passerby should wonder, Eva and Connie and Virginia were supposed to look like a trio of men on the road looking for work, who had stopped by the river for their noon meal. None of them had an appetite, but they lifted the sandwiches from the hamper and pretended to eat. The food attracted flies and other buzzing insects. One fly and then another landed on Eva's bare hand. Their bites felt like tiny stings, and she slapped at them, but the flies were already gone.

Virginia was positioned to see downstream where the bank slumped into the river. That's where Bill Davis had said to look for him. Eva saw her check the pocket watch that nestled in the little pocket of her trousers and then pull at the tight collar under her wool jacket.

In abrupt contrast to the cold weather a week earlier, summer had come, even though it was still spring. The day was hot and humid, and the sun beat down with an unreserved vengeance.

Eva found a piece of cardboard in the bottom of the hamper and fanned herself. She alone looked cool. Virginia kept one hand on the watch. Connie was cracking his knuckles, and Eva told him to stop. He gave her a hurt look, but she ignored it.

Time passed like a sunning turtle.

They saw Bill Davis before they heard him. He emerged from the trees on the bare back of a handsome chestnut stallion, and from a distance, he looked like some romantic figure from a movie reel.

He hailed them with an uplifted arm. The horse splashed into the river and forded it, and the pair disappeared on the other side.

"That's some horse," Connie said.

"The sheriff's pride and joy," Eva said.

Virginia pulled the watch out again and looked at it. "In ten minutes, that banker is going to be sorry he ever messed with Bill Davis and his neighbors."

21

Planning a bank robbery wasn't that much different from planning a school lesson. At least that's how Virginia looked at it. How to rob a bank in four easy steps.

Step one: assess the situation.

Virginia stood inside the doorway of the bank, Eva beside her, and looked around. The ceilings were high, as befitted a prosperous establishment, with a white, pressed tin ceiling and two rotating fans suspended from it. Lights on the wall shone out of ornate plaster sconces. Tall, narrow windows that were cut into the limestone walls afforded the only other light, making the interior dim and solemn.

Along the far wall, two tellers stood behind a counter that was enclosed with shiny brass bars, as though the bank clerks were caged animals.

A narrow door stood open behind the cage. Virginia guessed it might lead to the vault. An office that she took to be the bank president's was glassed in and shuttered and dark. Bill Davis's information was good. The banker always went home for dinner at midday.

Only a few customers were inside the bank. Virginia studied each one carefully. A stout man in a suit spit into a cuspidor. An elderly woman weighed herself on the heavy-duty scales while a younger woman held her parcels. The two male clerks engaged in conversation with each other on the other side of the teller cage.

The time for backing out had passed, but Virginia suddenly and completely realized the gravity of what she was doing. She was in too far to extricate herself.

It was like that long ago night when she had first seen Johnny Crow at the dance pavilion at Hyde Park and he had steered her into a dark corner and stroked the rounded curve of her breast. Something in her, some destructive longing, wanted his touch, wanted his smoky eyes to ignite with desire for her alone.

All she had done was agree to dance with him - something done on a whim, and now she had a choice: slap him or let him caress her. She had too much pride to do the first, and besides, she told herself, she was the one to blame for dancing with him. For desiring him. She should accept the consequences.

That's what she was doing now in the bank. Moving forward on pride alone. Paying the price for her decisions.

Think of Isabelle, she told herself. Focus on the reason you're here.

Step two: take control.

Virginia nodded at Eva, who gave her an unreadable look before moving into place next to the bank entrance. They both pulled out revolvers, Eva with Connie's unloaded Smith and Wesson, and Virginia with a Colt single-action Army revolver that belonged to Bill Davis. ("Called the Peacemaker, but I never knew why," he had said when he gave her a lesson on how to use it.) Unlike Eva's, Virginia's gun was loaded.

Virginia held the Peacemaker close to her body until she came to the tellers' cage. No one yet knew that anything out of the ordinary was happening. Just another peaceful day in Paradise.

The big ceiling fans swept the air overhead in an endless swishing sound. The air rustled the papers on the tellers' counter. Virginia held the gun up so the teller could see it, and said in a voice as low and rough as she could manage, "This is a holdup."

Step three: take the money.

There was a tight, clenched feeling in her chest, and the words didn't come out as loud as she had intended, but the teller heard her all right. He was a young man who wore a wedding ring, and his mustache was growing into a manly thickness. Behind round, wire-rimmed glasses, his eyes widened. He glanced at the other clerk next to him, who seemed frozen in place.

"I beg your pardon?" he said.

Virginia pounded the counter with the butt of the gun and then pointed it at him. "Put all your cash in bags. Now! Both you boys, get to work."

Behind her, the bank customers had begun to notice something was out of the ordinary. The stout man headed for the door to the street, but Eva stood in front of it, gun held up, and blocked the exit. The young woman began screaming.

Back to step two: Take control. Virginia grabbed the woman by her sleeve and shook her. "Shut up," she said. "You're scaring your mama."

The old woman stood next to her daughter, her eyes blank. Their parcels had dropped to the floor. The younger woman put an arm around the older. "Memaw," she said, "they're robbing the bank."

Step three: Take the bags of money that the docile tellers are handing through the window.

It was a moment frozen in time. A moment so silent that Virginia heard a mourning dove cooing from the eaves. A moment so still that the kaleidoscope shadows on the bank's wooden floor caused by tree branches swaying in the wind seemed fraught with meaning.

All eyes were on Virginia. She held two heavy canvas bags in her hands, and she tucked one under her arm so she could use the gun if need be. Everyone else stood still and watched her. Even Eva.

Step four: Make a getaway. Virginia pushed past Eva and said, "Let's go."

They walked through the heavy door of the bank into the bright sunlight.

A police siren wailed in the distance, but it was headed away from the bank. The citizens on the walkway craned their necks toward the sound of the siren.

"Put your gun away," Virginia said to Eva. "We don't want to draw attention."

Eva tucked the gun in her waistband and took the bag Virginia handed her. The car was parked next to the building - the engine running and Connie Yates at the wheel.

He watched them with a kind of manic intensity, as though his tension could hurry them. Virginia and Eva climbed into the car, and Connie released the clutch too quickly, almost killing the motor. He pushed it back in, the car coughed, and they jerked down the road.

"Slow and easy," Virginia said. "We don't need no Laws on us right now."

"They're all at the hotel, ain't they?"

"That's the idea."

"How'd it go?"

"Like butter on a hot biscuit. Let's find Bill Davis and get out of here."

Now that it was done, Virginia thought she might be sick.

The car rattled across the bridge. At the edge of the little roadside park, Bill Davis emerged from the trees and flagged them down. He slipped into the back seat beside Eva. He looked at Virginia, who confirmed their success with a nod.

Bill Davis's face was shiny with sweat, and on his shirt, damp stains spread under his arms. He smelled like horse.

He poked an elbow in Eva. "Well, Esther," he said, "now

you're a bank robber."

Eva glanced at him and then looked away, but a smile played at the corner of her mouth.

In the front seat, Virginia unfolded a Conoco road map, and traced their route. Dust billowed out behind the car, and dust from the cars they met enveloped them in a choking cloud.

The map wasn't really necessary. In this part of the state, Bill Davis knew every cat road, the twisty and narrow timber tracks and farm lanes. They'd be across the state line in minutes, and the Laws wouldn't follow them into Oklahoma.

After they crossed the line, and the Cookson Hills rose in front of them, Connie said over his shoulder to Bill Davis, "How'd you get that sheriff's horse on the second floor of the hotel?"

"They didn't have no elevator," Bill Davis said, "so we took the stairs."

"I never knew no horse would do that."

"You have to whisper in their ear. That one didn't think he wanted to go, but I told him about a mare waiting for him up there. He took those stairs two at a time."

"How they goin a get him back down?"

"That's their trouble."

Virginia began laughing. The small laugh grew into gales of laughter so contagious that they all joined her and became children again, giggling hysterically at their daring and luck.

22

The Paradise bank job had been textbook perfect, and when Virginia had stood with the gun in her hands and had seen how the tellers jumped to obey, she had felt a sense of power that she had never known before—certainly not as a schoolteacher in front of an unruly classroom. The feeling had warmed her, and at the same time, something welled up inside her, an instant addiction to the rushing feeling that had gone on in her head.

The day after the robbery was Saturday, and Virginia went about the business of living: preparing food, drawing from the shrinking reserves of water in the well, feeding old Red the dog, washing and ironing clothes.

While Virginia tidied up the house, Eva walked into Gilead to buy copies of the Fort Smith and Tulsa newspapers, although with all the other bank robberies, kidnappings and jail breaks going on, and the various political maneuverings of Franklin D. Roosevelt, Adolph Hitler and Huey P. Long, the Paradise robbery didn't even make the front page.

No Laws came to the farmhouse looking for bank robbers; no one seemed to suspect that its inhabitants had stepped beyond the bounds of civilized behavior.

When evening fell, Virginia sat on the porch and watched the darkening sky fill in the spaces between the hickories and oaks at the edge of the field. Finally the line between land and sky fell away as though all the earth floated in dark amniotic fluid.

She had a sense of precarious control, as though something could take her right over the edge to a place from which she couldn't return. The robbery replayed itself in Virginia's head in an endless loop: The look on the tellers' faces, the fear in the customers' voices, the feel of the gun in her hand. What if she had had to use that gun? What kind of person would that make her? Was any crime acceptable if it led her back to Isabelle? If there was some other way to raise the money she needed, she couldn't come up with it.

The bank robbery had gone off without a hitch, but the take had been disappointingly small. After it was divided, each had a nest egg, about $600 each for Virginia and Bill Davis, and $400 each for Eva and Connie.

Connie and Eva weren't happy about the way the money was divided, but Virginia wouldn't discuss it other than to say they were lucky to get as much as they did. As far as Virginia was concerned, the issue was settled, but that only went to show how little she knew about the workings of a teenager's mind.

Eva and Connie went to Connie's house in the dead of night and retrieved the phonograph and records and his few other belongings. The phonograph was now hooked up in the parlor, where Eva played the two records over and over until Virginia ordered her to stop the racket.

Eva wanted new records anyway. She was tired of the same old songs. And that wasn't all she wanted. Her share of the bank money was begging to be spent. She talked Connie into driving her to Tulsa so she could buy a new dress and take in some nightlife.

Before they left, though, Virginia had an errand to run. And she needed Connie's car to do it.

The robbery had left Virginia with one overriding desire: to find her child. Now that she had some money, she could pay Ned Bender, and he could tell her where to find Isabelle.

She couldn't wire the funds to him from the Gilead post office. People might wonder how Virginia Crow suddenly came up with the money. So first thing Monday morning, Bill Davis drove her to Muskogee to the Western Union. She left the office clutching her receipt as though it was a ticket to heaven.

Bill Davis and Virginia hadn't been home ten minutes before Connie and Eva piled into the little Ford and left for Tulsa. Virginia didn't like it, but who was she to tell Eva what to do? Even though the girl seemed like an adult in many ways, she needed a mother, someone she could go to for advice and someone who would tell her when she was headed for trouble. Virginia suspected it would only lead to more strife if she tried to assume that role. She had enough strife.

Besides, Eva was a temporary problem, one that would soon end.

That same day, a siege of restlessness hit Bill Davis, and he said he needed to go into Fort Smith. What he actually said was, "I aim to get me a new jug and drink till the world looks little."

"You don't have to go as far as Fort Smith to do that," Virginia said.

"Maybe not, Sister, but that's where I'm bound."

So he left with promises to return with a fresh supply of sipping whiskey for Virginia, and she was left alone in the house.

Virginia savored the quiet. After the morning chores were done, she sat on the front porch and tried to read, even though the only book she could find in the house was a Bible. She wondered what had happened to the other books her parents had once shelved in their room: Gibbon's *Decline and Fall of the Roman Empire*, Robert Louis Stevenson's *A Child's Garden of Verses* and John Bunyan's *Pilgrim's Progress*.

She remembered winter nights when her mother would read this very Bible silently by the light of the lamp. The leather binding was worn and cracked, the pages as thin as spider webs. In the front in black ink that had bled through the page were listed the names of her ancestors: the Sledges and Armistries and Watts and Hollifields. All those forgotten people. They were like a foreign language that her parents had never taught her.

A tasseled bookmark was placed at the third chapter of the first book of Kings. She opened the book there, and her eyes fell on the story of two harlots who came before King Solomon. Each claimed to be the mother of a boy child. Solomon had a sword brought to him, and said, "Divide the living child in two, and give half to the one, and half to the other." The real mother spoke up then. "Let this woman have her." Then Solomon knew who was telling the truth, and he awarded the child to its real mother.

"And they lived happily ever after," Virginia said. Her voice floated over the empty porch. That took no study, she thought. Of course the mother would choose life for her child.

She had a sudden and awful thought. What if Isabelle were dead right now? Would she somehow know? Or what if she was sick and needed her mother?

She wished Bill Davis would hurry back with something to drink, something that would deaden the fear for her daughter's safety, the fear that she would never see Isabelle again.

The heat rose in waves from the dry fields. After awhile, Virginia soaked a towel in water and lay on the porch with the towel draped across her face.

In summers past, when she was a little girl, sometimes her mother would fan her during the hottest part of the day. She could still remember the fan, a colored picture of a sorrowful-looking Jesus in the Garden of Gethsemane on one side and an advertisement for Tucker's Funeral Parlor and Wallpaper Coverings on the other. Evenings, her mother and Carolina and Virginia would sit on the porch and snap beans or shell green peas to prepare them for canning in the cool of the next morning. And at night, she would lie beside Carolina on a bed on the sleeping porch, a thin muslin sheet between Virginia's skin and the cooling night air.

Sometimes she longed for the simplicity of those days.

The sound of a car pulling into the yard roused her from a near-stupor, and she sat up and laid the towel on the porch. Under the porch, the hound dog didn't bother to venture out in the blistering sun to greet the visitor.

Virginia watched the man unfold from the black Plymouth. Sheriff Ray Callahan. He wasn't in uniform today, and he wore blue jeans, a white shirt and a narrow-brimmed Stetson that made him seem unnaturally tall.

A tow-headed girl peered out the open window and shyly ducked down when she saw Virginia looking.

The sheriff carried a brown paper package in his hands, and when he neared the porch, he shifted it to one hand and tipped his hat to Virginia.

"Afternoon, ma'am," he said.

Virginia's heart had been beating out of control when she realized who it was, as though he knew she had robbed a bank and had come to return her to prison, but what man would bring along a child on such a mission?

"Afternoon, sheriff."

He shuffled back and forth on his booted feet, and held out the package to her. "Some numbskull hit one of my steers with his car, then said I should pay for repairs because I shouldn't let my livestock wander free-range, so I been butchering all day. Bad time of year to put up meat. Thought maybe you and your niece could use some fresh beef."

Virginia accepted the package. It must have weighed five pounds. "Obliged," she said.

"It's a nice shoulder roast."

"We haven't had any in some time," Virginia said.

She stepped off the porch and into the yard, leading the sheriff away from the front windows. She had a sudden image of the pallet in the parlor where Connie Yates slept and the phonograph and who knew how many other pieces of evidence that people other than she and Eva stayed here. Bill Davis, thank God, slept in the barn, and he kept his belongings as neat as a pin. Had she taken his overalls off the clothesline in back, though? What would the sheriff see if he nosed around? There was no law against having company, but it could lead to questions, and the answers could lead to trouble. Virginia forced her attention back to Ray Callahan.

His eyes were a warm brown color, and they looked at her with a mixture of embarrassment and something else that Virginia couldn't define. "It's hard times," he said. He could have turned to leave then, but he paused. "About the time before." A scarlet flame spread across his cheeks. "My deputy, he gets a little official sometimes. I didn't like him being so hard on you. You've been through things no lady should have to endure."

"I didn't pay it any mind," she said. She didn't want him to know how deeply the deputy's words had wounded her. As though Virginia had given up her right to motherhood because she had been in prison.

Ray Callahan's thoughts seemed to be running in the same direction. "I have children," he said, glancing toward the car. "It ain't fair what they done to you and your little girl."

"Fair? That's a word I marked out of my dictionary."

Just then the little girl called from the car. "Daddy. Daddy, I'm thirsty."

The sheriff gave the girl an admonishing look. "We're fixin to leave, Cassie. You know you're not to interrupt."

"I'll get a glass," Virginia said.

"No need."

"I'll be right back." Virginia was almost running to the kitchen, wondering why she had opened her mouth. She wanted them gone. If the sheriff looked in the window, it would be over. But it was a brutally hot day and the little girl was thirsty. It wasn't her fault her father was a lawman.

Virginia splashed water in a glass and ran back out, some of it spilling on her hand. She was relieved to see the sheriff had stayed next to the car. He was saying something to the child, who looked chastened.

Nevertheless, the girl reached for the glass with greedy hands. Her eyes were a dazzling shade of blue. She couldn't be older than five.

"What do you say, Cassie?" The sheriff's voice sounded with a proprietary pride.

"Thank you, ma'am," Cassie said shyly.

She drained the glass and handed it back to Virginia. "My daddy makes ice cream with ice and salt," she said. "I like strawberry ice cream."

Virginia was charmed. "So do I," she said. "I surely do love ice cream." She reached out to tousle the girl's hair, but at the touch of the soft curls, she was reminded of Isabelle, and she jerked her hand away as though it had burned her. What was she doing? It was insane to be standing in the yard with the sheriff and his daughter, chatting as though they were at a social.

She backed toward the porch, and the sheriff followed her. She stopped, and he stood close.

He cleared his throat. "My wife," he said, "she went off last year. Said she couldn't take this life no more. Left me and four little ones. We live with my mother now."

Virginia couldn't bear to look at him. She didn't want anyone else's sorrows floating around this place.

"You need to go to church and find you a good woman," she said.

"Maybe that's not what I want."

Virginia looked him square in the face. "Ray, I have work to tend to. Thank you for the roast."

The sheriff touched her shoulder with a pressure no greater than a butterfly landing. They stood for a moment while the whole world unfolded. But the spell broke, and the sheriff turned abruptly and left.

As the car drove away, Cassie leaned out the window and waved to Virginia. Virginia lifted a hand and then let it fall to her side.

"Damn it," she said. "Damn it all to hell."

After Ray Callahan and his daughter went away, Virginia couldn't settle. The memory of the girl's soft hair and the look in the sheriff's eyes wouldn't leave her. She finally fled the house and walked into town.

Dusk was falling, and the cicadas were raising holy hell. Virginia went over the bridge and dry creek and past the cemetery where her parents and sister crumbled back into the earth and where a ghost-like figure sometimes showed itself, and she walked up the long hill into town.

In Gilead, the old men sat on the hotel porch. They called her name when she passed. "Mrs. Crow. Mrs. Crow. Come sit a spell." She pretended not to hear.

At the post office, she tried the door, but it was locked. She walked past the bank and grocery store and down a side street to the house where Pearl Whitesides lived. Pearl's mother answered the door, a worn woman wearing a flowered housedress and dirty apron. She wiped her hands and called Pearl's name.

Together Pearl and Virginia walked back to the post office, and Pearl dialed the phone number for her and stood outside while Virginia waited for Ned Bender to answer his phone. It rang and rang, a disembodied jangle of metal and rubber, but no one picked up on the other end.

Virginia watched Pearl lock the door and walk away, and then she stopped at the water fountain on the square and splashed water on her face and sat on a park bench. She was struck by a cold fear. How could she expect any good to come to her? Hadn't every moment of her adult life, even the happy moments, either been disasters or periods between disasters? And did she really deserve any happiness? Her husband had killed a cop, and she had robbed a bank.

She forced the fear away, forced herself to sit quietly and breathe in and out, deeply and slowly. When she felt a measure of stillness inside, she walked back to the hotel and went through the kitchen door.

Beulah Stivers was sitting at the table with a girl who was a younger copy of her. They were snapping beans.

She looked up when Virginia came through the door, and her face widened in a smile. "I hoped you'd come see me," she said. She stood and bustled around the stove for a minute, stirring up the coals to heat a pot of coffee. "This is my oldest girl, Irma," she said. "She's helping out here now."

Irma's face was broad and plain, and her eyes spaced too close together, but she had a wide smile, with strong, straight teeth. She ducked her head at Virginia, and went back to snapping beans. The wash pan was nearly full of glistening green pieces.

"I'm going to get my girl back," Virginia said. "I've got a man working on it."

A look of sadness crossed Beulah's face, but she smiled and said, "I wish you the best, Virginia."

They drank coffee and talked about the hotel and the old men who lived there. Irma left the room, and Beulah lowered her voice. "I heard they know who killed Al and that moonshiner."

Virginia felt herself grow cold inside.

"I can't think they're right, though," Beulah continued. "They're sayin J.P. Yates did it. J.P. is my cousin's boy, and I've known him since he was a baby. He don't have a mean streak in him to do something like that."

"Did the Laws catch him?" She had a sudden vivid memory of him stepping out of the barn through the smoke and the fire and yelling that all this was on Virginia Crow's head. If J.P. was in custody, that changed everything. He might talk about Virginia and Frank Pendleton and that day when all hell broke loose. She'd have to go on the lam then. The Laws would never believe anything she had to say.

"He's disappeared," Beulah said. "We got a passel of relations in these hills. No telling where he might be."

Virginia looked at Beulah's honest face. "Connie Yates. Isn't he your relation, too?"

"That rascal is my sister's boy. He worried her into an early grave."

"What do they say about him?"

Beulah leaned toward Virginia. "Nobody's paying him any mind since Al Bucklin got hisself killed. Sheriff has more important things to attend to than a petty thief like Connie Yates."

Virginia walked home slowly in the dark. When she arrived at the farmhouse, only the hound dog was there to greet her. He walked out to the road on stiff legs and waved his tail slowly like a solemn conductor. Together they walked to the silent house.

23

Eva and Connie hadn't been on the road five minutes before they began to pick at each other.

All Eva did was ask why Connie had headed the car south toward Muskogee, and he turned to her with a fierce look on his face and said, "Because it's too damn hot and dusty to drive on any road that ain't paved."

"But we're going to Tulsa." Eva said it firmly, as though there could be no question. Her confidence went no deeper than her voice. Connie could be unpredictable, and she hadn't been applying the appropriate incentives lately to keep him under control. She wished that she had gone to him the night before while he lay on the floor in the front room. It had been hot and sticky, though, and she couldn't bear the thought of flesh touching flesh.

Eva ran her hand up Connie's thigh to let him know she'd make up for the neglect when they arrived in Tulsa. She'd make up for other slights, too. Her aunt saw her as a child, and she yearned to be treated as an equal. She had stood beside Virginia in the Paradise bank robbery, and yet when it came time to divide the money, Eva and Connie had been treated as second-class. She was going to make sure that never happened again.

The first step in her plan required new clothes from head to toe. Hat, shoes, dress, undergarments, gloves, maybe even a new permanent wave in her hair. She would be a woman of the world before this day was through. First, though, she had to get to Tulsa.

Beside her, Connie kept his eyes on the road and his hands on the wheel. The early morning traffic consisted mostly of farm trucks and an occasional wagon and mule. Once they passed an old truck loaded with a family and all its belongings: kids bouncing on the mattress on top; a galvanized tub tied to the sideboards. The tires were bare; Connie said they wouldn't get far. Then he turned to her with a fierce look. "Why not Muskogee? What's wrong with Muskogee?"

"I've been there," Eva said. "I have to stretch my wings." What she didn't say was that Frank Pendleton was from Tulsa, not Muskogee. She knew this to be true, even though no one had told her.

"Stretch your wings and what else?" Connie said, as though he had read her mind.

Eva clamped her mouth shut and sat still. After the car crossed the Arkansas River bridge and Connie steered west onto U.S. 64, she breathed easier. The road stretched out across the flat countryside in front of them. To the south of the highway, rib-slatted cows grazed the sparse grass in pastures ornamented with oil pumps. The mechanical up-and-down motion of the pumps was the only movement in the expanse of prairie.

They drove through the all-Negro community of Taft, and then the highway turned northwest to Haskell. It was another 20 miles or so into Bixby. The towns were small, and the people and the houses alongside the road looked every bit as worn and poor as the people back in Gilead. Eva was disappointed. What if the whole world was just more of the same? She knew that couldn't be true, because she had seen the newsreels of places like Hollywood and Chicago and New York City. Someday soon she would find a place that had sparkle and glamour. Tulsa was just the first step.

When they drove into Bixby, a car pulled out in front of them, and Eva made the mistake of telling Connie to watch out.

"If you want to drive… " he said. It wasn't just the words. From the set of his mouth and indeed, from the tension pouring out of his entire body, it was obvious that Connie was angry and that he would find any excuse to lash out.

He was so caught up in his funk that he missed a turn, and they ended up going west instead of north. By the time he realized what he had done, they were in Glenpool, where the oil-soaked earth still bore the stains of unbridled development. Neither spoke. They rode in silence past the abandoned drilling rigs and rotting shacks. Eventually the highway swept across a hilltop and below they saw a vast refinery spread across the sand-carpeted river bottom—row upon row of white tanks punctuated with tall smoke-stained stacks. A white plume of smoke fell back to earth and shrouded the valley in a ghostly fog.

Beyond the refinery, like a golden city, rose a cluster of skyscrapers. Tulsa. A long-ago lesson from Bible school sprang into Eva's memory, and she thought about the vast desert and the river Jordan and the Promised Land beyond.

"It's beautiful," she said.

Connie had been to Tulsa before, but seeing it with the woman he loved, even though he was beginning to feel her pull away from him, softened him, and he put a hand on her knee. "We'll have us some fun in T-town," he said.

Eva glanced at him and then returned her gaze to the skyline. Connie had disappointed her deeply in the past few weeks. First in the way he muddled the hotel robbery and then in the way he tried to cozy up to her aunt and Bill Davis, as though they were the queen and king of the fucking outlaws.

She was surprising herself these days. Saying such a vulgar word, even if only to herself, would have been unthinkable not that long ago. When she was little and tagged along with her grandfather Finis, she heard lots of things she wasn't supposed to hear. She had worn the invisible cloak of the silent child while she shadowed him on his rounds.

She mouthed the words again, "fucking outlaws." She liked the way the words ricocheted in her brain like a rapidly firing machine gun. It made her laugh out loud, and Connie looked at her in surprise, and then grinned back, even though he didn't know why she had laughed.

It was in this spirit of misunderstood cease-fire that they crossed the Arkansas River into Tulsa at the 23rd Street bridge.

Eva looked at everything with avid curiosity. The buildings were modern monuments of carved stone and brick. They reached so far into the sky that she felt she was in a twilight canyon. No, that wasn't the feeling exactly. She had a thought so profound that she turned to Connie to share it.

"This must be what a cricket feels like in a graveyard," she said.

Connie frowned, his eyes on the traffic. "What? Like what?"

"A small creature wandering among the headstones. This must be what it feels like. Like you're so small and the world is so big."

Connie gave her a look of incomprehension, and Eva curled her lip and turned her attention back to the sights.

She had never seen so many cars in her life. Not only cars, but buses and taxis and people bustling in and out of them. Connie proudly named the makes of the automobiles: Oldsmobiles, Dodges, Chevrolets, Buicks and Fords, LaSalles, Cadillacs, Packards and Pierce-Arrows.

At the corner of Boston and 11th, Eva pointed out a convertible that seemed all silvery chrome on the front. "That's what I want."

"Cadillac convertible, 1931 model," Connie said. "V-12 engine, top speed 125 miles per hour, horsepower 135. That'll set you back about $5,000."

The driver and passenger looked carefree; the woman's silvery scarf billowed out behind her like a meteor's tail. Eva could hear her laughter as they passed.

"I guess we need to rob another bank."

"Or ten."

They rented a room in a hotel that was nicer than any Eva had been in before, except maybe the Hotel Severs in Muskogee. It certainly was nicer than that fleabag in Gilead where her aunt had worked. Then they ate lunch in a downtown diner, and Eva stared at the businessmen and secretaries rushing up and down the sidewalks while she chewed an egg sandwich and sipped a chocolate malted.

Connie was still drinking coffee and smoking a cigarette when Eva pushed her plate away. "I have to get going," she said.

"I'm not done." Connie signaled the waitress to refill his cup. He looked at Eva, a long, challenging stare that dared her to leave. The shadows under his eyes were more pronounced than usual, giving him the appearance of a hungover hound.

Eva returned his stare. "When you're done, you go on and do what you want to do. I'm shopping for new clothes, and I don't need no man along for that. I'll meet you at the hotel later, and we can go dancing."

She knew where she wanted to shop. Back when Eva still went to school, Shirley Jensen, the most stuck-up girl at Gilead Secondary, had bragged about a trip to Tulsa with her banker father and her weasel-faced mother. They stayed at the city's finest hotel, at least to hear Shirley tell it, where they dined on shrimp and Shirley tasted champagne. "The bubbles tickle your tongue," she had told the throng of girls who crowded around at lunchtime to pay homage to her new clothes. Eva had tucked away every word that spilled out of Shirley's thin, superior lips.

Her dress, Shirley had said, came from Miss Jackson's, and the girls admired the box-pleated skirt and fitted capelet with embroidered roses. "She carries only the latest fashions." Shirley prattled on, seemingly unaware that at least half the girls in the crowd would have gladly sacrificed Shirley to the volcano gods in order to have her new clothes.

Eva's ambitions were grander, though. She saw how small and insignificant Gilead society was, indeed, Oklahoma society in general was far too small to satisfy her desires. She would see what Miss Jackson's had to offer, but she knew that someday she would look back on it and laugh at how provincial it all was.

Across the table, Connie's face was a wavering map of emotions. "You've got it all figured out, don't you? Just tell me to jump, and I'll say, 'How high?'"

Eva adopted a conciliatory look and ran her hand down his arm. "Baby, I just want to surprise you. I'll give you the time of your life tonight."

"I'll go with you now."

"No."

"Why not? I want to."

"You'd be bored. Shopping is for women."

"Maybe I'll learn something." Connie tried a little laugh. He didn't realize he had already lost the argument.

"I'll meet you at seven," Eva said, "and we'll go to dinner. I'll wear a new dress that will make you lose your mind." She bestowed a dazzling smile that reached no further than her lips and walked quickly from the table.

By the time Connie paid the check, she had disappeared.

It took Eva two hours to complete her shopping. Miss Jackson's had not disappointed her. In fact, she had been dazzled by the array of dresses and hats and other accoutrements. So dazzled that she had spent half of her proceeds from the bank robbery before she knew what had happened. She directed the snotty sales clerk to send her purchases to the hotel, except for an afternoon dress in sheer white crepe with a pink pleated sash. And, of course, except for the small package she had retrieved from the back of Connie's Ford. He had never even noticed it was there.

In the dressing room at Miss Jackson's, she picked up the package and looked at it thoughtfully. Plain brown paper tied with string. And inside, Frank Pendleton's jacket, waiting like a time bomb.

Eva donned the white crepe dress and handed her old one to the sales clerk. "Donate it to the needy," she said grandly. She loved the feeling of largesse that went with such a command, as though she were in a movie where the rich heiress wears a new frock every day.

To go with the white dress, she selected white gloves that went halfway to her elbows and a white hat with a sweeping flat brim that was trimmed with pink flowers. Pink satin pumps completed her costume.

Eva stared at herself in the mirror, entranced by the new creature that was a more sophisticated version of herself. She didn't look like a little girl. Someday, she would be festooned with ruffles and feathers and diamonds like Mae West in "She Done Him Wrong." She lowered her lids in a sultry gaze. It always made the men go ga-ga over Mae. That air of knowingness. That's what the suckers couldn't handle. She freshened her lipstick and once again checked the address on the small slip of paper the sales clerk had given her: Ralston Brothers, 910 Boulder.

The name on the paper matched the label inside the lapel of Frank Pendleton's jacket.

At the tailor's shop on Boulder, a small balding man in shirtsleeves and garters watched her approach the counter. She felt him appraise her clothing, and for the first time, she felt confident that she would pass any inspection.

"I'm here to pick up Mr. Frank Pendleton's order," she said.

The man flipped through a stack of cards and stopped at one. "We don't have anything for Mr. Pendleton, miss. We delivered, let's see, a pair of trousers last week."

"I'm sure you must be mistaken. Won't you check in the back?"

The little man shrugged his shoulders and went through a curtained door.

The moment he left, Eva picked up the card and looked at it. Frank Pendleton. Hotel Ambassador.

It was as easy as that.

Now that she had what she came for, an uneasiness settled over her. What did she think she was doing? Frank Pendleton was a dangerous man. She had witnessed him shoot a man dead and set his body on fire. What if he hurt her? Or what if he wasn't even there? What then?

She stepped out the door and into the street and shook off the doubts. No one ever won a war by running the other way.

A shoeshine boy gave her directions to the Hotel Ambassador. It was several blocks away, so she tucked the package under her arm and caught a bus. Only five cents; she could afford that and more. She was proud of herself. So many adventures, so many new experiences, and no one observing her would imagine she was a country bumpkin who had never been to the city before.

Eva's first obstacle stood at the arched doorway of the Hotel Ambassador: a portly man garbed in a uniform replete with gilt braid and shiny buttons. He wore a cap on his head, which he doffed to a gentleman as he held the door open for him.

Do the little girl thing, she told herself. She went up to the man and focused on her feet like some demure country lass. "Mister," she said. "Mister, I'm looking for my uncle Frank Pendleton."

She didn't look him in the eyes. Instead she thrust out the package. "Aunt Vera said I was to bring him this."

The doorman reached for it and said, "I'll see he gets it, miss," but she drew it back.

"I'm supposed to deliver it to him myself. Aunt Vera doesn't like it when I don't do what she says." Eva's voice was low and trembling, leaving unsaid the horrible things the imaginary Aunt Vera had done to her. She sounded as though she might start crying at any moment.

The doorman bought it. Maybe it was the virginal white Eva was wearing.

"He's on the seventh floor, miss," he said, holding the door open for her.

The elevator was lined with dark mahogany and shiny brass rails. The black man who operated it bowed his head respectfully and took her to the seventh floor. As the cage rose higher and higher in the building, Eva felt herself expanding and aging, until by the time the door opened and she emerged on Frank Pendleton's floor, she was a full-grown woman.

She felt a heightened sense of danger, of the unknown. She remembered the look on Frank Pendleton's face as he set fire to the car with Al Bucklin's body in it. Cool. Dispassionate. As though he were burning a brush pile.

When she was 13 and her mama was still alive, Eva and Dodie Ashton had hitchhiked to Muskogee to see Paul Muni in "Scarface." Her mama wouldn't ever let her see a movie about a crazed killer who whistled a little tune before he blew someone to shreds. So she told her mama she was spending the night with Dodie.

Her favorite character in the film was Poppy, the woman Scarface fell for. Ann Dvorak had played Poppy. So calm and cool. When Scarface first met her in his boss's house, he had said, "Hi!" and she just said "Mmhmm" in a knowing way and studied her nails. She was the tough, beautiful broad that all the gangsters had to have.

Eva told herself to be Poppy, the only woman who could tame the handsome killer. She was standing on the edge of an abyss, and anything could reach out and pull her down. No looking back, she told herself. No looking forward. The time that matters is now.

She knocked on the door of 714.

He looked different than she remembered. Smaller and diminished in his undershirt and dirty pants. His face was narrow, and stubble shadowed his chin. She felt disappointment as though she had paid for something that turned out to be less pleasing than she expected.

A cigarette hung from his thin lips. He blew out a stream of smoke and looked at her through the contrail. Behind him, Eva glimpsed a large room with a clothes-strewn floor and unmade bed.

She decided to make the best of it. Be like Poppy, she told herself. Be like Ann Dvorak. It's just a part to play.

"Well. Ask a girl in."

He leaned against the door and studied her the way a cat studies a mouse.

"You can't expect me to stand out here in the hall all day."

He shoved off the doorjamb and motioned her in. "Do I know you?"

"Maybe I'm someone you want to know."

Eva stepped inside the room and looked around with avid curiosity. Two tall windows, heavily draped, limited the light. A fan stirred the air. The room was simply furnished: iron bedstead, wooden chest of drawers, two overstuffed chairs, a small table with a lamp. The table was littered with an overflowing ashtray, empty beer bottles and a crumpled racing form.

Pendleton closed the door to the hallway and grabbed Eva's arm in a grip so tight she almost cried out. "Cut the games. What's your grift?"

"It's not a game! I'm just returning something you left behind." She handed him the package, neatly tied in string. "Here. Take it. Open it."

He tore it open and stared at the jacket and then at her. "Where'd you get this?"

Eva looked at him through lowered lashes. "Why don't you offer me a drink, Frank?"

He blinked at the use of his name. "What do I look like, a nursemaid? I don't keep a bottle of milk on the premises."

"That's cute."

He pulled out a bottle and splashed some amber liquid into a dirty glass. "Drink up and talk to me."

Eva took a big swallow and turned away so he wouldn't see the face she made. The foul-tasting stuff burned all the way to her stomach. But its warmth spread quickly and left a pleasant buzzy feeling in her head. She turned back to him, bolder now, and took another swallow.

"I have a business proposition."

"I don't do business with kids."

"I'm no kid, Frank." Eva stretched her arms over her head, the Loretta Young look Connie always fell for. "Tell me what you like."

A hungry look narrowed his fox-like face. "What do I like? Fast cars, fast horses, fast women and a wad of cash in my pocket at the end of the day."

"I think you'd like me."

Pendleton sank into a chair by the curtained window. "Then come sit on your Uncle Frank's knee."

24

Bill Davis drove up to the farmhouse in a battered Dodge pickup on a Tuesday afternoon. He had left for his drinking spree in Fort Smith three days earlier. Virginia wiped her hands on her apron and watched him through the kitchen window as he climbed out of the truck and shut the door with a proprietary slam.

Over the past days, every sound of a motor had drawn Virginia to the window. She had been smoking one cigarette after another and willing Bill Davis to hurry back. She needed him now more than ever. She couldn't wait any longer for Ned Bender to contact her. She had wired the money on Monday, and it was now past midweek. She had heard nothing. The time for waiting was over. It was time to go to him and find out where Isabelle was. But she couldn't go alone. She needed someone she trusted completely. Bill Davis.

The day was sultry, and the leaves on the cottonwood in the yard hung silvery in the heat. The trio of remaining chickens drooped in its shade.

Behind her, Eva was talking. In fact, she had been chattering nonstop since she and Connie returned from Tulsa the day before. She asked Virginia's advice on clothes and cooking. She talked about movie stars and fast cars and the tall buildings in Tulsa. She wanted to know when they planned to rob another bank so she could get her hands on more money.

Virginia wondered what she had started. The girl seemed to have no second thoughts about entering a life of crime. What would Virginia's own parents say if they were alive to see the chain of events Virginia had set in motion?

It was too late now to undo any of that. The best Virginia could try for was to divert Eva's attention from robbery and toward more wholesome activities. Although, truth be told, she couldn't imagine the girl going on hayrides or to pie suppers and gospel sings.

Eva had brought Virginia a gift, a pair of silk stockings, which she badly needed. The new Eva wanted to help Virginia with her hair. A style that wasn't so old-fashioned. Virginia declined. She liked her thick mane of hair and the coil at the nape of her neck. The new Eva was easier to get along with than the sullen teenager who had left for Tulsa a few days earlier, but her ebullience made Virginia uneasy. There was something brittle about her gaiety, as though it were made of spun sugar that would shatter at the slightest touch.

In contrast, Connie Yates had been morose and withdrawn; something vital had been sucked out of him. He spent his time fiddling with his new purchase: a GE tabletop radio.

Its shape reminded Virginia of a tombstone, but its scratchy sound was hard to resist. At night, it brought in voices and music from all over the country: comedy and variety shows, advertisements and holiness preachers. Connie and Eva sat in front of the little box by the hour, as though they had been enchanted by the sounds that flowed from it, but Virginia held herself aloof. What right did she have to seek cheap entertainment while her daughter was missing? She couldn't afford to go soft now.

The only part of the radio that Virginia had anything to do with was the news announcements: tense tales of CCC boys killed while fighting California wildfires, the kidnapping of an auto executive, reports on Adolph Hitler ranting against

Poland and Russia. There was never any shortage of trouble in the world.

With Eva and Connie acting so unlike themselves, it was a relief to see Bill Davis walk through the door. Even though Virginia was bursting with the need to enlist Bill Davis in her plan to go to Oklahoma City to see Ned Bender, she forced herself to wait. Let things settle down. Allow the man to relax a bit. Talk him into it when the time is right.

Bill Davis took off his hat, and Virginia noted his freshly shorn hair. "Did you get your ears lowered?"

He smiled at her shamefacedly as though he were a wandering husband, and said, "Reckon they had too many sheep to shear to take much time over me."

"That's some kind of rattletrap you drove up in."

"It's all part of a grand scheme. Where's the rest of our notorious gang?" He winked at her when he said this, as though they shared a joke.

Virginia indicated the living room with a toss of her head. "They dragged in from Tulsa yesterday with their tails between their legs. Something happened there, but they're talking about anything and everything but that. Eva is, anyway. Connie's sulled up. I reckon I didn't miss out on much by being a homebody."

"How you been keepin yourself?"

Virginia shrugged. She hadn't told Connie or Eva about the sheriff's visit, and she wasn't going to tell Bill Davis. What was there to say, after all? That she and the old hound dog had shared a fine beef roast that the sheriff had left? That the sheriff was going all moon-eyed over her? It was nobody's business and nothing to take pride in.

Bill Davis pulled a flask out of his hip pocket. "Brought you some fine sipping whiskey."

Virginia took out the stopper and sniffed. "Aged more than 30 days," she said. "I appreciate it."

"Nothing but the finest. Let's have a snort then call the younguns in for a powwow."

"What are you scheming on, old man?" Virginia turned toward the cupboard and pulled out two glasses. They each downed a shot, and Virginia poured again. Somehow, it made the heat more bearable. It made everything more bearable.

Bill Davis looked at her across the table and lifted his glass to her. "Why don't you call in the children, Sister, and we'll have us a little talk."

Despite her worries, Virginia smiled. His good mood was infectious. "You go get them," she said. "This is your party."

They came in cautiously, Eva and Connie, as though they had been caught at something they shouldn't be doing.

They all sat around the kitchen table, and looked at the floor and at the walls. At the flies buzzing in the dirty window.

Bill Davis started in on Eva, whose fingernails were painted bright scarlet. "Catch your fingers in a door, Esther?" He winked at her.

Something flashed across Eva's face and then disappeared into vapid smoothness. She spread both her hands out for him to see. "It's called 'Mandarin Red.' I picked up a bottle in Tulsa."

He turned to Connie. "And what about you, boy? You like T-town?"

Connie scowled. "I reckon it was swell for some."

"Got you a new noise box out of the deal."

"I did that."

"Well I had me a good trip," Bill Davis said, settling back in his chair. "Saw an old friend who had some ideas in his head. Good ideas. He has a boy that works for the Purity Oil Company out of Tulsa. Business is booming, and he says he can get us men folk a job."

The three looked at Bill Davis. A job?

"I know what you're thinking," he said. He leaned his chair

back against the wall. "But you'd be wrong. We'd work just long enough to get the lay of the land. They got a big payroll, just waitin to be plucked. I tell you, it's like smelling whiskey through a jail-house window. So close. We just have to find the key. And the old man is going to help us."

"It's a smooth-graded road down to hell," Virginia said.

"What's that s'posed to mean?"

Virginia's fingers drummed on the table while she struggled to articulate her thoughts. "It didn't seem like such a crime to rob a bank. Everybody knows bankers would steal the roof over the heads of widows and orphans, but now we're talking about taking the pay of working men with families to feed. What's the reasoning to make that okay?"

Bill Davis sat his chair down with a thump. "No workin stiff is goin to lose his pay, Sister. Them oil barons can't afford for 900 men to riot. They'll take the loss and make it up to the workers. They'd be damn fools not to. Anywho, it's ever' dog for his dinner. It's gettin harder 'n' harder to separate out the deserving from the undeserving."

Virginia and Eva scatted up some supper while Bill Davis and Connie Yates put their heads together under the hood of the pickup.

While she worked at the stove, Virginia's thoughts raced. How would Bill Davis's new scheme fit in with her need to go to Oklahoma City? Could she convince him to hold off on his payroll plans for a few days?

"He said the payroll was more than fifty thousand," Eva said dreamily. "A person could go far on that." She had paused in setting the table and was looking through a Sears, Roebuck & Co. catalog. "Lookit here. You can mail order a fur coat or a gun. Or both. If you just had the money."

"Your mother would cry to see what's become of you."

"I haven't done a thing except carry on in my grandpa's tradition."

Virginia turned on her. "Don't you talk about my father that way. Finis Watts was an honest man."

"Doc was a moonshiner and a horse trader."

"There's no sin in that. He made the finest whiskey in these parts. A man should take pride in his work."

"I saw him break a man's arm once. He had a big heavy bar in his hands and he smashed that man's arm. I heard the bone snap like a tree branch."

"You're a little liar," Virginia said. She felt the heat rising in her, rushing to her face. "My father did no such thing."

"I saw him. He didn't know I was looking, but I saw him."

The potatoes boiled over on the stove right then and the sputtering, foaming pan diverted Virginia's attention long enough for her to control her anger and to realize there was nothing she could say to change the mind of a girl as opinionated and stubborn as Eva. She might as well stand on the porch and yell at the wind to stop blowing.

As it turned out, convincing Bill Davis to take Virginia to Oklahoma City was as simple as saying the words.

After dinner, they sat on the front porch, sipping the fine whiskey Bill Davis had brought with him, and when the mood had reached the proper level of mellow, Virginia told him what she needed.

"I knew that was eatin at you, Sister," Bill Davis said. The rocking chair creaked as he shifted position. "I'll take care of you. I promised Doc I'd do that."

Virginia reached out in the darkness and took his hand. Its callused roughness comforted her.

25

The tall limestone buildings of downtown Oklahoma City rose before them, and Bill Davis intoned, as though he had been waiting for the moment, "If I find in Sodom fifty righteous within the city, then I will spare all the place for their sakes."

Virginia followed his gaze to the west. "You sound like your brother the preacher."

"We were raised on the same mother's milk."

"All his talk about hellfire and damnation. I don't like it."

The crinkles around Bill Davis's eyes deepened into a smile. He patted Virginia's hand and said, "Well now."

Connie's little Ford had made good time from Gilead. They left in the cool, dark morning before the chirpy birds were awake, and they had rushed through the dawning day into the long afternoon. Central Oklahoma was hot and dry and flat, and they drove with the windows down. The heated air beat against them like the blast from a furnace.

Virginia felt wilted, but as they neared the city, a current of electricity ran through her. Deep inside she knew they were closing in on Isabelle. Maybe this was the day she would be reunited with her daughter.

In the maze of downtown, Virginia pointed the way to Ned Bender's office. Bill Davis expertly guided the car to a parking place in front of the Chinese restaurant, and together they mounted the stairs. The stairs were dusty and the door at the top locked.

Bill Davis cupped his hands on the glass and peered through. "No one home."

The electricity in Virginia drained away and left her feeling sick. "We have to find him. He has to be around here somewhere."

But like a searchlight shining on a dead body, she suddenly saw the truth of it. All her hope had been wasted. All her naiveté, all her belief in a happy ending, all her refusal to look reality in the face. How could she have been such a fool? Why had she ever trusted Ned Bender?

Bill Davis took out his pocketknife and poked the blade in the keyhole. He delicately picked at the lock while jiggling the doorknob, and the door swung open.

Virginia shoved past him and ran into the room. Ned Bender's desk sat in the middle of the floor. Its top was bare, and the chair behind it sat crookedly, a leg broken. The telephone was gone, as was the fan and the other chair.

From the restaurant below, the odor of garlic and ginger floated up, perfuming the air with an exotic aroma.

It was obvious no one had been in the room for days.

Bill Davis opened the desk drawers, one by one. Most were empty. A few scraps of paper lay in the middle drawer, but nothing of interest was printed on them. The final drawer held a collection of empty whiskey bottles.

"Rent it to you cheap," a voice said.

Bill Davis and Virginia turned in unison to face a monster. At least that was Virginia's first impression. The man was a giant in all ways: girth and height and head. His face was wide and ruddy, a map of hard living, and a patch covered one eye.

Bill Davis was the first to recover. "We're looking for Ned Bender," he said, walking toward the man with a hand extended. "Mr... "

The giant didn't offer his name, but he took Bill Davis's

hand in his own. "I'm the landlord."

"The landlord." With an effort, Bill Davis retracted his hand. He flexed his fingers as though they had been melted together.

"Ned Bender skedaddled," the big man said. He frowned, and his whole face, eye patch and all, crumpled into a concentrated scowl. "Owes me money, too. Rent for two months. Anyways, I get first shot at him." The giant cracked his knuckles one by one.

"I sent him money," Virginia said. She paced the room like a caged animal. "He told me he would find my daughter." She thought if she saw Ned Bender right now, she'd kill him with her bare hands.

"Found his way out of town, I judge."

Bill Davis put a hand on Virginia's arm. "We'd best be going," he said.

"He said he'd help me!"

"Just let's go." He guided her through the door and down the stairs. By the time they reached the car, tears were running down Virginia's face.

"I want to kill him," she said. "I can't take anymore."

Bill Davis sat in thought, tapping his fingers on the steering wheel. "Wait here," he said, and he slid out of the car and went in the restaurant.

He returned shortly clutching a piece of paper in his hand. After he started the car, he touched Virginia's shoulder. "It's a long shot," he said, "but we'll go to his boarding house."

Through the long afternoon and into the evening, they followed a ghost, from boarding houses to speakeasies to burger joints, but Ned Bender had disappeared, taking Virginia's money, and her hope, with him.

All leads exhausted, Virginia and Bill Davis rented rooms in a downtown hotel. The hotel was somewhere between drab and seedy, and the desk clerk leered at them knowingly. Neither cared.

Bill Davis left to find some whiskey, and Virginia lay on the worn chenille spread that covered her narrow bed.

In one hand, she clutched Isabelle's picture. She had learned a lesson that she couldn't afford to learn. Some lessons don't enlarge your world; some grind you down and make you smaller.

When Bill Davis returned with two bottles, Virginia looked at him wordlessly and took one. In the darkened room, the neon lights of downtown blinked on and off through her window, like a semaphore's plea for help. She drank the whiskey straight from the bottle.

It may have been the next day or the one after, Virginia lost track, when Bill Davis pulled her out of her bed. He stripped off her filthy clothes and sat her in the bathtub and poured warm water over her. Then he dressed her as gently as if she were a baby.

"We're going to find your little girl," Bill Davis said. "I promise you that."

Virginia looked at him with dull eyes. What was his word worth?

It was as if Bill Davis read her thoughts. "Maybe you look at me and see a broken down old man," he said. "And maybe I am. But I promised your daddy I'd look after you and the others. Carolina's dead, and I don't know where your brother's gone off to, but you're here. You're my promise. And I aim to keep it."

He said the words with such conviction, that something inside Virginia began to pulse, some of the rage melted away and was replaced with a faint ray of hope. The image of Isabelle that she held inside her began to take shape again.

Bill Davis hadn't finished what he had to say. "You gotta do your part, Sister. Be the mother that your little girl deserves."

He turned his back. "She don't need no drunk."

Words of self-defense leaped to Virginia's lips, but she swallowed them back. She suddenly saw herself clearly, as though the Lord himself had held up a mirror for her to look in, and she knew Bill Davis was right. Isabelle deserved better.

"Let's go home and follow your plan," she said, "the one about the payroll. We're going to need more money."

For a day after her bender, Virginia couldn't hold any food down. She sat at the kitchen table, her hands trembling, as she lifted glass after glass of water to her lips. Eva worked around her as if she wasn't there.

Virginia slept a deep and dreamless sleep that night, and the next day when she got out of bed, she went about her daily chores as if the events of the past week had never been. However, a shadow hung over her, and it cast a shadow of its own.

Bill Davis and Connie left for their new job two days later, driving the rusty truck. The plan that Bill Davis had hatched in Fort Smith was on. They all needed more money: Virginia to find Isabelle, Bill Davis to buy a farm for his family, Eva to go to Hollywood and become a movie star, and Connie, well who knew what Connie wanted, least of all, Connie himself. He just wanted to be a part of whatever was happening.

The two men planned to board near the oil field and stay the week. They might even be gone two weeks, Bill Davis said. It depended on how quickly they could learn the lay of the land and the payroll truck schedule; it depended on the inspiration of a plan to liberate the money from the Purity Oil Company.

In the meantime, Eva and Virginia were left with Connie's

car. Their task was to learn how to drive it. That was Bill Davis's idea. He said that the more skills each of them had, the better their chance of success. What was left unsaid but clearly understood was that someone could get shot or even killed, and they dared not risk capture for lack of a driver.

Eva and Virginia had each been given brief lessons before the men left.

Eva caught on quickly. Soon, she was releasing the clutch and engaging the gears all in one smooth motion. The little car purred for her, and her delighted laugh rang out while she steered it around the barnyard.

For Virginia, it was a different story. When she tried to drive, the car would lurch forward and then choke and die. The gas fumes rose around her in a toxic cloud. She finally was able to get the car to go, but she was tired and hot and cranky, and she felt no triumph over the machine.

After Bill Davis and Connie left, Eva said she was going to drive down the road a piece, and Virginia watched her go. Good riddance, she thought. Good riddance to all the annoyances in her life past, present and future.

Virginia lay on the living room floor, the coolest place in the house, and watched dust blow in the windows and across the floor. She couldn't remember the last time it had rained. The well her father had dug behind the house years before Virginia was born was deep and steady, but how long could it last when no water replenished the earth? The steady, reassuring creak of the windmill floated through the windows.

Already, she had heard, many of the neighbors' wells had run dry, and they had to abandon their farms or pay to have water hauled. Pay for water. Imagine that. Was this land destined to become a desert that grew only tough and spiny plants like the badlands out west? Even now, the fields were burned to nothing but rocks and dry ground. It was enough to make a body dream of the ocean. Her body felt heavy, and she fell asleep and dreamed of a younger Virginia and Isabelle at the ocean's edge, watching the endless waves wash against the sand.

26

Eva sat on the edge of the bed and pulled on her stockings. She was not in a good mood. It turned out that all men were alike, caught up in their own self-importance and pleasure and power, and women meant nothing more to them than arm dressing. It required that women be smarter than men, so men wouldn't even suspect they were being led around by their body parts.

Frank Pendleton, for instance, liked to talk even more than Connie, and his favorite subject was himself. He lay back on the rumpled sheets, hands folded behind his head, and his mouth kept moving.

"Only a sucker works for a living," he was saying. "I wasn't cut out to work steady. I could make more chips running a craps game or playing poker. My old man put me to work at the stockyards when I was twelve. I was there a few years too many. One day I went to work with sixty-five dollars in my pocket. Been up all night playing craps. I wasn't in no mood to work, and the boss was riding me.

"I don't take that off nobody, see? Especially not with green stuff in my pocket. So I took a sawbuck out and lit it with a match. Then I used that sawbuck to light my cigarette. Took my sweet time about it. The boss is going crazy. He says, 'Pendleton, you're fired. Get your time and get out.' I say, 'You can't fire me 'cause I already quit.' I never looked back. Only a sucker looks back."

"You're sure no sucker, Frank," Eva said. She was more than a little bored, but she let him light a cigarette for her, and she inhaled tentatively. All the actresses in Hollywood smoked, and it was time she learned how. She coughed when the harsh smoke burned her lungs, and Pendleton laughed.

"You're just a kid," he said. "The old man will take care of you. Just you stick with Frank."

She tried to sound adoring. "You have connections, Frank. You must know all the important people in Tulsa." She wished he would brag a little about who those important people were. She'd like to leapfrog on past Frank and meet the real power in town.

She saw how her words swelled him up. He took the cigarette from her and sucked on it. "After this is over, baby doll, we'll be rolling in dough. We'll live the life of Riley."

"I told you, Frank, I don't know when it's going to happen. The old man hasn't set a time yet. But I'll let you know."

"And I'll be there to collect when the time comes. Your aunt owes me after that little stunt in the back woods. She almost got me killed."

"And then we'll go to California."

"When the time is right, we'll blow this joint."

Eva didn't like that part. When the time is right. That sounded like the kind of run around she had gotten all her life. What it really meant was Frank thought he was in charge. He had a thing or two to learn about Eva Wilder.

Eva had told Pendleton her version of the events that had led to her returning his jacket. She sanitized the details. In her story, she hadn't been watching from the top of the bluff that day as he walked toward Al Bucklin's body, firing shots into him. In her story, her aunt had come home wearing the jacket with some harebrained tale about a gun battle and a fire.

There was more Eva didn't tell Frank. Lots more. He didn't

know about her mother and how Eva had to wrap her body in a quilt and hide her in the corn crib. He didn't know about the bank robbery and the part Eva had played. It was best he stay in the dark about what she was capable of. Let him call her baby doll. Let him feel protective and call himself her daddy.

"I have to get going," Eva said. "Aunt Virginia probably won't believe me, but I'll tell her I went to see a friend and had a flat tire and Dodie's father had to patch it. I had to stay the night. If we had a telephone, I coulda called her. What's she going to say?"

Eva started gathering her belongings. Her lipstick and comb went into her vanity. Her gloves. The keys to Connie's car. Frank Pendleton's phone number. She had accomplished her purpose. The pieces were in place, and someday soon, the story would play itself out, and she would live happily ever after.

27

Bill Davis paused outside the church and listened to the singing that poured out the open windows. "On a hill far away stood an old rugged cross..."

The land swelled around him, rising and dipping like a brown ocean, but there weren't any hills in sight in the fading light. Nor any trees that looked like timber for rugged crosses. Only a herd of bedraggled cows in a barren pasture and a few cars parked in jigsaw fashion on the verge of the road. People were still coming in after a day's work in the fields, looking for a bit of redemption at the revival meeting.

The twilight fell on the fields like a blessing, its earlier harshness replaced with a soft glow as if atoning for its excess.

The song ended, and Bill Davis heard his brother's voice from the pulpit. "Brothers and sisters, from Hosea 8:7, 'For they have sown the wind, and they shall reap the whirlwind.'"

Bill Davis smiled, a grim, humorless smile, and he ground his cigarette butt into the dirt and went through the doors.

The chapel was plainly adorned. Whitewashed walls and an unpainted wood floor. A wide aisle led to a long pine altar, where the sinners could repent and find Jesus. Behind the altar was a low platform with a lectern. Bill Davis's brother had set the lectern to one side, and he paced from one side of the platform to the other, looming over the congregation, his heavy brow furrowed with the weight of hell and damnation.

On the wall behind the preacher hung a large cross of rough-sawn pine, attached to the wall with spikes. It was the only decoration.

The pews were filled with farm folk. Bill Davis took a seat in the back and studied the people while he listened to the rise and fall of his brother's voice.

On the pew directly in front of him, a young farmer sat close to his sweetheart, not touching, just yearning. Next to them sat what he supposed to be the girl's mother and father, and a passel of tow-headed boys and girls stair-stepping down to the end of the row. Over their shoulders, he could see an old woman, her bald head topped by a hat, seated beside an elderly gent.

The church was filled with hardworking farmers and sharecroppers, roughnecks and ne'er-do-wells. All searching for an evening of entertainment or grace.

Bill Davis's brother was dressed in black, tall and gaunt, his eyes burning with an inner fire.

"From Jeremiah," he thundered, "'For the land is full of adulterers; for because of swearing the land mourneth; the pleasant places of the wilderness are dried up.'"

Bill Davis knew where the sermon was headed: How man's wickedness had brought on drought and famine and how only a return to righteousness would bring back the rain. He reckoned he parted company with his brother on that score. He didn't believe in a God who punished good people along with the bad. He thought that if there was an all-powerful God who could look into a man's heart, then surely he could dispense punishment with an even and just hand.

But did he deserve punishment? Bill Davis mulled over the question. He had done things deemed wrong in the eyes of man and the law, but what did God have to say? He closed his eyes for a minute and tried to hear or feel the touch of something holy. But his brother's voice was all around him.

"Brothers and sisters," the preacher said, his voice now low and seductive, "The Lord Jesus knows your hearts, and He knows your secret thoughts; He knows them that work iniquity, and He knows the evil that we do. He is a just God, and He will bring down swift and terrible punishment, but He is a loving God, too, and He will bring peace to those who sorrow and sustenance to those who hunger and rest to those who are weary."

Bill Davis slipped out the doors and waited in the shadow of the church. He smoked one cigarette after another and crushed the butts into the dry earth with his boot heel. A bat swooped across the light that streamed from the windows and faded back into the night. In the distance, a cow bellowed for its calf.

Eventually the congregation sang another song and there was a long, drawn-out altar call, "Oh Lamb of God, I come, I come," and he heard the sounds of weeping and shouting before the worshipers finally filed out into the night. Their eyes were red-rimmed and they talked in hushed tones as though they had witnessed something solemn.

After the crowd dispersed, Bill Davis walked around the corner of the church to where his brother stood on the steps. He waited until the last man left and then he stepped forward into the light. His brother saw him then, and he didn't seem surprised.

They clasped hands, and the preacher said, "Brother William, are you right with the Lord?"

"We don't have no quarrel," Bill Davis said. He didn't think it was any of his brother's business how he stood with God, but even when they were small boys, his brother had felt he had a duty to set everybody right.

"I heard you'd be here tonight," Bill Davis said. "I was wondering if I could get you to do a little something for me."

His brother's eyes narrowed, and some of the fervor that

always gathered in them when he preached faded.

Bill Davis reached in his jacket pocket and pulled out an envelope. "I need you to take this to Maisie and the boys. Will you do that for me?"

The envelope was thick with money, and the preacher weighed it in his hands. Bill Davis pulled out a thinner envelope. "Something for the Lord's work," he said, handing it to his brother.

"Is this blood money, William?"

"I worked for that money. I'm a working man." He had toiled for two weeks, and he had drawn his pay just like the other men at the oil field.

"Why don't you go home, William? Give this to your wife yourself and see your boys?"

"I hope to do that soon, but I have some business to tend to first."

"I'll be praying for you."

Something clutched Bill Davis's heart then, a fear that he might never see his family again, might never know the peace of waking in bed with his wife beside him and hearing the boys stir in the next room. He was a man in exile.

28

The plan was a good one. They had rehearsed it and timed it and talked about everything that could go wrong and what they would do if this happened or that happened. The only question was figuring out who would do which job. But even that was decided without too much fanfare because each task seemed best suited to one and only one person.

Bill Davis was happy because he might get to blow something up. He'd always wanted to play with dynamite, and now with the sticks he'd stolen from the Purity Oil Company, he had his chance.

Connie was happy because he didn't have to go to work every morning at 7 a.m. and hoist heavy tools and equipment until dark. No, his working days were over.

Eva was happy because she could dress up for the occasion. No more men's clothing for her. The only catch was that the pretty white dress she bought at Miss Jackson's might be ruined, but with the money they would come away with, she could buy a hundred white dresses if she wanted.

Virginia was relieved because they were finally moving forward again. The past two weeks of inactivity had been more than she could deal with. She wanted to see some progress, to feel some hope.

For the robbery to succeed, it required a fine level of teamwork and communication. And no small measure of luck.

Every Saturday morning, the armored car left the City National Bank in Tulsa at 10 a.m. and arrived at the Purity Oil Company field office an hour later so the paymaster could pay off the men at noon. It held two men: a driver and a guard. Both were armed - the driver with a Colt .45 semiautomatic, and the guard with a sidearm and a shotgun. The guard could lock himself in the back compartment from the inside, and with the steel-reinforced sides, bottom and top, he held a nearly invincible position. Nearly.

The route took the vehicle through the gently rolling hills south of Tulsa along well-traveled roads. The way Bill Davis figured it, the best place to make a move was along the five miles of gravel road that led from the highway to the oil field offices. There, amidst the rolling swales and creek bottoms, the terrain perfectly suited their needs.

They were in position by mid-morning. The slanting sun beat down on Virginia. She wore her father's suit again, disguised as a man, perspiring like a woman. Her thick hair was gathered under the crown of a hat. She wiped the moisture from her face with a red bandanna, carefully avoiding the ribbon of mustache over her lip, the same thin strip of raccoon skin she had worn in the bank robbery, and then she looked again at the hilltop to the south. There, atop a rock outcropping, Connie would wave a flag when he saw the armored car approach. A white flag meant the vehicle was by itself and the heist was on. A red flag meant something was wrong, and they'd have to wait to try again the next week.

Virginia didn't think she could wait. The oatmeal and bacon she had eaten earlier lay on her stomach like a tumor, and her tongue felt thick and furry. She needed a drink. It wasn't water she craved.

Connie's Ford coupe was hidden in the brush next to the road. No need to raise questions from the locals if they saw an unfamiliar vehicle on this little-used road, and Virginia had positioned herself behind a thick growth of oaks on a gentle rise where she could glimpse the hilltop to the south.

A memory of Eva painting the detour signs made her smile. The girl couldn't spell even simple words. "Detur. Bridge out." she had laboriously penciled onto the wooden signboard. When Virginia corrected her, Eva blushed and muttered something about the stupid way people spell things with extra letters that serve no useful purpose.

Eva had painted the signs with an artist's precision, and from a distance they looked like the real thing.

There was nothing to do now but wait. Virginia pulled out her pocket watch and checked the time. The second hand moved forward in maddening ticks, in tiny mechanical jumps like a flea on a leash. Whose idea had it been to measure time in such small increments, she thought? And what if time could be measured to an even finer degree? Would that change the way lives were lived? Could it extend that final breath if time could be broken down in smaller and smaller bits, to a half of a half of a half and so on? Could man in some way cheat death by parsing out his last moment into infinity?

In the forest around Virginia, the crickets and locusts made their own ticking sounds; so fast did they tick that they created a hypnotic hum that became the noise of the summer forest. She craned her neck to get a better view of the hilltop where Connie waited.

They were all waiting now: Virginia on her little hill, Connie on his taller one, Eva down by the bridge, and Bill Davis at the crossroads. When Connie signaled, they would go to work like well-oiled machines. All with their part to play.

In the meantime, Virginia wished she had a drink. Just a small swallow of something to take the edge off. What was it Bill Davis liked to say? "It takes gizzards and guts to get along in the world." Right now, Virginia's guts were all tangled up.

Connie waved the white flag at 10:45. Right on schedule. They had no more than 10 minutes to get in position. Virginia ran down the hill. Long spider webs hung between the trees, breaking on Virginia's face, and she swiped them aside. When she was near the car, she parted the brush and looked both ways down the road. No traffic. Perfect.

She pulled the rough sawhorses out of the brush one at a time and blocked the side road with them. Then she attached the detour sign with a piece of wire. The traffic on the road had been almost nonexistent that morning, but it was best to discourage any passersby.

She jumped in the car and started it. In her excitement, her foot slipped off the clutch and the motor coughed to a stop. She took three slow, deep breaths and started it again. This time she carefully put the car into gear, and it lurched forward onto the road.

A half mile down the road, she came to the slope that led down to the bridge. It wasn't much of a valley, just a dip the sluggish stream had carved out of the surrounding farm land over the years. On the other side, she could see Bill Davis and Eva getting the truck into position. She waited on the top of the grade to see whether they would need the chain in the trunk of the car.

While Virginia watched, Eva stood at the side of the road. Bill Davis was at the wheel of the old pickup. He aimed it toward the bridge and let it build up some speed. When it neared the bridge, he opened the throttle and jumped clear.

All eyes were on the pickup. It hit a rut in the road and took a nasty hop before crashing into the abutment. The truck spun around in the center of the bridge and came to a rest on its side. The motor died and silence descended.

The trap was laid.

Virginia turned Connie's car around and parked it out of sight above the bridge. Then she stuck the Colt single-action revolver in her pocket, picked up a gunny sack that held two tomatoes and went to join Eva and Bill Davis. She circled around the truck, which smelled of gasoline and oil. Eva was tugging the driver's door open.

It fell onto its hinges with a thud and gaped open like a hungry bird's mouth.

"You ready to begin your acting career?" Virginia said to Eva.

"I never been more ready."

Eva had rehearsed how she would drape herself on the battered truck, but the truck had been upright. No one had expected it to fall on its side. They didn't plan to take the truck with them anyway, so it didn't matter, but its position presented a small problem for Eva, who now had to adjust her pose for maximum stopping power.

She made little sounds of disgust while she tried to find a comfortable, provocative and heart-stopping way to pose in the doorway of the broken truck.

In the meantime, Bill Davis tested the length of the safety fuse on his bundle of dynamite. It had to be long enough to reach the middle of the road while providing him the protection of the trees. He found several places near the bridge where he could hide, and he chose one and hunkered down behind a tree to wait. Virginia could see his squirrel rifle sticking out, and she motioned for him to lower it.

"We don't have all day," Virginia said, turning back to Eva.

Eva pouted. "This damn running board is getting my dress dirty."

"I'll buy you a new one." Virginia grabbed the collar and pulled down, ripping the fabric and revealing a large expanse of Eva's creamy skin.

"Hey!" Eva said. Her head popped up.

"Shut up," Virginia said. "I hear them coming."

Virginia took a ripe tomato from her gunny sack and squished it between her fingers. The juice ran down her hand, and the pungent smell of tomato filled the air. She pushed Eva's head down and smeared the tomato pulp on her neck. Eva lay half out the door, one arm dangling, and her torn white dress fluttering in the wind. From a distance, the pulp glistened like a fresh wound.

"Do you have your gun?"

"Yes." Eva's voice sounded smothered, but an undercurrent of excitement ran through it.

Virginia ran across the bridge and slid down the embankment just as the armored car rounded the bend and geared down for the valley.

The car was a shiny black affair, with sturdy little windows in the back and white lettering on the side that said Hollingsworth Security Services.

Virginia could see the vehicle through the shielding branches, but she was afraid to watch it too intently, as though the driver might sense her stare. She heard it slow and then stop, the motor still running.

They waited, listening to the hum of the car. Apparently a conversation was going on inside because for the longest time, the doors stayed closed.

Virginia risked another look as the driver cautiously opened the door and stood beside the car. "Miss?" he said. "Miss? Can you hear me?"

Eva stayed still as a statue.

"Miss? Are you hurt?" The man took a few tentative steps toward her, his hand on the holstered revolver, and then he seemed to come to a decision and walked rapidly to the truck. He put one hand on her bare skin.

Before he had a chance to realize the blood on Eva was in fact tomato pulp, she reached up and grabbed the back of his shirt. Her right hand came up with a gun in it. She held it against his head.

"Don't move," she said, "or I'll blow you to kingdom come."

This was Virginia's cue. "I've got you covered, mister. We don't want to hurt you. We just want the payroll." She kept her voice low and harsh. No need to let him know he was being held up by two women. They might not get the proper respect.

At the sound of Virginia's voice, the man's head jerked around. Eva tapped him with the gun butt to remind him that she was in charge. "Take your gun out cautious-like," she said, "and drop it on the ground." She waited for him to comply. The gun hit the dusty road with a dull thud. "I'm climbing out of this truck," Eva said. "And if you pull any funny business, my partner will feed you a few."

By this time, they were certain they had the attention of the man in the back of the armored car.

In order to divert the driver's attention from the car, Eva kept talking to him. "See that row of bushes over my shoulder?" She jerked her head in Virginia's direction. "My partner is over there, and he's a dead shot. I don't want to see anyone killed, but he's a mite trigger-happy."

Virginia was torn between admiration for Eva's coolheaded demeanor and a sudden sick realization that things could go to hell in a handbasket. Until now she had focused on the plan and managed to keep a clinical detachment. All that was stripped away in the harsh glare of the sun. Just a few feet away, Eva was holding a gun to a man's head. Someone could be shot. Someone could die. This was so much worse than the bank robbery. These people were trained to deal with armed robbers. She clutched the gun in her hand more tightly. Breathe, she told herself. Just breathe.

Eva climbed out of the truck, keeping the gun trained on the driver, and keeping his body between hers and the armored car. No point in making a target for the man still inside. She swooped down and snatched the driver's gun off the ground. Now she had a gun in each hand. She tucked one into the sash around her waist.

"The guard. He's got orders to lock himself in the back when anything like this happens. You won't get in there." The driver's voice was shaking, but his eyes searched the brush behind Eva for the hidden shooter. Virginia shook the bushes beside her to give him something to look at. Then she moved farther under the bridge.

"Guess we have us a little standoff," Eva said.

While this conversation was going on, Bill Davis ran doubled over to the back of the armored car, the bundle of dynamite in his hand, and the fuse spooling out behind him. He scrambled under the car and attached the package to the undercarriage. Then he ran back to the protection of the trees. The whole process took less than ten seconds, less than the time Bill Davis had to stay on a bucking bronco at the rodeo.

From the trees, Bill Davis's voice boomed out through a megaphone, which made its source hard to locate and also made him sound more threatening. The megaphone had been Eva's idea.

"There is one pound of dynamite stuck to the bottom of your car," he yelled.

The guard's head whipped around toward the direction of Bill Davis's voice.

"It's in a steel box so the force of the explosion will be directed upward. It has a forty-foot safety fuse, which means that twenty seconds after I light the fuse, your armored car is going to blow sky high. Come out now with your hands up, and no one will get hurt. Stay inside, and you'll eat dinner in hell."

It was quite a speech, and it vibrated in the heat rising off the road.

One of the windows in the back of the armored car had a small opening in it, like a rifle port. The nose of a gun stuck through the port and a shot rang out. Dust rose next to the safety fuse. Another shot rang out and then another. The safety fuse remained intact, but now Bill Davis was angry.

He aimed at the window with his squirrel gun and pulled the trigger. The booming explosion made the earlier gunshots seem like rain splatters.

Virginia wondered if the man inside had been deafened by the firing of his own gun. And then she wondered if Bill Davis knew what he was doing. What in God's name was she doing here? She had to stifle the impulse to run away.

But something held her in place, and in the silence that followed the gunshots, she heard the slow click of a bolt being drawn. The back door opened, and a man stepped down to the ground, his hands over his head.

He was cursing in a low and angry voice.

Bill Davis rushed forward, a bandanna covering his lower face, just like a highway robber of old, and patted the man's sides to see if he had any weapons, and then he nodded to Eva. "Good work," he said. "Bring the other old boy over here, and we'll hogtie 'em."

While Bill Davis and Eva secured the two men, Virginia climbed onto the road from under the bridge and looked in the back of the armored car. Inside were stacks of bulging canvas bags. She felt her heart stop and then start again.

She boosted herself into the car. The ceiling was low, and she could stand only by doubling over. The walls were lined with dark oak, and Virginia shook off the thought that she had stepped inside a casket. A small padded seat was bolted into the wall behind the driver's side, and she sat on the seat and pulled a gunny sack open. In the bottom of the sack was a second gunny sack. She shook the second sack open, too, and began loading the canvas bags into it. The weight of each bag was uniform. Virginia smiled grimly as she thought of the careful counting and banding that had gone on at the bank.

Her hand felt something hard, and she picked up the guard's gun, some kind of revolver that she didn't have time to examine. She dropped that in the bag, too.

She worked methodically and efficiently. When the first sack became too heavy to easily heft, she filled the second. The small space reeked of gunpowder, and the air was stifling. The black suit and hat Virginia wore added to her discomfort. She was grateful to finish her job and escape from the armored car.

She pulled the bags out behind her, and they fell on the ground with a satisfying thud. Eva stood to the side of the armored car, holding a gun on the driver and guard, but her vigilance wasn't necessary because Bill Davis had tied their hands behind them and hobbled their feet. Both men were gagged.

He looked up from his work and his eyes sparkled at Virginia as though they'd just won a competition at the county fair. "It's time to vamoose," he said. "We'll put these boys inside where they'll be comfortable for a spell. I had to muffle them because they had more to say than a rooster at break of day."

"I took his weapon," Virginia said, nodding toward the guard. "Cleaned out the back."

"Shotgun, too?"

She frowned and climbed back in the car. She soon emerged with the guard's shotgun.

Bill Davis took it from her and slid back the bolt to make sure it was loaded. "A sweet little sure-shot," he said. "Short-barrel 12-gauge Winchester. All you have to do is point her in the general direction and the rest will take care of itself."

He snapped the bolt back in place and handed the gun

back to her, and Virginia held it carefully, as though it might fire of its own accord.

Bill Davis hoisted the men into the back of the armored car one at a time as easily as if they had been sacks of chicken feed and then crawled under the car to retrieve the dynamite. He handed the steel box to Eva, saying, "Take care of this, Esther," and then he went around to the driver's side and started the engine. He drove it slowly off the road and down into the creek bottom, where the tires sank into the shallow water. The armored car settled under the bridge with a small scraping noise.

Bill Davis emerged grinning and yelled at Virginia to bring him a board. They had hauled two extra boards in the back of the pickup just in case they needed to use them as levers, and now he took one and wedged it tight between a rock and the back door handle. Even if the men managed to free themselves from the ropes, they would be stuck inside the armored car until help arrived.

Privately, Virginia thought the extra precautions were wasted. Anyone who came along would see the pickup on its side in the road and stop to investigate.

She didn't say anything, though. So far, Bill Davis's plan had been as good as gold, and she wasn't going to tell him what to do.

Connie chose that minute to come barreling down the hill above the bridge. He had been positioned a mile away, and even if he had run cross country to get here, Virginia reckoned that not more than fifteen minutes had passed since she had set the detour sign across the road.

It seemed like an eternity.

Connie Yate's face was red in the heat, and he stopped at the edge of the road and sucked in deep, sobbing gulps of air. "I blocked the other end of the road with the detour signs," he gasped.

"You missed the excitement," Bill Davis told him. "It's time to skedaddle."

Connie's face fell in disappointment. Virginia handed one of the sacks to him. "Help me with these."

He smiled when he felt the weight inside. "Whooee. We're rich!"

They loaded the burlap bags, the dynamite and their gun collection into the car, and the four of them took off down the road with Connie driving, headed back to their hideaway where they could divide their spoils and celebrate their success.

All they had to do was get there.

29

"It ain't even noon, and we're rollin in clover," Connie said.

He perched in the driver's seat with the window rolled down and his head in the wind like a dog.

Bill Davis sat in the passenger's seat. Virginia and Eva were in the back. The little car was filled with the musky odor of success.

Eva relived her triumph as an actress. "Did you see that man's face?" she said to no one in particular. "I thought he was going to pass out from shock."

"He thought you were going to clean his plow all right," Bill Davis said. Both his hands were in his lap and his eyes were straight ahead. He wasn't ready to relax yet.

The road was rough, and the tires threw up a spray of dust and rocks.

Virginia was locked in her own thoughts. She watched the landscape roll by: gray farmhouses, untilled fields, listless stock. In the north, a bank of gray clouds loomed. Maybe they'd finally get some of that rain.

Maybe with the money her thoughts could return to such mundane things. Water, food, air. Isabelle. If everything had its price, Virginia had paid and paid. She would pay again with her share of the money. She would find a better detective. And then she would find a way for her life to return to normal. It didn't matter where she was. All that mattered was that she and Isabelle would be together. Her heart skipped a beat.

Beside her, Eva clapped her hands. "We got us a regular arsenal now," she said. "Connie's Smith and Wesson, the Colt, the squirrel gun, and those guns we picked up today. It's about time I had one of my own."

Bill Davis looked over his shoulder. "Esther, with the money we made today, you can buy yourself one of those itty-bitty pearl-handled derringers the ladies favor. It'll fit right in your handbag."

"You don't call me Esther anymore." There was a dangerous note in Eva's voice. "I don't like it when you call me that."

"Lissen at that. No tellin what she'd do with a loaded gun," Connie said to Bill Davis.

Eva thumped Connie on the head. It looked playful, but it shut him up.

Connie slumped the driver's seat and pouted.

They crossed the Arkansas River north of Haskell and, staying on a back road, drove south past the site of the Old Blue Creek Mission. The boarding school for the Creek Indian children had burned years ago, and on the grounds, scrub brush grew and overtook the crumbling walls. Green clumps of mistletoe clung to the tops of scrubby oaks, sucking life from the drought-stricken trees.

The four were quiet until they came to the end of the back road they had been traveling and the car nosed onto the highway east of Muskogee. They weren't far from home now, and they breathed a collective sigh of relief.

Along the brush-choked fence row, a line of Burma-Shave signs stood in snaky order.

Bill Davis read them aloud with gusto.

"His face was smooth
And cool as ice
And oh Louise!
He smelled
So nice."

He poked Connie in the ribs and glanced back at Eva. "Is that right, Eva? Does Connie smell so nice?" He exaggerated the pronunciation of her name.

Eva looked out the window. "He's got that Gilead stink on him," she said. "You all smell like a hick town in the middle of nowhere."

"And you smell like a whore," Connie said, twisting in his seat to look at Eva.

To Virginia, Connie's face looked like a puppy that had been kicked. He was her boy right then, and she suddenly hated Eva for her casual cruelty.

Any spat that may have developed had to wait. With a sound like the explosion of a gun, one of the rear tires burst. The road curved, and Connie cursed and fought the wheel while the car rocked back and forth like it was trying to shake itself loose from the string of highway.

The car came to rest in the ditch, amidst a cloud of dust and broken weeds. The sudden quiet seemed to go beyond silence; it was the waiting kind, the hole that needs filling, the secret longing to be told. Off in the distance, thunder growled, and the wind quickened.

"It wasn't my fault," Connie said. His voice was thick as though he were fighting tears. "Them tires were bound to go."

Bill Davis was the first to shake it off. "That chat eats them up," he said to Connie. "We'd better fix 'er fast before that storm hits."

Connie nodded, and the two men got out of the car.

From the back seat, Virginia and Eva watched them examine the damage.

Bill Davis directed the operation. "Esther at the wheel. Sister and Connie back here with me. We're going to have to shove her back on the road."

While the three of them grunted and pushed, Eva steered the car. The ditch wasn't that deep, and the red dirt was dry.

They soon had the car back on the shoulder. Bill Davis removed the spare tire from its bracket.

While he and Connie worked to change the tire, Virginia brushed the dirt off her trousers and studied the sky. The wind was blowing harder, and the dark clouds seemed to be rushing toward them. The temperature was dropping, which was a welcome relief.

An old black man happened by in a Model T and offered to help, but Bill Davis waved him on. "We've almost got 'er," he said.

Out of the thick woods nearby, a dirt track joined the highway. Virginia realized with a start that it was the road that led to the cabin where Slick and J.P. had brewed their moonshine. Where Frank Pendleton and Al Bucklin had their shootout. Where fire had consumed the dead bodies. It seemed to Virginia that the approaching storm was coming right down that narrow lane.

She wished she had a bottle with her. Just one drink would dilute the memories and foreboding that threatened to envelop her. But there was nothing to drink.

Virginia stuck her head through the open car window and spoke to Eva. "Your dress is torn. You should put on that suit you wore for the bank robbery. If anyone else happens by, they shouldn't see a girl in a torn dress. That's what those men in the armored car are going to remember. A girl in a torn dress."

Eva's dark eyes looked at her steadily. "I think I like my torn dress."

"This isn't the time for your nonsense. Do you think I like wearing this phony mustache?" She unconsciously fingered the ridge of hair across her upper lip. "It's about as comfortable as a corn cob. Anyway, that's not the issue right now. If the Laws picks us up, who do you think will get your share of the money?"

Eva sullenly turned away and dug on the floorboards for the packet of clothing. She untied the strings slowly and shook out the trousers and shirt. The heavy shoes thumped on the floor.

"Where's the jacket?"

"I don't need it."

Virginia remembered Frank Pendleton and the look on his face as he emptied his gun into Al Bucklin's body. She had been wearing his jacket that day. She shivered. "You're getting a womanly figure. The jacket will hide it."

Eva held up her sash. "Help tie this around me. It can flatten me out."

"Where's the jacket, Eva?"

Something flashed in Eva's eyes. "I don't know."

The men had lowered the car off the jack, so Virginia climbed back inside. She cinched the sash tight over the camisole that covered Eva's breasts, and Eva put on the shirt and wriggled into the trousers. She tucked her hair under a cap, and the shoes she left on the floor. She looked at the dress thoughtfully, then wadded it up and thrust it under the seat.

By this time, Connie and Bill Davis were throwing the tools in the trunk that was strapped on the back of the car. They'd soon be on their way and no harm done.

Down the road, down the road where Slick and J.P. once lived, a distant movement caught Virginia's eye. A car barreling toward them.

The wind caught the dirt kicked up by the car before it could form a tail. The swirling dust formed a haze around the car as though it were wrapped in dirty gauze.

As the car neared, Virginia saw it was black, a big black Plymouth with insignia on the side. In the windy, wavering light, it was hard to tell how many were in it. The car skidded to a halt across the road from the Ford, and it wasn't until then that Virginia recognized the driver.

Sheriff Ray Callahan. Beside him in the front seat sat his deputy. Another man sat behind them.

Virginia felt the blood rush from her face. Her hands were ice.

She was dimly aware of Connie backing around the end of the Ford, away from the side that faced the sheriff's car. Bill Davis stayed put, hoisting the ruined tire in its bracket.

Virginia put a warning hand on Eva's arm. "It's the sheriff and his deputy."

"What'll we do?" Tension clutched Eva's voice.

"Sit tight. See what happens." More than anything, Virginia wanted to get out of the car and run across the field to the safety of the hills beyond. Just keep running.

"I won't let them have my money," Eva said. "We need our guns."

"Leave this to Bill Davis to handle."

Eva's breath made a sound of explosive impatience. "That old man."

At her feet, Virginia was aware of the burlap bags and the money they held.

The driver's door of the Plymouth opened, and the sheriff stood beside the car, shielded by the door. His deputy stayed put in the passenger seat. Another face pressed against the back window. The face was a thinner version of Connie's.

"J.P." Virginia felt the shift in gravity as the world dropped beneath her.

"What?"

"J.P. Slick's running buddy. Connie's cousin. He's in the back seat."

Eva seemed unaware of the new danger that J.P. posed. "They caught a little fish. Maybe that'll hold them for a bit."

"Don't you remember? You were there. He stood down in that holler with the fire all around him, and he shouted 'Virginia Crow, this is on your head.'"

"Criminy."

Hardly daring to breathe, they watched Ray Callahan cross the road. His lanky body was decked out in full sheriff regalia: crisp khaki shirt and trousers (Had his mother starched and ironed them?), black boots, Stetson hat, Sam Browne belt across his chest and a pistol hanging from his hip. There was a look of casual inquiry on his face. Just a man of the law wanting to help citizens trapped before the oncoming storm.

Virginia was aware of Connie pressed against the car beside her. She rolled down her window a few inches.

"Stay calm," she said. "They might not recognize you."

"I'm about as calm as a tornado."

"Don't ruin it now."

"I tucked my gun under the front seat." He looked at Virginia, keeping his voice low. "Can you reach it to me?"

By now Callahan was face to face with Bill Davis, and the two men shook hands.

"Obliged. Just a bit of tire trouble." Virginia heard Bill Davis say in response to Callahan's question.

"Give him his gun," Eva hissed to Virginia.

Virginia looked straight ahead and ignored her.

The voices of Bill Davis and the sheriff dropped to a murmur and then the sheriff turned toward his car. Virginia swiveled to watch him go, and her eyes met the eyes of J.P.

His widened in recognition while she shrank back in the seat.

"He saw me. Damn! He saw me."

It happened fast. At the same time, each second seemed trapped in amber.

J.P. lunged over the front seat and with one arm put a choke hold on the deputy while the other hand grabbed for the deputy's gun. J.P. had the advantage of surprise and position. The deputy struggled fiercely and when he continued to fight, J.P. raised the gun and shot him in the head. Something dark splattered across the inside of the windshield.

At the same moment, the sheriff crossed the road in a loping run, fumbling in his holster for his gun. J.P. saw him coming and dived out of the car, rolling to a crouch. He lowered his gun toward the sheriff and squeezed off a round. A rose-shape bloomed on the sheriff's thigh, and he dropped to the ground. His gun fell and skidded across the pavement.

Virginia had been frozen in place, but now she felt released from a spell. She reached under the front seat and felt Connie's revolver. Bill Davis's head and shoulders stuck through the front window; he was looking for his gun. Virginia handed him Connie's Smith and Wesson.

Their eyes met in an instant of understanding.

Before Bill Davis could use the gun, though, J.P. was coming for them. He charged across the road like a crazy man, yelling at Virginia. "You bitch. You turned me in. This is your fault!"

Virginia heard Eva cry out behind her. Connie darted around the end of the car and ran toward his cousin.

"J.P.," he yelled. "No. Don't do it."

J.P.'s eyes burned, and he didn't seem to hear Connie. He stopped and raised his gun toward the window where Virginia sat.

Connie rushed toward him and into the line of fire. A single pistol shot rang out, and Connie fell.

Bill Davis aimed and squeezed the trigger of his gun.

From inside the car, Virginia heard a solid thunk as a bullet hit home. But J.P. was a wild beast. He kept walking and firing his gun. His aim was erratic, though, and the bullets whistled into the distance.

Bill Davis pulled the trigger again, and this time J.P. fell and stayed still.

It was Eva who broke the sudden silence. "Connie!" she screamed. "You idiot!" She jumped out of the car and threw herself on him.

Virginia was close behind her, and she heard Connie moan.

"Connie," she said, leaning over him, "can you hear me?"

Connie lay face down on the rough pavement. "Damn," he said in a voice soft as feathers. "He shot me. My own cousin kilt me."

"We'll get help for you," Virginia said. "We'll take care of you."

Eva stood aside while Bill Davis and Virginia turned him over as gently as possible, but Connie screamed nevertheless. Blood soaked the front of his shirt and mixed with the road dust that had ground into him when he fell.

They were oblivious to the sheriff behind them, who was painfully pushing himself across the pavement toward his gun.

"We've got to get him in the car," Virginia said. Her voice came from a dream.

Eva was no help. She cursed Connie and told him again that he was a fool, as if he could take back the moment when he had thrust his body in front of J.P.'s gun. Virginia pushed her aside, and then Bill Davis and she half-lifted, half-dragged Connie to the back seat. Connie was silent. Virginia wedged in the back seat beside him and laid his head on her lap.

"It's better he's out of it," Bill Davis said. "It's a long way to a doctor hereabouts."

He turned to look at the sheriff then, who was closing his hand over his gun.

"Don't think about it," Bill Davis said. "There's enough dying here today."

Bill Davis held his gun loosely by his side, and when the sheriff turned and saw, his hand dropped away from the gun on the ground.

Bill Davis walked over and picked up the sheriff's gun. He looked in the car at the deputy, who was sprawled across the front seat. There was no doubt he was dead.

"My deputy's gone," Ray Callahan said. "He has a wife and three children. Because of you he's dead."

"Your prisoner killed him. That no-good son-of-a-bitch went crazy and started all this. You better remember that if you want to see your own children again." Bill Davis's voice was low and intense, and he seemed to be fighting off a fury deep inside.

The sheriff tried to get to his feet, but the pain forced him back down. His trousers were torn and blood-soaked, and he looked down at them with a curious detachment. "I need a doctor."

"You ain't the only one."

A car could come down the road any minute. It was a miracle that none had come by while the shooting was going on. Maybe the approaching storm had kept them all home. Bill Davis looked around him and took in the possibilities: the dirt track winding into the hills from the direction the sheriff's car had come, the highway going both east and west, the barren and wide-open fields all around.

Behind him, over the growing sound of the wind, he could hear Eva crying.

"We gotta get out of here," he said to the sheriff. It was as though Bill Davis sensed the sheriff would be his ally in survival. "The storm's going to hit us. We're going to have to work together for a time until we get this sorted out. We can't leave you here."

The sheriff nodded and allowed Bill Davis to help him to Connie's Ford. The sheriff's right leg was useless, the bullet must have broken a bone, and sweat shone on his face. Bill Davis put him in the front seat next to Eva, who scooted aside as though the sheriff had something contagious.

Bill Davis touched Eva's hand. "It'll be better soon," he said. "You keep an eye on him while we clean up this mess. If he gives you trouble, holler."

"Take him out and shoot him," Eva said. "Then won't no one have to keep an eye on him."

Virginia raised her head. "He said it right a minute ago. There's been enough killing."

Bill Davis gestured to Virginia to help him, and she laid Connie's head on the seat and climbed out of the car. Together they dragged J.P.'s body to the sheriff's car. They lifted him in the trunk and then Virginia got behind the wheel of Connie's Ford. She followed Bill Davis, who was driving the sheriff's car. Bill Davis had asked Virginia to drive the sheriff's car, but when she saw the congealing blood on the seat, she balked. "I want to do what I can," she said, "but I don't think I can stomach all that blood."

"You'll have to make sure the sheriff don't cause no trouble while you're driving."

"I can handle him."

Bill Davis hid the sheriff's car with the bodies in a thick growth of cedars. After pushing the broken cedar branches back into place, Virginia slid into the back seat of the Ford, once again cradling Connie's head in her lap, while Bill Davis took the wheel. Connie moaned when she settled in the seat, but he didn't seem to be aware of his surroundings.

There was plenty of blood in the back seat with Connie, blood that was thick and viscous like slow death. It spilled over the seat and pooled in the floor, staining the burlap bags. Connie's face was pale and waxy, and his breath rattled.

"We have to get this boy to a doctor," Virginia said.

Before Bill Davis could reply, the storm burst on them. Not rain, but a black wall of dust that rushed across the land like coal smoke.

Bill Davis turned the car toward the hills. "We'll be afoot if we don't find shelter. These dust storms eat right into a motor."

The sheriff spoke for the first time since he had been put in the car. "That boy we arrested was living in a barn up that road."

Virginia remembered the barn. It had stood behind the burning cabin the day Frank Pendleton had invaded the little valley. "It's no more than a falling-down shack," she said.

"That's more than we have now," Bill Davis said. "I can't see a goldurned thing in this dust. It feels like hell ain't a mile away and the fences all down."

The light had vanished from the sky, and they were surrounded by a howling black beast. The road was visible only a few feet ahead in the weak glow cast by the headlights. The dust filtered through the windows and formed a gritty cloud that burned their eyes and noses and throats.

Virginia rubbed her eyes, and felt the tears well up. They were scratchy tears that ran down her cheeks and left a trail in the dirt on her face.

She was trapped in a nightmare from which she couldn't wake. She tried to focus on Connie, but the dust in the air and in her eyes blurred her vision. His face seemed softer and younger than she remembered. The scrunched-up, anxious look he usually wore was smoothed out.

She saw that he needed a haircut, and she brushed the bangs off his forehead.

At her touch, his eyes fluttered, and he said, "Mama?"

"I'm here, boy."

She had to lean near his lips to hear him.

"Mama. I didn't aim to do nobody harm."

"You're a good boy," she said.

He didn't say anything more, and a moment later Virginia felt some essence leave his body.

Virginia didn't say anything to the others. She looked through the haze at the backs of their heads: Bill Davis hunched intently over the steering wheel, Eva's blue cap erect in the center, Ray Callahan's Stetson crushed as his broad shoulders and head slumped against the door. Virginia thought that if she spoke, if she told what she knew, she might start screaming and never stop. It wasn't fair. It wasn't fair. It was more than not fair. Bad luck had cast a net around them and was playing its fickle game.

30

The wind pried through the cracks in the barn walls, carrying a dark river in its wild currents. Bill Davis and Eva found the corner where J.P. had lived, little more than an animal's lair, but at least it provided protection from the full force of the storm.

The sheriff and Virginia waited in the car, which Bill Davis had pulled partway into the open side of the building. After a long silence, the sheriff turned in the seat and stared at Connie.

"I reckon he's dead," he said, looking then at Virginia.

"Yes."

"I'm sorry. I heard you call him son." Ray Callahan's face was gray with pain, and when he shifted in the seat, he groaned.

"He was someone's son. He was a good boy."

"He saved your life back there."

"That's a heavy debt to bear." She wondered how it was the sheriff didn't seem to recognize her through her disguise. J.P. had seen right past it. But Ray Callahan didn't give any sign that he knew who she was. For that small thing she was grateful.

Even in his pain, the sheriff couldn't set aside his job. "That boy we were takin in. He wanted to kill you."

"He must have mistook me for someone," Virginia said. "Or maybe he was just crazy." She thought about the hat on her head and the line of mustache above her lip, that little strip of coonskin, and she wondered how J.P. had seen straight to the heart of the matter.

Comfort was a relative term. The walls of the barn shielded the refugees from the force of the wind, but it did little to hold back the dust. All of them, Bill Davis, the sheriff, Virginia and Eva, wore makeshift masks over their noses and mouths to protect themselves from the onslaught of the fine powder that hung in the air and settled on every surface.

Earlier, Bill Davis and Eva had returned to the car to help move Connie, but they took one look at Virginia's fierce face and knew the truth.

"Leave him be," Virginia had said. "Just leave him be."

She tenderly laid him out in the back seat of the car, his arms folded over his chest as though he were resting. Then she found a piece of cloth in the barn, a rough and dirty piece of burlap, and she draped it over him. To protect him from any who would look.

Outside the barn, the wind still howled, and darkness descended on the corners and rafters of their shelter.

J.P. had made a corner of the barn into a home, of sorts, and it held an iron stove and a table and two rickety chairs. They were singed and smoke-stained, as though he had pulled them from the fire Frank Pendleton had set. A wooden shelf held cracked pottery and dented pans and a few essential food items: coffee, Vienna sausages, beans. In the corner, a cot, covered with stained and ragged quilts, completed the furnishings.

Eva appropriated the least offensive of the quilts and sat against the wall, the covering pulled over her head. She had been silent since they arrived, and it was hard to know if Eva was grieving for Connie or if she had been unnerved by the gun battle or if she was just persevering.

Virginia couldn't spare pity for her. She had her own concerns. Having Ray Callahan as a hostage changed everything. He would be able to identify them. They could never return to Gilead. Yet, leaving him behind hadn't been an option: an injured man with a storm bearing down. They might be criminals, but they weren't that kind.

Bill Davis helped the sheriff to the cot, where he lay down and closed his eyes.

"I heard the old boy that lived here was a moonshiner," Bill Davis said to the sheriff. "Reckon he left a little somethin laying around?"

With his eyes still closed, the sheriff said, "We tore down his still and axed his barrels."

"Maybe he had some stashed away. I could use me a stiff shot right now."

Bill Davis searched the barn, turning over farm implements, reaching down into stalls and stanchions, emptying a stack of boxes. The boxes were filled with trash: old newspapers, rolled balls of twine, emptied feed sacks, flattened cans, moth-eaten wool goods. Bill Davis kicked the boxes away in disgust.

Virginia did what she had seen her mother do so many times before in the face of catastrophe. When a neighbor's child was stillborn or the prize bull died or when hail beat down the crops, she made food. It wasn't easy to start a fire in the storm, but Virginia used some of the old newspapers that Bill Davis had strewn about and coaxed the flames to life. A covered pail of water stood nearby, and Virginia filled a pot, scooped in some coffee from a tin and set it on the stove to boil.

She glanced at Ray Callahan, who appeared to be sleeping. He looked harmless, lying there on the dirty cot, but to Virginia, it was the false security of a trapped snake. Don't open the lid, don't give it a chance to strike. Because that's what it's waiting for. One false move.

She wished for the power to roll the clock back. If only she hadn't looked through the window and met J.P.'s eyes. Then Connie might be alive now. They might be back in the farmhouse at Gilead, dividing their money and waiting for the storm to pass.

Or if she could roll the clock back even further: If only she hadn't gone with Frank Pendleton that day. If she hadn't put in motion the events that led to Slick's death and the fire, then J.P.'s glance would have gone right past her. Just a face in the window. Nothing to do with him.

If she had the power to recapture time, how far back would she go? To that day in Kansas City when Johnny Crow killed the cop? Knowing what she knew now, could she have prevented that from happening? The moment that began this long chain of disasters?

But how could she find that one pivotal moment in time? Did it all really begin that night years ago at the dance on the pavilion at Hyde Park in Muskogee? When Johnny Crow held out his hand and she took it? Though how could she want to take back that moment? Then there would be no Isabelle.

She considered the thought. No Isabelle. Whoever would have guessed that a tiny creature could hold your heart hostage and magnify your fears until each fragile little cough that came from her body was an occasion for Virginia to imagine the worst. The worst, of course, being no more Isabelle.

But what if there had never been an Isabelle? Would Virginia be free? Would she be a different person? Perhaps she would still be teaching in that tidy one-room school, where the oldest boys were as big as she, and the youngest children looked at her with a mixture of fear and worship that filled her with responsibility and pride.

She hardly remembered how that had felt. And something

about her life up to that point had left her empty. Why else would she have taken Johnny Crow's hand and let him sweep her onto the dance floor?

The fire sputtered and smoked, and as Virginia coaxed it back to life, an idea came to her. An idea that would provide some small measure of redemption. It wouldn't undo anything, but she knew deep in her heart it was the right thing. Connie Yates should be buried in the family plot next to Finis and Araminta Watts, next to Carolina and the space left empty for Virginia.

It might provide comfort to Connie's family to have him properly buried, to know that he had been cared for at the last. Later, when Virginia was established somewhere else, she could arrange for a stone to be erected. Whatever money was left from Connie's share after that, she would send to Beulah Stivers to give to his family.

She turned to tell Bill Davis her thought, and she saw him holding a bottle aloft.

"Victory," he said, smiling. "The devil's own elixir, nectar of the downtrodden, medicine for them that ails."

Ever so briefly, Virginia remembered that she had vowed to stop drinking. That she would be clean and sober for Isabelle. These were extraordinary times, though, and such promises could be kept later. She and Bill Davis each took a drink of the vile brown liquid directly from the bottle. It burned Virginia's throat and stomach, but she craved that sensation of her head floating away from her heart. That's what whiskey provided: an insulated door that tempered the pain.

She helped the sheriff into a sitting position, where he sipped and choked on the moonshine. When he had enough, she tore the lining of one of the quilts into strips and found a couple of short boards to splint his leg.

Ray Callahan grunted and turned white when Bill Davis

pulled his leg straight, but he didn't scream. It would have been the natural thing to do when the broken bones scraped across the nerves; however, the sheriff lay rigid and clutched a stick so hard it snapped in half.

When they finished, the sheriff took another swallow of whiskey and lay back. He placed his hat over his face as though to keep the light from his eyes.

But the light was long gone from the sky. Even had there been no dust in the air, it was now night. Virginia opened the firebox to throw a little glow into the room, and Bill Davis found a couple of candle stubs. He lit one and put it on the table.

Its wavering light was a small victory.

Bill Davis and Virginia drank the dregs of the bitter coffee she had brewed earlier, ignoring the grit that went down with it.

"Whyn't you get some rest, Sister?" Bill Davis said. "I'll wake you when the storm lets up, and we can get out of here."

Virginia nodded and made a pallet in the corner, next to where Eva huddled, and eventually she fell into a fitful sleep.

Much later, a sound awakened Virginia. Perhaps a shift in the wind or the rise and fall of the men's voices nearby. The memory of a dream trailed away. Something about her father. She had been crying in her dream, now she remembered. She had been inconsolable, and her father, with his big meaty hands, had hugged her and patted her back, saying over and over, "There, there, child. Don't you cry."

He had been like a bear, her father Finis Watts. Big and hairy and gruff. She tried to pull the comfort of his memory closer, but the misery of the present distracted her. Something was poking her in the back, and she shifted on the worn blanket until all she felt underneath was the smooth, packed-dirt floor of the barn.

She nearly drifted into sleep again and felt the wetness on her cheeks. The tears in her dream had been real. But who was she crying for? For poor Connie Yates? For her lost daughter? For herself? She longed for her father's bear-like arms to once again enclose her and tell her everything would come out right.

She had made mistakes that were perhaps beyond remedy. Now a boy and a deputy were dead. Someone would probably even mourn J.P.

Virginia rolled over and tried to sleep. She dreamed again, and in her dream, she and the sheriff were alone in the barn. Sunlight streamed through the cracks. Virginia was wearing her man clothes and her mustache, and while the sheriff sat with his arms folded and watched her, she took off her disguise, piece by piece, and revealed to him the truth.

He didn't seem surprised. When she stood alone in her nakedness, he stood and began taking off his clothes. He, too, wore a disguise. Under his sheriff regalia, he was a boy, a manchild, with soft peach fuzz over his body.

He looked at her shyly, a smile on his lips like those of the mischievous students she once had taught, and she drew him to her and stroked the soft hair on his back.

Next to Virginia's sleeping body, Eva stretched out. She snored lightly, like a moth beating its wings against a window. Above and around them both, the wind blew.

31

While the women slept, Bill Davis and the sheriff kept watch. It was as though they were soldiers keeping a vigil for their fallen comrades and guarding their small encampment from further attack.

Bill Davis stirred the dying fire and heated two cans of beans that he had opened with his pocketknife. The men dug the beans out with their fingers and drank the broth. They had little appetite, but they understood it was important to keep up their strength.

The sheriff lay back after eating half the beans in his can and let out a heavy sigh. "I never thought it'd come to this," he said.

Bill Davis assumed the sheriff was referring to the events of the day, and he felt obliged to defend himself. "My daddy was an honest man," he said. "A farmer. When I was a boy, he'd hitch his plow mule to the wagon every Sunday, and we'd go to church. We was faithful to every revival and camp meeting that come near."

He paused and rolled a cigarette for the sheriff and then rolled one for himself. Talking made him crave the smoke, and he had a point he wanted to make, even though the dust-filled air made his lungs ache.

"My parents tried to get me to walk the straight and narrow, but when I got older, I started watching those men of God. I saw them preach water and drink wine.

"I ain't a bad man," he said, drawing on the cigarette. "I ain't never killed a man before today, and even though I didn't have no choice in the matter, it don't set well.

"I saw things a man's better off not seeing. I worked on a farm in Kansas. In '32 I think it was. Come summer, it was hotter'n the devil. The cows would stand under the cottonwood trees and pant in the heat. And no rain. You could see the wheat burn in the field. In the garden, the potatoes and the corn and the beans were wilting where they stood. Do you know what that feels like, to see next winter's hunger?

"We were fools there, praying on our knees day after day for rain, and no rain comin at all. It was then I knew God had turned his back on us.

"The farmer had some young ones, and I'd see his wife put the food from her plate onto theirs. They was lucky to eat twict a day. They couldn't work me no more, so I went down to Oklahoma City. Things weren't no better there. The soup lines longer than the Canadian River.

"And the wind kept blowin and the dust storms kept comin. And there wasn't no rain. There was a joke going around that a farmer went to a bank for a loan and looked out the window and saw his farm blowin past."

Bill Davis put his boots up on the stove and leaned back in his chair. In the dim light, with his kerchief pulled down so he could smoke, he looked like a traveler come in from the night.

"The politicians, they said there was work for them that wanted it, but it was a lie. They were takin the relief money and using it for their own ends. Finally, a bunch of us had enough, and we marched on the City Hall. I ain't sure how it come about, but we went in a grocery store nearby and started helping ourselves. After a bit the Laws come, and they hauled us down to the jail. At least they fed us there."

Bill Davis paused to see if the sheriff was awake. The sheriff's cigarette had gone out and dangled from his fingers.

His eyes were closed. Bill Davis took the cigarette and placed it on the edge of the stove for later. The sheriff's eyes opened, and he said that he was still there, listening.

"I met this old boy in the jail," Bill Davis said. "He'd been in the Bonus Army and he'd rode the rails from one end of the country to the other. He'd heard folks talk about justice, and he knew we weren't gettin any.

"He said that people make laws for their own personal gain. They're tryin to stay in charge of us lesser men. Cause they fear if the mob ever got in charge, the bankers and the politicians would be hanging from the nearest tree.

"The only laws we have to follow, the man said, are the laws in our hearts: the natural and God-given laws that are based on justice and fairness."

"Who gets to decide what is just and fair?" The sheriff's voice was tired, as though this was a question he had played over in his mind many times.

"We decide what's fair. And justice? What is that? Maybe a sense that some kind of balance has been reached. Nature cares nothing for justice. It only seeks to continue."

"Do you believe in God?" the sheriff asked.

"I reckon I do."

"Then you believe in law because the only other side is evil. It's darkness and fear and crime." The sheriff raised himself on one elbow and looked at Bill Davis. The intensity in his eyes shone through the dusty air. "I don't know what all you and those folks with you done, but it damn sure ain't Sunday school stuff."

"Hell, sheriff, all I do is rob the rich, and robbing the rich ain't hardly no crime a'tall."

"You ain't in no position to talk about it," the sheriff said. "There's three men dead, and I don't know about two of them, but my deputy was a good man." He turned his back to Bill Davis and pretended to sleep.

Bill Davis picked up the cigarette butt from the stovetop and looked at it a long moment, and then he threw it into the open firebox. As the paper caught, a bright flame flared and then died.

32

Eva awoke in a foul mood. Not awoke really. That would have required that she had first slept. Wrapped in the smelly quilt, she had alternately dozed and brooded on the hard floor of the barn while the storm raged outside.

It had been a long, black night. Beside her, her aunt had tossed and turned, reeking of whiskey, and on the other side of the room the sheriff and Bill Davis had conducted a gabfest. All the while, in the back seat of Connie Yates's Ford, Connie Yates lay dead, shot down like the common criminal he was.

Part of Eva couldn't believe Connie was really dead. She expected him to walk into the barn any minute with that goofy grin he sometimes wore. He'd kiss her cheek and say, "Bet I had you worried, huh?" Eva didn't know yet if she missed him. In some ways, she had already said goodbye. She knew they wouldn't be together after the money was divided, and yet she couldn't rid herself of the image of Connie laid out on the back seat of his car, all bloody and still. Was that what it was like when Bonnie and Clyde were gunned down near Arcadia, Louisiana? Pools of blood and bad smells and nothing glamorous about it at all?

Weeks ago, when Frank Pendleton had emptied his gun into the still body of Al Bucklin while she watched from the distance of the bluff top, it had seemed dreamlike. Unreal and distant like a movie on a big screen. Yesterday, though, that was a different view entirely. From where she lay on the barn floor, Eva kept hearing echoes of the gunfire in her head, and she had to stand up and get moving to escape it.

She rose slowly so as not to wake her aunt, who sprawled on the floor like a broken doll. The mustache Virginia had so painstakingly glued on the day before was half torn off. What a useless disguise. Even that ignorant J.P. had seen right through it. Eva saw the sheriff on the cot. His eyes followed her as she moved toward the open side of the barn.

Bill Davis had disappeared.

Eva's mouth tasted like the inside of a rusted can, and under her cap, her hair was matted with dust. To top it off, she was still dressed in the stupid boy clothes her aunt had made her wear. She stepped out into the swirling light of morning.

The storm had ended, but dust floated in the air, obscuring the early sun, pulling a gauzy curtain over the bluffs. Everything seemed out of focus: the hills on the other side of the valley, the dry creek bed filled with waves of sand, the dilapidated barn and the road that led out of the hollow. She walked to the burned-out hulk of J.P. and Slick's house. The blackened framework of burned timber looked as though it might topple at any moment, and shapes that may once have been furniture hunkered on the ground.

A flat steppingstone lay where the porch had been, and a single sunflower grew next to it. The yellow bloom was dull, and its weight pulled the weak stalk over. Eva saw it as a sign. It was telling her that she was a wilting flower, and if she didn't get out of here soon, she would be as rooted as that sunflower.

She had a sudden thought, one that struck Eva so forcefully that she involuntarily turned toward the car. Why not leave? Right now. The money was in the car, nestled in the gunny sacks like trussed chickens ready for market. What did she owe Bill Davis or Virginia? Even if they were blood kin, she didn't owe Virginia Crow anything. What had the woman done for her besides lead her into a life of crime? It would serve them all right if she disappeared with the money, leaving them here to deal with the wounded sheriff.

The thought of Connie's body lying in the back seat stopped her. It creeped her out to think that maybe his ghost was hanging around the car. Anyways, she couldn't just roll his body into a ditch along the highway and go on.

Best to bide her time, she thought, and let the plan she had hatched with Frank Pendleton unfold.

Bill Davis materialized from the thicket of cedars that crowded the bluff, and Eva watched him walk toward the barn. He was joined by Virginia, who was shaking the shawl of dust off her clothing. They put their heads together and began to talk.

Eva was damned if she was going to let them leave her out of whatever they were planning. She joined them just in time to hear her aunt say something about burying Connie at the Old Taney Grove Cemetery.

Eva pictured the cemetery in her mind and imagined Connie lying there next to her mama. Would his ghost join the others then? The one Virginia had claimed to see and the one Eva had seen next to the barn? The woods were filled with ghosts if a person had eyes to see. What did they want, these ghosts? Eva felt a chill run down her back.

"Sister, your heart's in the right place," Bill Davis was saying, "but we can't go back there. The Laws will be breathing down our necks."

"I won't have anyone else on my conscience."

In the morning light, Virginia's face was haggard and lined, as though she had aged a decade in one night. The pasted-on mustache had fallen off entirely.

Eva saw an opening for her plan and put in her bid. "Aunt Virginia's right," she said. "The only decent thing is to bury the man I loved in the family plot." She allowed her voice to catch; she played the part of a heartbroken girl who was trying to put on a brave face. Even if it wasn't a perfect act, her audience was ready to accept it. It was enough.

Bill Davis put an end to the argument. He patted Eva on the shoulder and said, "We can't figger out anything on an empty stomach. Doggies! My belly thinks my throat's been cut."

Eva knew what that really meant. That Virginia would get her way. She always got her way, and Eva might as well be a piece of stump wood for all the consideration she got. But this time she didn't mind.

33

Bill Davis and Virginia and Eva forced down some food from the remaining stores on J.P.'s shelf: beans, coffee, Vienna sausages. The sheriff turned away when they offered him a share. His face was pale and pasty, stained with beard stubble. He needed to get to a doctor.

Their preparations to leave were those of an army unit readying for battle.

"The Laws might be looking for the sheriff or for the armored car robbers," Bill Davis said out of the hearing of the sheriff. "We have to be ready for whatever comes our way. They bushwhacked Pretty Boy Floyd. They didn't give him a rabbit's chance."

He assembled their small arsenal. It had grown considerably in size and stopping power in the past twenty-four hours. There were Connie's guns, of course: the Smith and Wesson double-action revolver and the Winchester 12-gauge autoloading shotgun. Bill Davis's two weapons: a Colt single-action Army revolver and a squirrel rifle that was so worn only a firearms expert could tell its provenance. Then, there were the two revolvers and the shotgun they had taken from the guards at the armored car robbery the day before.

Bill Davis checked the ammunition in each. He tucked one of the guard's revolvers into his waistband, and the other he handed to Eva. Since Connie had died, he had treated Eva more gently, Virginia noticed. He wasn't calling her Esther now, and his sometimes abrasive teasing had been replaced with a solicitous concern for her comfort.

Eva smiled with genuine pleasure when she took the gun. She turned it over in her hands and then aimed it at the distant hillside.

"Bang! Bang!" she said.

"It ain't no toy, girl," Bill Davis said. "We're in a mite of trouble here."

"Don't you worry about me."

"I don't know how to do otherwise," he said simply. "You're Finis Watts's grandbaby. I'm obliged to worry."

Eva gave him a look that said he was talking nonsense, so Bill Davis set aside the sentimental feelings that had suddenly appeared from nowhere, and he showed her how to release the safety on the gun. "Then you pull the hammer back with your thumb," he said, "and she's set to go."

Virginia had the guard's Winchester shotgun. She tested its cool heft and tried to act as though it were a natural, everyday occurrence for her to pack a gun. True, she had carried a gun in the two robberies, but that was more for show. Now she felt like she had stepped up to a whole different level of criminal mayhem. The muscles in her shoulders and neck tightened, and she had a sudden vision of the three of them as seen from above. A small band of criminals on their way to the next round of trouble.

Bill Davis took no notice. "It's more reliable than Connie's auto-loader," he said to Virginia. "They call it a riot gun. With that 20-inch barrel, all you have to do is point it in the general direction. Just hold it firm against your shoulder and let 'er go."

The remaining weapons Bill Davis placed on the floorboard on the passenger side. He covered them with burlap sacks from the barn.

Connie's body in the back seat had stiffened, and in order

for the three of them and the sheriff to fit in the car, it was necessary for Bill Davis to lay Connie flat on the floor in the back. Fortunately, he wasn't a tall man. This was the first time anyone had thought his lack of height a fortunate thing.

Connie's body lay atop the bags of money. Virginia shielded him from view with one of the quilts from J.P.'s hideout. It did little to smother the stink of death. But at least they didn't have to look at his body, which no longer looked like Connie. Before Virginia had looked away, she had glimpsed his face - waxy, almost translucent. The once-healthy pink of his cheeks was now purplish and blotchy.

The aroma that rose from his body was hard to identify. Burned coffee. Potted meat. Sickroom. Rotting garbage. Fox den. Dirty diapers. Some of all of those, but worse. A whiff of destiny.

They decided to stretch out the sheriff on the backseat, so his broken leg would be cushioned.

When it came time to get him to the car, Virginia and Bill Davis made a sling from one of the quilts and carried him. This time he didn't try to hide his pain, and he cried out when they picked him up and again when Virginia stumbled and his leg bumped against the open door of the car.

They rode with the windows down, and no one spoke. Virginia sat in the middle, next to Bill Davis, who drove. Eva was next to the door, and she kept her face turned to the open window.

Virginia hadn't been afraid the day before when the gunfire erupted. There hadn't been time for fear; it had happened so quickly that instinct had taken over and protected her. Now, a tight feeling clenched her chest. The shotgun wedged next to her poked her leg, a constant reminder of its purpose.

Disaster could strike any moment. They didn't need the presence of Connie's decomposing body to remind them of that.

However, Virginia thought, if this was all the punishment they had to endure, they were getting off easy. Maybe that's why she was so nervous. She was learning that punishment was never simple, and that it ran its own course, regardless.

They reached the highway without incident. The sun was high in the sky, but the haze persisted, and even though they were off the dirt road and now driving on pavement, the dust followed them and preceded them and swirled all around them.

It seemed odd to return to the ordinary world. It seemed like the dust storm should have swept away the familiar sights and replaced them with something new. Or perhaps it was death that changed Virginia's perception. Nevertheless, the car passed ordinary houses and ordinary barns and ordinary farmers in fields, and they were soon on the outskirts of Muskogee. They hadn't seen a sign of any Laws.

Bill Davis spoke for the first time since they began their journey. "We have to stop for gasoline. Listen to me. I'll keep the pump jockey busy. You two will have to make sure the sheriff here don't cause no trouble."

He turned his head to look at the sheriff, who slumped with closed eyes against the door. "Sheriff Callahan."

The sheriff's eyes opened slowly.

"Sheriff, we're stopping for a bit. If you try to raise a ruckus or call for help, someone else might die. You don't want that, do you?"

The sheriff shook his head to show he understood, and then his eyes closed again.

"We have to get him to a doctor," Virginia said.

"He's a tough bird."

"Even so, there's just so much a man can bear."

"He ain't nearly reached his limit."

Bill Davis drove the little Ford onto the busy streets of Muskogee. Everywhere, merchants were sweeping dust from the sidewalks in front of their stores, and shoppers walked quickly with scarves and kerchiefs covering their noses and mouths. Virginia thought that people could simply look at them and know they were wanted by the Laws. Any moment the cry would go up. But no one paid them any mind. They had their own worries.

Bill Davis pulled the car into a Conoco. A broken-down looking truck stood on the opposite side of the pump. It was heavily laden with household goods, and a boy in overalls perched atop the load. Next to the truck, a worn man counted out change from a pocketbook. The attendant stood close by, watching as though the man might try to cheat him.

"Kin we fill our water jugs here?" the man asked.

"It's a nickel a gallon."

"A nickel!" The man's shoulders slumped. "We ain't never paid for water before."

Bill Davis unfolded his lanky legs out of the Ford. "Give him the water," he said. "I'll pay for it."

The man faced Bill Davis. "I ain't a beggar."

"And I ain't no Andrew Carnegie. I just want to help a guy out."

"Well, I thankee."

The attendant scowled, but he didn't stop the man when he took his two jugs to the side of the building.

Eva opened the door of the passenger side and started to climb out.

"Where you going?" Virginia said.

"I gotta use the facilities," she said. "I got the cramps somethin awful. But I ain't goin in this dump. I'm goin over to the hotel. I been there before, and their facilities are sanitary."

For Eva, who usually limited her conversation with Virginia to one or two words at a time, it was quite a speech. After she delivered it, she wheeled around and walked away quickly toward the massive brick facade of the Hotel Severs, which loomed a block away.

"We don't have time. Eva! Wait!"

But she was already gone. Bill Davis, jawing with the attendant, didn't even seem to notice. It appeared that it was up to Virginia to keep an eye on the sheriff.

The sheriff seemed to have the same thought. He spoke from the back seat. "I know who you are, Virginia. If you turn yourself in now, I can help you."

Her heart beat like a captured bird. He had known all along who she was. He had just been waiting for his moment. And she had fooled herself into thinking she could get away with her silly disguise.

"You can give up the old man. Tell how he's a cold-blooded killer. Tell how he forced you to take part. Nobody wants to lock up a pretty woman."

Virginia turned to look at him. His face was gray with pain and exhaustion, but his mouth was resolute.

"I'm not going back to jail," she said. "I have a little girl out there somewhere, and I'm not stopping until I find her."

"You can't hide from the law these days. I don't know what all you're running from, but I know you're a good woman. You're not meant for life on the run."

"I don't have a choice."

His voice was earnest and confidential. "Now they got that J. Edgar Hoover in Washington and the Bureau of Investigation. Used to be, you could cross the state line and start over again. It ain't that way any more. In '34, they hunted down Bonnie Parker and Clyde Barrow. Texas outlaws, shot down like dogs in Arcadia, Louisiana. Our own Pretty Boy Floyd tracked all the way to a field near Clarkson, Ohio. It's a different world, Virginia."

"Let me tell you about the world, sheriff." The words fell off her lips like bitter tears. "I had a little baby girl, and I left her in good hands, I thought. That woman sold my Isabelle.

Where's the right in that? Where's justice?"

Virginia stopped abruptly, realizing that her voice was rising. She took a deep breath and said. "I'm going to find her, Ray. Don't try to stop me."

The sheriff was quiet for a long time, and then he said, "I have children. I know it's hard."

Virginia sank back in her seat and watched Bill Davis walk into the Conoco with the attendant. "I reckon you do," she said.

He leaned forward to touch her shoulder, even though it must have hurt his leg to do so. She flinched away, and then she turned again to face him.

"How do you expect to help me, sheriff, when you can't even help yourself?"

Whatever energy had sparked the sheriff faded, and he lay back on the seat with his eyes closed.

Bill Davis returned to the car with bottles of Grape Nehi so cold that beads of condensation coated them.

When he saw that Eva was gone, his eyebrows drew together. "Where is she?"

He handed a Nehi to Virginia and another to the sheriff, who took it with both hands.

"She had to use the facilities," Virginia said. "I couldn't stop her, could I?"

"We don't have all day."

"We have more time than you might think. The sheriff here knows who I am. We might as well go on home before we take care of our business."

Bill Davis gave her and then the sheriff a long look. "I reckon we're in it now," he said.

"We always were."

The Grape Nehi slid down Virginia's throat like icy vapor, and she forgot for a moment the body that lay behind the seat and the miles they still had to go.

Across the street, Eva appeared. She waited for a car to pass, and then she crossed the street and joined them. The car door slammed shut behind her.

"All better," Eva said. She looked like she had been laughing.

Bill Davis handed her the soda pop without comment and they were on their way.

34

They decided to wait until dark to bury Connie Yates.

After the sun went down, the mail road that went past the cemetery was seldom traveled, and darkness would hide their work.

The panic and despair of the past twenty-four hours ebbed once they were at the farmhouse. The previous day's dust storm had left its mark there, too. Miniature drifts of sand piled against the foundation of the house, and dust frosted the flat surfaces a dull gray. However, the familiar surroundings, the four rooms, the barn, the creaking windmill, all seemed to offer a cloak of protection.

Even if a search had been launched for the sheriff, even if the victims of the armored car robbery had been freed, and even if the bodies of the deputy and J.P. had been found, what was there to link Eva and Virginia and Bill Davis to the crimes? Only the sheriff, and for the time being, he was with them.

When drove up to the house, the old dog crawled from under the porch to greet them, but when he smelled the odor emanating from the car, he growled and the hackles rose on his back.

Virginia led him around back and gave him some scraps of food and water. She felt a moment of regret that they would have to leave him behind. Finis Watts had taken great pride in his hunting dog. When Red was younger, he could sniff out squirrels and anticipate which tree they would jump to next.

Now he was old, though, and in Virginia's future, there was no place for a dog.

She patted his head and told him he was a good boy. The dog, lapping water, wagged his tail.

Bill Davis pulled the car close to the back door so they could move the sheriff into the house. First, though, they had to prepare a place for him. Virginia took the quilts from her bed outside to shake off the dust that the storm had laid there, and then she joined Bill Davis.

Since he had spoken to Virginia at the Conoco station, Ray Callahan hadn't said another word, and when Bill Davis told him they'd have to move him one more time, his lips tightened in anticipation of the pain.

Together, Bill Davis and Virginia carried the sheriff into the house and put him on Virginia's bed.

Eva disappeared into her own room the minute they reached the house. Her bedroom door was closed tight.

The sheriff rallied when he saw where they put him. "Never thought I'd be in this bed," he said.

Bill Davis grabbed the sheriff by the collar and jerked his head up. "I don't like to kick a man when he's down," he said. "But that ain't no way to talk in front of a lady."

"Leave him alone," Virginia said. "He can say what he wants."

Bill Davis released the sheriff's shirt and let him fall back on the bed.

Ray Callahan took a deep breath and said, "My apologies, Mrs. Crow. I reckon I'm out of my head a bit."

They left him as comfortable as possible, with water to drink and a pillow for his head. The door they kept open.

Bill Davis drove the car into the barn. Just in case, he said. Given their recent string of bad luck, who could say that any number of precautions were too many? If anyone should happen to stop by, Connie's body and Connie's car would be well out of sight.

The house was filled with reminders of Connie: his radio, his phonograph and records, the pallet he had slept on, a neatly folded pile of clothing in one corner of the front room. Virginia rolled the clothing into the pallet and pushed the bundle behind a chair so she wouldn't have to see it. The radio, however, she turned on.

Bill Davis, finished with his chores, sat on a chair and watched her from the kitchen. "What you want that racket for?"

"Time to catch up to the modern world," she said. "There might be some news. We need to know if they're looking for us."

She moved the needle up and down the dial. This time of day, though, the stations didn't come through. Static, snatches of music and voices, more static. Virginia turned off the radio and joined Bill Davis in the kitchen.

Everywhere, dust formed a dull coat. Virginia herself was grimed with dirt, but for the time being, she ignored it. She was relieved to be leaving this place, to not be responsible for cleaning the mess left behind by the storm.

Bill Davis pulled out a bottle and poured the last of it into two glasses.

"Sister," he said, "get some rest. We're going to have a long night."

The whiskey freed Virginia to think about things she had tried to avoid. "After we bury him," she said, speaking of Connie, "what then?"

"Then we drive as far and as fast as we can."

"And the sheriff?"

Bill Davis gave her a long look. "We'll make a phone call when we're a safe distance away and tell them where to find him."

He rolled a cigarette for her and then one for himself, and

they smoked in silence. The only sound was the rhythmic protest of the windmill, drawing water from deep in the parched earth.

The afternoon crawled by. Virginia found herself watching the clock as she pumped water in the kitchen and built a fire to heat the water and as she packed the few items she wanted to take with her. From Eva's room, silence reigned.

The realization that she could never return to this place where her parents had worked and died and where she had spent the first two decades of her life left Virginia feeling melancholy and spent.

It hadn't felt like home for many years now, but it held memories, memories that cascaded through Virginia's mind as she worked. Araminta in the kitchen kneading bread. Virginia and Carolina on the porch shelling peas in the cool of the evening. Her father and her brother, Charles, mowing hay in the back forty. Evenings in front of the fire while Finis spun his ghost stories and played his fiddle and her mother's knitting needles clicked away.

The later years, those after Charles left for California and after Carolina married her traveling man, Virginia didn't think about at all. Only the good times were allowed in her memories of this place. The days when life was safe and predictable and there was no doubt the sun would break the next morning on a day much like all the others.

Where was her father's fiddle, anyway? It seemed like something that should not be left behind. It was tangible evidence of a man's life that she might someday want to pass on to her daughter.

She hadn't seen the fiddle or its cracked leather case since she had come back home. But, then again, she hadn't looked for it. Virginia viewed the front room with fresh eyes. Bill Davis had rolled out Connie's pallet and lay with his hat over his face. The family Bible sat in its usual place on the fireplace mantel. How could she leave that behind? She wrapped it in a clean tea towel before placing it in her valise.

There weren't many places to search. The wood box next to the heating stove had been cleaned out for the summer. The corner behind the overstuffed chair was bare. The curio cabinet Charles had made for his mother stood in another corner. Virginia opened the glass doors and looked inside. A china shepherdess, with chipped bonnet; two empty flower vases, one glass and the other painted pottery; embroidery scissors and red thread; a cross-stitch project Carolina had never finished; a calendar dated 1931; a cigar box.

Virginia took out the cigar box and looked inside. It was filled with family photos. She added the box to her valise.

Her search for the fiddle led her to her own bedroom, where Ray Callahan dozed on her bed. He started when he heard her footsteps, and his eyes watched her as she moved around the room.

She opened the cedar chest and looked inside, even though she was sure the fiddle wasn't there. No harm in checking once more. The baby blanket that her mother had started knitting for Isabelle lay on top. A pang of guilt stabbed Virginia. She had intended to finish the blanket as a sign of her love for Isabelle, but somehow she never had gotten around to it.

The rest of the items in the chest she pulled out one by one: her mother and father's old clothing, a pair of unfinished quilt tops, a flannel nightgown. She replaced them all in the cedar chest and gently closed the lid.

Searching the wardrobe was equally unproductive. The only place she hadn't looked was under the bed. She lowered herself to her knees and peered underneath. Nothing but dust balls.

Beside her, she heard the sheriff's voice.

"I'm not myself right now," he said, "or I wouldn't have said what I did before."

Virginia straightened and found herself at eye level with him. She guessed he meant the thing about lying in her bed. "Don't think about it," she said.

"I'm not myself."

"None of us is. We're just doing the best we can, so let's leave it at that."

She stood and turned away from him, searching the familiar corners of the room for her father's fiddle. She found it helped to be angry at the sheriff. Who did he think he was, bringing his mooning eyes into her bedroom? It would be easier if he were cursing them for the pain they'd caused. Pity, though? No thank you. It was a feeling she couldn't afford.

However, she decided, she could extend a little kindness.

"I'm heating some water," she said. "I'll bring you a wet cloth so you can wash your face. It'll make you feel better."

"Sure," he said. "That'll make it just like none of this ever happened."

After Virginia took the washcloth to the sheriff, she knocked on Eva's door. She interpreted the grunt on the other side as an invitation to enter.

A tornado had struck Eva's room. Her clothes were strewn over the bed and floor, and a valise stood open on a chair. One of the dresses she had purchased at Miss Jackson's, a black gown with a plunging back, lay atop the clutter. Eva herself was still dressed in the boy clothes she had worn the day before, and to Virginia, her lank hair and thin body made Eva look like one of the orphan children that she had seen in newsreels after the Great War had ended.

She felt a sudden motherly surge. "There's hot water in the kitchen if you want to bathe," she said.

"I don't know what to take with me," Eva said. "We're never coming back here."

"No."

The next words came out haltingly. "I saw mama's ghost once. After she died. Next to the barn. Old Red scared her off. What if she had something important to say to me?"

Virginia was reminded of the white mist she had followed down by the cemetery, and for the first time, she wondered if the ghostly figure was no more than the shape of a person's longing.

"If your mama wants to tell you something," Virginia said, "she'll find a way to do it. Now we have work to do."

She looked around the small room. "I'm looking for your grandfather's fiddle."

"You're wasting your time. Mama sold it."

"Sold it?"

"To Pecky Johnson's son, Abner. He's in a string band. She got five dollars. Bought groceries with it. The hens were still laying then, so we had a regular feast." Eva paused, then added, "A little sorghum molasses to pour on the biscuits would have been good."

Virginia sighed. She wouldn't expect a teenage girl to understand the importance of her grandfather's fiddle, but Carolina should have held on to it.

"Your water's getting cold," she said to Eva. "I'm going to heat some for myself, and then we have to get Connie ready to bury."

Virginia remembered the first time she had gone with her mother to a neighbor's house to help lay out a body. She had just passed her fourteenth birthday and was a woman by all physical signs. It was time that she learned the ways women kept a community together.

The dead woman had been ill for a long time, Granny Wilson, everyone had called her, so even her children and grandchildren said it was a blessing that she had gone to her Heavenly Reward. Nevertheless, there was a proper way to do things, Araminta told Virginia. Before the stiffness set in, the women washed the body and dressed Granny Wilson.

Granny Wilson had made her own burial clothes years earlier, and since that time, she had loved her bacon and biscuits too much. The women had to slit the backside of the dress to fit it on her. After she was arranged in the pine coffin, they brushed her fine, white hair and put silver dollars on her eyes to hold them shut.

Araminta and Virginia and the other women sat up with the body until after midnight. Carolina must have been there, too, but Virginia couldn't picture her among the women, couldn't remember any words they had exchanged. She and her mother joined with the others to sing "Shall We Gather at the River," one of Granny Wilson's favorite hymns, before going home.

You had to treat the dead with respect. Virginia knew that with a deep-rooted understanding, and she felt bad that Connie's body lay on the floor in the back of his car. It wasn't right. But so many things weren't these days.

After Virginia washed her hair and put on a clean dress, she went to the barn to figure out what to do next. As soon as she pulled the quilt back from Connie's face and touched his skin, her good intentions flew out the window. The day was warm, and Connie's body, which had already brewed its own distinctive blend of aromas, was now in full flower. Not only that, but when she tried to move one of his arms, she discovered it was as stiff as a tree trunk, and if they were to dress him in clean clothes, they might have to break his limbs. The thought turned Virginia's knees weak. She had been through too much in the past two days to add any more bad memories. The best they could do, Virginia decided, was wash his face and wrap him in their best quilt. Araminta wouldn't mind if her handiwork was used to lay the boy's body next to hers.

35

The graveyard bristled with strange whispers and ghostly shadows. Wind combed the parched sycamores, clattering the leaves, mimicking the panicked sound of rising birds. The dense thicket of blackhaw and chinkapin cloaked the dry creek bed.

Then the wind died, and there was just enough humidity in the cooling air to form mist. The low haze pressed down on the valley and smothered it in a filmy cloud.

From deep in the lonesome woods, a hoot owl called.

Of all the things she'd done, Virginia thought, this somehow felt like the worst. And it probably wasn't even that illegal. Burying a friend in the dark of night. But it felt like a betrayal. They were denying a good boy a proper burial. In the cemetery, she stood knee-deep in the hole in which they would lay Connie Yates.

He had been elevated to the position of friend in her mind in the past few hours. Before, Connie had just been a background noise, a sometimes unruly youth who needed to be watched. A driver for the getaway car, a sprawling boy who took up space in an already too-small house. Now Virginia saw him a good kid who, like the rest of them, had only wanted a few things out of his reach. His heart had been in the right place. He had proved it by offering his body to take a bullet meant for her, and that fact alone eclipsed everything she had known about him before.

After full dark, the three of them, Eva, Virginia and Bill Davis, had packed their few belongings into Connie's Ford, along with a shovel and a heavy pry bar with which to force rocks out of the clay soil.

Bill Davis raised his eyebrows at Eva's choice of attire. "Esther," he said, "right now you look like the prize chick in the hen house, but you try to dig a hole in that get-up and you'll look like you been a'sortin wildcats."

Eva wore the black evening gown that Virginia had seen on her bed earlier. It was sleeveless, and more appropriate for a nightclub than a makeshift funeral. Black kid gloves reached above her elbows. She had washed her hair, and arranged it in an upswept, Mae West style. She looked much older than her fifteen years.

"I'm wearing black out of respect for Connie," Eva said. "It's him we're puttin in the ground. Not you. And don't call me Esther. Don't call me that name anymore." Her voice was suddenly intense and filled with venom.

Bill Davis tipped his hat to her.

The three of them were standing beside the car in the barn. Virginia wore a sensible traveling dress and sturdy shoes. Bill Davis was dressed in the same clothes he had worn for two days or more, and he was tarnished with dust and sweat.

"There's no point in arguing," Virginia said. "We have a night's work ahead of us."

Eva turned her back on Bill Davis. "I'm not riding in that car."

Connie's body emanated a toxic cloud that escaped the car and hung in the barn air around them.

"We'll walk down and meet you there," Virginia said to Bill Davis.

"Don't never argue with a woman," Bill Davis said. "Maisie taught me that one." He was in good humor. They'd soon be on the road, and before long he could to return his wife and two boys, the debt discharged that he felt he owed Finis Watts and his family. He and Maisie and the boys could pack up their belongings and start a new life in Oregon. He'd wanted to go to Oregon since hearing tales as a boy of wagon trains going to the promised land of the Willamette Valley.

He backed the car out of the barn and headed down the hill.

"You go on ahead," Virginia said to Eva. "I'll catch up to you."

Eva looked at her questioningly, but Virginia nudged her in the direction of the cemetery, and she began walking.

Virginia watched her go, and then she returned to the house.

The sheriff lay in the bed where they'd left him, and he raised his head when she walked through the door.

Virginia launched into her rehearsed speech. "Sheriff Callahan. Ray. I have come to ask a favor. And I know I'm not in any position to ask anything of you."

He looked at her, a dazed expression on his pale face, and she wondered if he could even take in what she was saying. Blood stained the coverings on the bed, and Virginia felt a pang of guilt. They should have taken him to the hospital.

"It's the old dog. Can you see he's cared for? My father set great store by him."

The sheriff's voice, when it came, was slow and husky. "My little girl, she's good with animals. He have a name?"

"Red."

"Red. That's a fine name."

"You're a good man, Ray. Thank the good Lord for every minute you have with your children." Suddenly tears were running down her cheeks.

She turned to go, but his voice stopped her.

"Your father was a respected man hereabouts, Virginia. You don't want to take that away from him."

Virginia brushed the tears from her face. "My father's dead, and if he's looking down on me from heaven, he knows what's in my heart. Anyways, there's no help for it. What's done is done, and there's no turning back. Sometimes you start down a path not knowing where it leads, and when you figure it out, it's too late to go any other way. It's like they already spotted you at the end of the path, and they're beckoning you to them. You don't want to go there, but what choice do you have? Which way should you run? Every direction is just a new path. A new path that may lead to somewhere worse."

She wanted him to understand, but she didn't wait for his response.

Now it was full night, and Virginia and Bill Davis sweated over the fresh hole next to Carolina's grave. The night was humid and warm, and every motion felt like swimming through soup. The full moon diffused its light through the mist, just enough to work without extra lights.

Eva stood off to one side. There was no point in trying to force her to help. That would have wasted energy they couldn't spare.

When the hole was four feet deep, they stopped to rest. Virginia squatted down, using her mother's headstone for balance, stretching her aching back. Beside her, Carolina's grave lay stark and unprotected. A faded bouquet lay near Carolina's head. Virginia wondered if Eva had placed it there.

The cemetery was awash in bittersweet memories, and the lone owl resumed its call. Hell might be like this, Virginia thought, all dark sorrow and no relief.

To Eva, the graveyard was a place where anything could happen, none of it good.

As usual when she was nervous, Eva became talkative. She turned to Virginia. "Dodie Ashton told me her mother was headed home late one night from the Wilson's. She's a midwife, you know, and she'd just delivered Miz Wilson's eighth baby. And she was walkin over the creek," Eva tossed her head to indicate the dry creek bed behind them, "and she seen a little baby without nothin on layin on that big flat rock in the middle of the creek. When she went closer, the baby rose up and flew away. It had wings."

Bill Davis had been leaning on his shovel and listening. "We don't need no haint stories," he said. "We have some work ahead of us."

"Dodie's mother saw it!" Eva's voice rose, as though her passion could make them believe.

Bill Davis lay his shovel down. He took Eva's elbow and guided her to the car. "You can make yourself useful by keeping an eye out for real-live people," he said. "You take that gun I gave you earlier and you keep watch for us."

He opened the trunk and handed her the revolver. A small smile played across Eva's lips and she took the gun and moved to the dark shadows.

Bill Davis threw down the cigarette he had been smoking and said to Virginia, "Let's get back to it."

Together they pitched in. Virginia chipped away at the baked earth with the pry bar, and Bill Davis scooped the loosened dirt out of the hole. When one tired, they exchanged places and worked other muscles. Virginia wore gloves, but still her hands ached, and the dust they stirred up tickled her throat and made her cough. They were so intent on their work that the shadow above them went unnoticed.

"Put 'em down easy," Frank Pendleton said.

He stood at the edge of the open grave, a revolver in his right hand. The quick flare at the end of his cigarette when he inhaled threw a flicker like lightning across his shadowed face.

The blank look he wore frightened Virginia more profoundly than anything she had seen in the past two years. It held no humanity, no thought for anything except its own desires.

Deep below the fear, Virginia felt a stab of helpless fury. To come so far and have an animal like him take all they had worked for was more than she could bear. She used the pry bar to steady her as she stepped out of the grave.

"What are you doing here?"

Pendleton ignored her and trained his attention on Bill Davis. "The shovel, partner," he said. "Toss it over there."

Bill Davis gave him a long, hard look and dropped the shovel. "Who the hell are you?"

"I'm the ghost of the Old Taney Grove Cemetery," Pendleton said, "come to relieve you of your burdens."

At the same time, Virginia said, "Frank Pendleton." A look passed between her and Bill Davis. She had told him about Slick's murder and the fire. And how Pendleton had shown no mercy to Al Bucklin.

Bill Davis climbed out of the hole, and he kept it between him and the other man.

Virginia began backing away, one tiny step at a time. Where was Eva? Where was Eva with the gun? Virginia tried to spot her without moving her head or attracting attention.

Bill Davis held Pendleton's gaze. "We're having us a funeral here, as you can see. You got no invite."

"But I do have an invite." Pendleton laughed then, a short, harsh sound. "Eva, honey! Show them my invite."

Eva emerged from the shadows and into the misty, swirling moonlight to stand beside Pendleton. She kissed him hard and swift on the mouth and then smiled at Bill Davis and Virginia. A triumphant smile. But her whole body trembled. She gripped her gun tight in her hand.

"You're livin in a fool's paradise, Esther, if you think this slick will share any money with you." Bill Davis's voice was low and persuasive.

A shadow passed over Eva's face. "Tell him, Frank. Tell him how it is."

Pendleton locked on that one word. "Esther?"

"Don't you ever call me that!" Her reaction was sudden and fierce. "My name is Eva Opaline Wilder. Don't you ever call me that name."

"Esther," he said again. "Esther." And he laughed.

She backed away and pointed the gun at Pendleton with both hands. Her hands shook, and the gun wavered back and forth. "You're not going to take me with you, are you, Frank? You're going to leave me here to be a ghost with my mama."

"Put the damn gun down, girl." He reached an arm toward the gun. "Don't be a fool."

Eva looked at something beyond him. A wisp of mist, a flash of silver. "Mama? Is that you?"

Pendleton grabbed for the gun, and it went off. The sound was sharp and final. A look of surprise crossed his face. His pistol fell, and he sank to his knees and slowly rolled to one side.

"Oh my God, oh my God." Eva's voice was a prayer.

Bill Davis was the first to react. He rolled Pendleton over and felt for a pulse, and then he looked up at Eva. "You drilled him proper," he said.

Virginia stepped forward. "Frank Pendleton would have robbed us and then planted us in that hole we just dug."

Eva stood in a trance, the gun limp at her side. Virginia approached her as she would a strange dog, slowly, gently, and took the gun from her hand.

After her niece was disarmed, anger washed over Virginia. "You called him," she said. "When we stopped at the Conoco in Muskogee, you called him."

"We were going away," Eva said dully. "I was getting out of here forever."

Virginia raised her hand to slap Eva and then let it fall back to her side. What was the point in inflicting a small amount of pain when the crime was so huge?

Bill Davis was the first to shake off the shock. He said, "We'll have to get out of here pronto in case anyone heard that gun go off."

"I didn't mean to," Eva said. "He shouldn'ta called me that name."

They finished Connie's burial in hurried silence. Without discussion. Bill Davis and Virginia dragged Connie's body to the hole, and they filled it in, a bit more of Connie disappearing with each shovel full of dirt until he had vanished.

Off to one side, the lump of flesh and bone that once was Frank Pendleton lay in shadow, an inert substance like the dirt it lay on. Yet, it was a constant reminder of how quickly things could go wrong. Out of the tail of her eye, Virginia would catch a glimpse of his body, and a chill would creep over her as if she were the one whose body heat was rising in the night air.

While they worked, Virginia and Bill Davis kept an eye on Eva. She sat next to her mother's grave, staring at the mist rising off the bottoms and seemingly oblivious to the activity around her.

The last words for Connie were spare and spoken by Bill Davis. He leaned back on his shovel. "There ain't much to say. He was a good boy, and he didn't deserve to die the way he did. I reckon the Lord will take that into account."

They stood in silence for a moment, and then Virginia took the tools and put them back in the car. No matter what level of disaster they faced, her father had taught her to always clean the tools and put them away. There was some comfort to be found in small routines.

"What now," she said to Bill Davis when they had finished.

He looked over at Eva. "She's a piece of work."

"My own blood."

"There's that. Let's find his car."

Bill Davis walked over to where Eva sat and yanked her to her feet.

"We're going on a walk," Bill Davis said, "and we can't leave you without supervision. No telling what kind of trouble you'll stir up next."

He dug in the pockets of the dead man and came up with a set of keys, which he placed in his own pocket.

Eva's face was pale and pinched in the moonlight, and she limped along after Bill Davis, her fancy shoes making her stumble as she tried to keep up with him.

Virginia walked on the other side of her, and the three of them marched up the road together.

The car wasn't far. It was parked at the top of the hill, not even hidden, where crumbling walls and a chimney marked the spot where a mansion had once stood.

"Ain't that sweet," Bill Davis said to Eva. "Your grandpa used to tell a tale about this place, about a woman and her two sons. Didn't come to no good end, neither."

He looked in the open windows of the car. "Always wanted me one of these Packards," he said, running his hand across the brushed upholstery. "Let's see how she runs."

The three of them crowded in the front seat, Eva once again flanked by Virginia and Bill Davis. The car rolled slowly down the hill, like a stately dowager descending a grand staircase.

When Bill Davis stopped the car in the cemetery, next to Connie's Ford, Eva suddenly came to life. "What are you going to do with me?" she said. "I worked hard for that money, too. Some of it's mine." Her hair, falling out of its upswept bun, curled in tendrils around her face.

"One thing's for sure: I ain't never calling you Esther again,"

Bill Davis said, and the three of them erupted into laughter, the unbearable tension finding a release.

He watched Virginia's face, on the other side of Eva, as he spoke. "You think we're not mad at you, girl, because you're still alive? Your Mr. Pendleton would have cut our throats for two bits and give fifteen cents of it back. We'd all be in that hole with Connie Yates. It's no small thing you've done."

Above, them a truck topped the hill, its headlights cutting through the mist. The three of them watched the truck rumble down the hill. Virginia recognized the vehicle as it passed the cemetery, its flatbed piled high with hay.

"Old Harp Cousins is taking hay to his cows." She hadn't realized until then that she had been holding her breath.

"Every minute we stay here is a danger to us," Bill Davis said. "That sheriff is a tough buzzard. He might be out on the road now flaggin down your neighbor and tellin him the whole story."

"So say it," Virginia said. "What you have in mind."

Bill Davis scratched a match along the Packard's upholstery and ignited a cigarette. The quick sulfur flare lit their tense faces.

"I'm not a man of violence," Bill Davis said. "I've been giving some thought to your question, Eva, about what to do with you, and if Virginia agrees with me, here's my idea of justice. You can take your Mr. Pendleton and his fine Packard and go wherever you damn well please. I'd say I wish you the best, but it wouldn't be sincere."

Virginia nodded her agreement.

"I need my share of the money," Eva said.

"You spent that and then some, girl."

"You can't just cut me out!" The first note of desperation sounded in her voice. She looked first at Bill Davis, and finding no sympathy there, turned to Virginia.

"Aunt Virginia, grandpa wouldn't want you to do this to

your own flesh and blood." A single tear, like a loose diamond, rolled down Eva's cheek.

"There's no time for discussion," Virginia said. She was already stepping out of the car. "You're lucky to be alive. You're damn lucky. Keep that in mind."

Part of her stayed with Eva, though. Part of her pricking conscience, part of her heart. Where had she gone wrong? Was there something she should have done differently? If she had paid more attention to the girl, would this have happened? Eva had needed a mother's guidance, and where had she been? With her head in the clouds, thinking only of her little Isabelle.

A deep heaviness settled over Virginia, and she thought that whatever happened next and everything that happened after, no matter how sweet or how terrible, this moment would always be a part of it. She had failed Connie, and now she had failed Eva.

Bill Davis conducted a quick search of the Packard and came up with a sawed-off shotgun. Its thick black barrel looked ugly and lethal. He added it to the pile of weapons in Connie's Ford, where the bags of money from the armored car robbery lay as a mocking testament to why they were there.

A string of profanity erupted from the front seat of the Packard where Eva sat.

Bill Davis and Virginia ignored her while they dragged Pendleton's body to the Packard and heaved him into the trunk.

"In that kind of mood, she's likely to head back up the hill and do more damage to the sheriff," Virginia said to Bill Davis as he slammed the trunk shut. "We can't leave her here."

He nodded his agreement. "You take the Ford and follow me. We'll get her a piece down the road before we cut her loose."

Instead of taking the mail road into Gilead, they drove west into the darkness, Virginia following Bill Davis and Eva. Ahead of her, the Packard turned a corner, and Virginia temporarily lost sight of it. Her headlights bored a velvet-lined tunnel through the dark. It seemed like the road might run through the end of the light into black space. Into black space where anything could rise up out of the darkness and be revealed.

She had to force aside the anguish and remember why she was here, remember that what she was doing right now might lead her back to her daughter. She had to hope that someday she and Isabelle would disappear together into that perfect black night.

36

Money can buy the answers to many questions. Where was the landlady who had sold Isabelle? Give me some money and I'll find out for you. Don't want to talk to the landlady? I'll get the name for you. The retired Pinkerton detective that Bill Davis knew in Oklahoma City was secretive about his methods. Whatever they were, he got results.

Virginia had thought to ask Bill Davis why they hadn't gone to this man before. On that black day when they had discovered Ned Bender had taken her money and disappeared, she could have used a little help. She was learning, though, that there are some questions you don't want answered. And if Bill Davis had held out on her for reasons of his own, it wasn't any use digging out those answers and holding them up for inspection.

The detective had a mean streak. When he reported to Bill Davis and Virginia, he couldn't resist twisting the knife a bit.

"She said, your old landlady Iona Tweedy said, you reminded her of her sister's girl. She says the sister had two boys from her first husband, and then when she married again, she had a baby girl. 'The boys was raised up right,' Mrs. Tweedy said, 'but the girl was yanked up by her hair.' Yanked up by her hair." He repeated the words with relish.

"Skip to the breaking news," Bill Davis said.

"Take it easy. I'm pals."

The three of them, Bill Davis, Virginia and the detective,

sat in the dining room of the Cattlemans' Hotel, near the Oklahoma City stockyards. Best not to let the man know too much of our business, Bill Davis had said to Virginia when he set up the meeting. He might find someone to sell that information to.

Virginia thought of Eva when he said that. The last time she saw her niece was at a roadside pullout west of Wagoner on Highway 51. It was well past midnight, and the traffic was nonexistent. Eva had stood beside the car in silence as Virginia and Bill Davis pulled onto the highway in Connie's Ford and left her with the Packard and Pendleton's body. Eva wasn't left destitute. Virginia had reached in one of the bags and pulled out a packet of bank notes.

She saw Bill Davis watching her. "Take it out of my share," she said.

He shook his head. "If you hadn't, I would have. We're just a couple of saps."

Not saps enough, though, to forgive Eva for her betrayal.

The two of them drove through the night. In the light of dawn, as the sun's rays glittered off the tall buildings of Tulsa in the distance, Virginia finally lay her head on the seat and slept.

They stopped in Tulsa to make a phone call to the Gilead sheriff's office and to get rid of the bloodstained car that had belonged to Connie. Bill Davis bought another: a 1930 Model A Ford with a Cyclops-eye speedometer and stainless steel brightwork. They could have afforded something flashier, but Bill Davis said there was no need to draw attention.

In the new Ford, they made their way to Oklahoma City and found lodgings. They were quiet and brooding in those days after leaving the farmhouse, and Virginia wondered if Bill Davis, too, felt bad about Connie and Eva, if he thought he had failed in some way. That she had failed them she had no doubt. If she had paid more attention, she thought. If she had only asked the right questions, known the right answers. She asked Bill Davis once if he was all right, and he smiled at her and said, "Right as rain."

What could that mean, she wondered, when there was no rain?

They divvied the money from the armored car robbery, saving out a portion for Connie Yates's family, and Virginia felt rich.

In the newspapers they learned that Pendleton's body had ended up in a ditch not far from where they left Eva. Virginia saw no mention of Eva even though she read every page of the news. For a brief time, the Oklahoma City newspaper, the Daily Oklahoman, was full of stories. The initial discovery of the dead man hadn't merited much space, but after Pendleton was identified as "a well-known figure in the Tulsa underworld," speculation had run wild about why he was killed and how his body had ended up beside a lonely country road east of Tulsa.

An enterprising reporter connected Pendleton's death to the dead deputy, the sheriff and J.P.:

"The plot of a gangster to free his friend in crime from arresting officers ended in a hail of gunfire. Sheriff Ray Callahan was shot, according to statements attributed to him, while attempting to shield his deputy from the gun of J.P. Yates, a local rumrunner and convicted felon. Deputy Cletus Baker was killed by a single gunshot to the head. The two had arrested Mr. Yates earlier that afternoon and were later accosted by a man who was thought to be Frank Pendleton. Mr. Pendleton is said to be an associate of criminal elements, including the Barker-Karpis outfit."

Virginia closed the paper and sat deep in thought. Was it possible that Ray would play it that way? That he would allow her this small amount of grace after what they had been through?

Now, a week after Virginia and Bill Davis had arrived in Oklahoma City, talk about the dead men was fading away. Two less criminals for the Laws to worry about.

The sudden flicker of a match drew Virginia's attention back to the interior of the Cattleman's dining room. The Pinkerton detective, whose belly pushed against the buttons on his vest, touched a flame to the end of his cigar and puffed on it.

"You want to talk business, pardner?" He emphasized the word. "There's the matter of my fee."

Bill Davis pulled out his wallet and counted out the bills.

The man made no move to reach for them until Bill Davis added another bill to the stack.

"Green. My favorite color," the detective said, rolling the bills together and stuffing the roll in his pocket.

He slid a piece of paper across the table to Bill Davis, who glanced at the words written on it and then passed it to Virginia.

Virginia picked it up, her heart beating like a trapped bird, and saw an address and a name. She was hardly aware that she had stopped breathing until she drew a deep breath.

Bill Davis took the detective by the arm. "This better be the real goods," he said. "We come a long ways for this."

The detective winced and tried to pull his arm away. "Satisfaction guaranteed," he said.

The following day, Bill Davis and Virginia went their separate ways. Bill Davis had offered to stay with Virginia until she had Isabelle, but Virginia knew the final part of her journey had to be taken alone.

The two of them stood at the Union Station and clasped hands.

"There's been too many goodbyes," Virginia said. "I'm not ready."

Bill Davis's faded blue eyes studied hers. "I told you I'd stay."

The train pulled in. In a few minutes Virginia would board it and head west to Denver where her daughter now lived. "You've done more than my father ever asked of you. It's time to get back to your own family."

He adjusted his hat as though it were too tight. "You're my family, too, Virginia Crow."

She was in his arms then, and they hugged wordlessly for a long minute. This was what family felt like, Virginia thought, that almost forgotten pressure of strong arms around you with that little extra squeeze that said, I'm here for you. She felt the sting of tears, but she fought them back. No tears for Bill Davis.

"Where will you go?" she said, stepping out of his embrace. "How will you spend your money?"

His lined face smoothed as he thought about her question, and he smiled. "I'll get some five-dollar shoes for my boys," he said, "and a pretty calico dress for Maisie. I'll buy a fine farm where I can raise some cows and ride a high-steppin horse."

"I hope you have all that and more."

"You and Isabelle come see us."

"Yes. We'll do that."

The porter was waiting for her to board, and she handed him her valise and stepped onto the train.

The last time she saw Bill Davis, he was standing tall beside the tracks, watching the train disappear into the western sun.

37

Denver was a revelation. Seventy miles out, the conductor drew the passengers' attention to the west with two words: "Pikes Peak." After the flatness of the eastern Colorado plains, the jagged wall of the Rockies seemed to be crushed upward into the clouds. Virginia marveled at the clouds sitting atop the mountains until she heard a man say it was snow.

In Denver, the air was so clear and light that Virginia felt like she could leave her hotel along Colfax Avenue and be in the foothills in half an hour. The only walking she was interested in, though, was along the street where Isabelle lived with the man and woman who had paid money for a child not their own.

After she settled into her modest downtown hotel, Virginia went to a nearby five-and-dime to buy a city map. She had thought about what she would do when she arrived in Denver while the train chugged across the miles of drought-stricken prairie. She would be infinitely patient. She would wait and watch until the time was right because she might have only one chance to reclaim her daughter. She would be as light and wraith-like as a ghost.

On the city map, she marked the block that would become her territory. Isabelle's new family lived on Eighth Street, east of the gold-leaf domed Capitol. Virginia first walked past the house when dusk was settling on the city, obscuring her features from other passersby. The house, when she saw it, surprised her. She had expected something pretentious, but it was small and neatly kept, a clapboard-sided bungalow along a row of larger redstone houses. A tall blue spruce stood like a sentinel by the front door, and a row of hollyhocks lined the brick walkway.

Through a lighted window, Virginia caught a glimpse of a woman working in the kitchen. She appeared to be washing dishes, and as Virginia watched from the sidewalk, the woman stopped and cocked her head as though she listened to another voice. She smiled and knelt out of Virginia's sight for a moment.

Virginia's heart thudded painfully. Isabelle, her baby, was on the other side of the wall. She walked away quickly, not trusting that she could stop herself from flinging open the door and grabbing her daughter. It wasn't time. She would wait for the right time. No matter how hard it was, she would wait.

In the days that followed, Virginia established a routine that was built around the schedule of the residents on Eighth Street. She rose early in the cool Denver morning, and ate a breakfast of oatmeal and coffee at a small diner. The waitress wrapped an egg sandwich for her in wax paper. Then Virginia went to Eighth Street to keep watch. A small city park lay down the street from the house. It was little more than a vacant lot, overgrown with tangled bushes and a narrow irrigation ditch running through it, but from its cover, Virginia could see the front door of the house on Eighth Street.

The man the Pinkerton detective had identified Isabelle's "parents" as Allan and Sheila Palmer, but Virginia thought of them as "the man" and "the woman." He left for work promptly at 7:45 a.m. in a blue Buick, shiny and new, and wore his hat cocked at a jaunty angle.

After her first day's vigil, Virginia hired a car so that she might park along the street and more easily blend in with the other cars parked there. From her car, she could watch the comings and goings from the house.

When Virginia finally saw Isabelle, she almost overlooked her. Even though at an intellectual level she knew that babies grow into children, she wasn't prepared for the sight of an elfin girl with curly brown hair and short, chubby legs.

It was mid-morning, and Virginia was half-asleep in the warm car. The door of the house opened, and a child and woman emerged. The girl clutched the hand of the woman, and together they walked down the sidewalk to a neighboring house, where they disappeared inside.

The realization that the child was Isabelle jolted Virginia. A current shuddered through her. Even after her daughter was no longer in sight, Virginia stared at the route Isabelle had walked. Such short, precise steps she had taken. How solemn she had looked. How daintily dressed she had been in a Shirley Temple frock and brown buckled shoes. Virginia's breath came in short gasps, and something in her chest felt like stones grinding against each other. She splashed her face with water from a jar that sat on the floor of the car.

"It's okay," she said aloud. "It's okay." But she didn't feel okay. The world had tilted and wouldn't right itself. She thought she might be sick. She struck her hand hard on the steering wheel and said, "Damn you! Be tough. Be Bill Davis tough."

The incantation of his name calmed Virginia, and after a time, she felt that she could watch her daughter walk down the sidewalk holding the woman's hand without rushing out to take her away.

On the third day that Virginia watched, the woman and Isabelle boarded the trolley on Colfax and went downtown. Virginia followed them from a distance. They went to the Daniels & Fisher Tower, where a giant of a doorman seemed to know Isabelle by name. Virginia was close enough to hear his voice when he squatted down to shake her daughter's hand and say, "Why here's Miss Emily come to visit."

Isabelle giggled and hugged the man's neck.

Emily. That's what the man and the woman called her Isabelle. Isabelle Crow was now Emily Palmer.

"Come, Sweetheart," the woman said. "We have a long list of tasks today."

They disappeared down the long aisles of dry goods, and Virginia shadowed them while the woman held swatches of fabric up against Isabelle and finally chose one to sew into a dress.

Virginia was learning to be invisible. She trailed the woman and Isabelle through the late-summer afternoon while they went to Bauer's for an ice-cream soda and then to the Denver Public Library, where they checked out a stack of books. All the while, Virginia watched her daughter with hungry, devouring eyes, noting every little mannerism: the way she covered her mouth when she laughed at something the woman said, the sober way she looked inside her little cloth purse and withdrew a handkerchief. Never once did she cry or whine or act like a spoiled child. She was exactly the kind of child Virginia had hoped she would become.

After Isabelle and the woman returned home, Virginia waited in her parked car through the long evening until the man went through the door and eventually the lights flickered out. She thought maybe her heart was breaking.

Sleep wouldn't come, and Virginia left her hotel room to wander the late-night streets of downtown Denver. It was Friday night, and music tinkled from the speakeasies along Larimer Street. Men on the bum drank from bottles in paper bags and watched her pass. One said, "Hotcha, hotcha," as she walked by.

Her thoughts were free-floating, and images rushed past chaotically: Isabelle with her new mother, Connie's head in her lap, Virginia's mother smiling at something her father said, Eva crying by the side of the road. It seemed like all life was chaos, and nothing existed to straighten it out.

Virginia went into a saloon for a drink. The large room was dimly lit and crowded and noisy with music and conversation. She shouldered up against the dark wood of the bar to catch the barkeep's attention.

While Virginia waited, she looked around the bar. Over the heads of the customers, the walls were lined with the mounted heads of antelope, deer and elk, their glass eyes staring sightlessly at eternity. Creatures of beauty turned into wall decorations. She lost her desire for a drink so abruptly and so completely that it occurred to her as she walked out of the bar that she might never drink again. The thought made her want to laugh. Such a small miracle in a world desperately in need of larger ones.

Virginia was at her post in the rented car along Eighth Street promptly at 7:30 Saturday morning. She watched the man get in his car at 7:45 and strained to hear what he said to his wife who stood in the door of the house.

She thought she hadn't heard the words at first, but the interpretation came to her as the sounds replayed in her memory: the monkey island at noon.

It seemed like a strange code the man was speaking, but when Virginia followed the woman and Isabelle to the zoo at mid-morning, the meaning became clear.

The Denver City Zoo lay in a large park, with a lake in the center and massive civic buildings ringing it. After the months of drought in Oklahoma, the green lawn and blooming flowers seemed like a piece of paradise.

However, the sun was a smoking ball in the sky, and no matter what folks said about the low humidity in Denver, the day was hot. In the shade of the cottonwoods, there was a brief respite, although biting flies lay in wait there.

The zoo was crowded. The central promenade swarmed with children and their parents, with music and vendors. At each cage that held an animal, a crowd gathered.

Virginia trailed a distance behind Isabelle and the woman. They stopped to admire the long-necked giraffes and the black bears. The alligators and the snake house they went past quickly. Along the walkways, ducks and geese and pigeons begged for handouts, and Isabelle and the woman stopped to feed them bits of bread.

Isabelle wore a light-colored frock with a big bow tied in front under her chin. A brimmed straw hat protected her from the sun. She trudged along with the woman and pointed at the animals and laughed, but after awhile, it was evident she was tiring.

The woman sat Isabelle on a park bench and told her to wait while she stood in line at a nearby vendor's cart. Flavored ices, the sign on the cart said.

What happened next, Virginia couldn't have planned more perfectly. It was as though she had an accomplice. A boy darted up beside the woman, grabbed her purse and disappeared into the crowd.

For a second, the woman stood as though frozen, and then she screamed, "Stop! Thief! He stole my purse!"

Some of the men in the crowd ran after the boy, and everyone who was left behind craned their necks to watch the action.

Isabelle was alone on the bench, and the woman was distracted. If ever there was a time to act, the time was now.

Virginia sat beside Isabelle on the bench, her heart beating crazily.

"Hello," she said. Her voice was rusty.

Isabelle looked up at her through long lashes. Her skin was creamy brown, and her cheeks round and fat. Virginia thought she couldn't bear it.

"I've lost my puppy," Virginia said. "Can you help me find her?"

The little girl nodded trustingly, and slid off the bench with Virginia.

With one last look at the woman, who was still anxiously watching the running men, Virginia took Isabelle's hand and led her into a grove of pine trees. Her hand was soft, softer than the finest silk, as soft as a pillowy dream. The trees sheltered them from the crowds, and the air was quiet and cool. However, Virginia's face felt flushed, and goose bumps ran up her arms.

Together they walked through the pines and away from the crowds, Virginia talking all the while about the puppy she had lost. She paused for a moment next to a cage that housed lions. At least that's what the sign said, though none were in evidence.

Isabelle spoke for the first time, and her small, clear voice startled Virginia.

"Does your puppy miss its mama?"

"What?" Virginia knelt beside her daughter and held her shoulders.

"I want my mama," Isabelle said. Her lip puckered out, and then she was crying and she said again, "I want my mama." Tears hovered at the edge of her eyes like sparkling diamonds and rolled down her cheeks.

It was time for Virginia to pick up Isabelle and run away with her. Run to a place where no one could ever find them. It was time to reclaim her stolen daughter.

But instead, Virginia felt something like a rushing wind passing through her, taking with it everything she thought she had known and felt and believed. She didn't examine the moment. She only knew with a sudden clarity that all her plans from the time she had found that Isabelle was gone had been made through a dark glass, and that until this moment, she had not seen clearly.

Virginia saw that she had had her turn at motherhood. So many chances. First Isabelle and then Eva and Connie. And each time the gift had been offered, she had in some way failed the test. It was time to learn from her mistakes and pay the price.

Virginia picked up Isabelle, who seemed as light as a puff of air, and she said, "Let's find your mama."

The little girl's arms crept around Virginia's neck, and she held tight while Virginia carried her back through the pine grove to the trees' edge.

Virginia saw the woman and set Isabelle down. "There's your mama," she said. "Go to her."

Isabelle gave Virginia one last dazzling look and then darted toward the woman. Virginia stood quickly and turned away. Maybe she had done the right thing, the only thing, but there were some things a person shouldn't have to witness.

She walked away from the animal cages, down the brick walkway and through a manicured hedge. On one side of the wall of green, an elephant trumpeted—an exotic promise of other places, a whole other world out there.

The walkway arched over a stream, and Virginia paused for a moment on the bridge to look down at the clear, flowing water. Polished stones lined the stream bed, their embedded mica glinting in the sun like jewels waiting to be discovered. Without thinking why, Virginia leaned over the bridge and reached down to pluck a stone the size of a quail egg from the water. In her hand it felt like a talisman, and she rubbed its hard, smooth surface until the water evaporated.

Her father's words came to her: *If you cross a stream of*

running water, no ghost will be able to follow. Virginia looked over her shoulder, at the crowd of people who shielded her view of Isabelle-Emily and her other mother, and then she straightened her shoulders and crossed to the other side.

Letha Albright, author of the critically acclaimed Viv Powers series, has worked at newspapers, in a sawmill and as a wilderness guide. She lives in Columbia, Mo., where in her free time, she climbs rocks and hikes.

The debut of *Tulsa Time* made the list of Best Books of 2000 in *Mystery News*, who called it "a dark, gritty, hard-edged first novel." Letha's second mystery, *Daredevil's Apprentice*, won accolades from the *Detroit Free Press* as "a subtle, suspenseful, well-plotted mystery with a stirring evocation of Cherokee history and culture." The third book in the series *Bad Luck Woman*, was also published by Avocet Press.